WHITE MARBLE LADY

BOOKS BY ROI OTTLEY

NEW WORLD A-COMING
BLACK ODYSSEY
NO GREEN PASTURES
LONELY WARRIOR
WHITE MARBLE LADY

WHITE MARBLE LADY

by Roi Ottley

FARRAR, STRAUS AND GIROUX
NEW YORK

To my daughter LYNNE ROYCE

PUBLISHER'S NOTE

When Roi Ottley died of a heart attack in 1960 he had virtually completed the book he called *White Marble Lady*. After some time his widow, Alice, with the assistance of the publishers, selected the final form of the book. *White Marble Lady* is a work of fiction in which there is mention of a few known public names.

PART ONE

I

Jeff Kirby had felt the nudge of the crisp air; and now, having finished a satisfying meal of curried lamb, rice, chutney, green lettuce, and beer, he had a luxurious feeling of anticipation—of what, he hadn't the faintest notion. He pushed back from the table, leaving an accumulation of dishes for the waiter to take away.

It was the spring of 1938, and the animation and dazzle, the half dark, the tobacco fumes and women's scents, and the thousand sounds of the Harlem night—all had a curious effect on him. He looked admiringly into the face of a young woman he though he knew. He realized his mistake and quickly turned away.

The girl, who had been wandering around drink in hand, joined the crowd at the old, hand-me-down mahogany bar. Jeff idly looked at the absurd, badly painted mural on the long sweep of wall behind, with its slant-eyed nymphs, nude, golden brown, and gaily festooned, mirthlessly cavorting in a muddy green forest. Whenever he noticed the painting he had a kindly feeling for the artist because of the spectacular lack of talent. He was sure the manager had fixed the price tag at a skimpy quota of free meals.

Jeff had taken a table directly facing the bandstand, which was covered with worn red carpeting. He had been hearing music, vague and vapory, but now it began to form a melodic line in his mind; a four-piece combo seated opposite the bar was playing softly, as if in no expectation of being listened to, so that the ebb and flow of voices mingled with the fanciful harmonies and improvisations, making everything seem undefined.

Of all the places in Harlem, he liked best to come here, to The Back Door, a tavern whose glittering neon letters spelled the way to a basement deep in a gray, beaten tenement building on a Lenox Avenue intersection—a very important thoroughfare to those who lived in this part of Harlem. On opposite corners, jostled by countless shops crammed with a variety of bogus merchandise, were Bethel A.M.E. Zion Church and Public School No. 89 and the glass-and-iron, house-shaped enclosure of the subway entrance. Harlem Hospital stood in grim cleanliness about a block away.

The Back Door completed the scenic design of this small but almost self-contained community. The tavern had a dozen or so tables covered with red-checkered gingham, surrounding a tiny dance floor. Sectioned off from the room was a makeshift alcove of booths and benches covered with striped red and yellow imitation leather; and behind them were the public toilets. The food was heavy, ample, and well-seasoned; the music rhythmic, often experimental and earthy.

The men and women who visited the tavern in the daytime were unhurried by the shrill pace set by a depressed, frenetic New York. They had no worlds to conquer, no big deals to consummate, no cosmic questions to settle. When not dozing in the sun, they sat idly in The Back Door and nursed solitary drinks. For some, nothing existed but the enchantment of alcohol and music, but a few listened to the old, garrulous bartender Jake who had inherited wisdoms handed down by generations of his race.

—2—

The people who began to come in now were a different, more affluent group from the afternoon crowd. For the most part, the daytime customers were unemployed and bought drinks from what they received as government aid. When this was gone they spent the small change they begged, borrowed, hustled, or stole. But in the evenings the management justified doubling the price of drinks because of the entertainment. This discouraged them.

The manager, Perkins Sparhawk, "Perky" for short, was a black, balding man whose five-foot-four height was deceptively powerful. He dropped heavily into a chair opposite Jeff. His shiny gold tooth, which Jeff always watched as a barometer of the manager's feelings, usually had the bright glitter of dime-store jewelry. He perspired freely, and exuded the proprietary air of men who are self-conscious about their possessions.

He looked at the empty plates, as his huge fist set down, with exaggerated care, a tall glass of whiskey.

"How's the eats?" he asked. "Man, you ain't left a speck for your friends." He spoke with the remnants of a Southern accent.

"They'll be along soon," Jeff said, ". . . but not from hunger." Then he looked at his watch anxiously.

From the kitchen they heard the West Indian cook's angry shouts, pointed up by her shrill, sort of hybrid Cockney accent reminiscent of her native Montserrat.

"Squashie's been in an uproar all night," Perky said, add-

ing mournfully, "That monkey-chaser mus' have the curse."
He turned back to Jeff. "How's Juilliard!"

"Okay, okay."

Perky lit a cigar and wagged his head dubiously, prepared
to sidestep the subject if the young man became belligerent,
as he sometimes did. Jefferson Kirby, Jr., not yet twenty-
seven, hoped to become a serious musician in opposition to
all logic and practical advice, and was studying composition
at the conservatory.

"A composer!" Perky frowned and looked at Jeff through
a squint. "Ain't it tough enough considerin'—" He did not
complete his thought about discriminations against Negroes.
"But a composer!" He suddenly felt sad for the young fellow
seated opposite him. He looked at his tense but handsome
brown face and saw the slight streaks of gray in the close-
cropped coal-black hair. "Man, you sure as hell buying yourself a boatload of grief.

"Another drink?" he suggested.

"No booze. Coffee for me—black," said Jeff.

The waiter, Floyd, hovered into view. His tired, flat-footed
shuffle, like a distinctive signature, reflected the millions of
miles his occupation had required him to walk across the
dining rooms of America.

Perky Sparhawk ordered and Floyd dutifully cleared away
the dishes and served them both. Jeff caught the odor of
licorice clinging to the waiter; probably Floyd had been
drinking Pernod again before his late arrival at The Back
Door.

"Lots of new faces tonight," Jeff said, casually surveying
the long, rectangular-shaped room.

"Yeah, but your overhead eats you up alive—specially
since I don't sell none of them kick-your-mammy brands! So,
you hafta wait for nights like this so you can meet them

[6]

bills." He paused reflectively and added, "Man, believe me, there ain't nothin' so regular as the first of the month."

He watched the cash register jingle and thought of his limited seating capacity, the cost of entertainment, rent and food, and the hundreds of additional expenses of such an unpredictable enterprise, like the five dollars in graft he had just given a building inspector for closing his eyes to The Back Door's faulty electrical wiring which violated the city ordinances.

Perky had always been a free-wheeler and it was history that had shaped his free-wheeling policy.

Harlem during the 1920's became something of a vogue as "Nigger Heaven" after the publication of Carl Van Vechten's novel of that title. Perky Sparhawk's place, actually a speakeasy in those days, attracted many white people who genuinely loved jazz and colored entertainers. But among the crowds there were, of course, men who chased after the jazzy Jezebels, and their Negro counterparts who hunted foot-loose white girls.

The police authorities began watching this sharply to discourage them from coming to Harlem, and unescorted white women or those escorted by Negroes were harassed and embarrassed on the streets en route to The Back Door. The more timid were frequently turned back as they came from the nearby subway station; and if mixed couples walked the streets any distance, patrol cars bore down on them with sirens screaming and red lights flashing, the police pursuing, mauling, and dragging them as if they were criminals.

Sparhawk's perverse soul relished the pain his policy caused skin-proud white men. However, he had wit enough to realize that if he were to continue operating he must find a dodge, at least to muffle the bias of the police officers who walked the beat in front of The Back Door. He therefore came to terms with their superiors and was able to transform

[7]

his place into a "club" to which, in theory at least, one had to be a member to be admitted. Thus he was able to bar anyone. He not only excluded the rank-and-file patrolmen, but if the whim took him, he turned away trashy whites and round-heel blacks.

But lately he had had to cut corners. After the brief heyday after Repeal, beginning with the economic debacle of 1929, which produced a black, crepe-hanging period in Harlem, there had been a steady decline in goods consumption; and now, nine years later, many of his customers were still hard pushed for the price of a meal, and were in an ugly, frustrated mood, which had already erupted in mass rioting, the angry destruction of property, and in scores of people being carted off to Harlem Hospital.

—3—

Jeff sat drinking another cup of coffee, studying Perky. The man's big, round proportions gave him a fictitious bulk; indeed, at first glance this, plus his work-worn hands, beady eyes and bullet head with a slanted forehead, seemed to mark him as an unfeeling peasant; but they were not accurate reflections of the man's inner yearnings.

He had been born and reared, actually, near a little town in South Carolina named Beaufort, which he pronounced Bewferd, and as a boy he had helped his father work the land. He had watched the brightly colored trains speed by, biding his time until he grew big enough to satisfy his ambition to wear the spic-and-span blues and shiny silver buttons of the Pullman porters, a uniform that afterward made him feel like "somebody." From then on, up the ladder to The Back Door.

Jeff asked, "How's Sherri?"

They had been quarreling, Perky admitted, bristling.

"Man, that woman jes won't do right—much as I've done for her. Why, her drawers were more holey than righteous when I met her. Now, she wants to floor-show me!

"I don't know what's come over women," Perky went on, his voice hankering after the girls of the tasty buffet-flats back in the days when snowfalls used to pile belly-high to a man. "Never had no trouble with them; maybe this one has it too good, an' is spoilin' for—"

Jeff interrupted. "Maybe she's just waiting for you to make the first move—toward a make-up."

Perky emptied his glass with one gulp. "I've tole her more'n once, we can't make it, let's forsake it!"

"Anyway, she's got guts," said Jeff fervently, recalling the built-in problems she had stoutly faced.

"You mean—gall!"

—4—

Perky had both exploited Sherri, known as "Sherl," and loved her, in a way. As he shared her with other men, his resentment and violent temper often showed. But as an entertainer she was important to the success of The Back Door. Her attraction was decidedly not talent. This fact the Negro women who frequented the place quickly and jealously recognized. Even so, she brought the customers flocking because rumor had declared her to be a white woman who was passing as a Negro, a not uncommon switch in Harlem, and the insinuation had excited lingering curiosity. She had, too, a valuable gift as an experienced, amiable trouper; she was capable of the snappy comeback to drunks and hecklers without taking or giving offense.

Sherl enjoyed a position in Harlem far out of proportion to her actual social and personal worth, and she had guile enough to develop a peculiar folkway that assigned romantic qualities to white women which they possessed in no more abundance than other women. Perky, whom her theatrical manager-agent, Knox Gilbert, often described as a "black barnum," had shrewdly invented and furthered her harmless hoax, and afterward danced attendance to her in a manner that was as gallant as it was threatening. To complete her novitiate as an authentic jazz singer, which she believed she could become only by intimacies with the high priests in the jazz temples of Harlem, she was hard pressed to withstand the prerogatives that Perky had insisted upon as her "sponsor" and employer and yet also to satisfy the demands of Knox Gilbert for time in bed.

–5–

Jeff liked Perky Sparhawk, but some of his antics irritated him. The proprietor's abuse of white people was sometimes shocking. One night, for example, Perky had torn up the bill of a protesting customer and hurled the pieces in his face, shouting, "If white men could castrate all Negro males, they'd be no race problem. It ain't nothin' but sex competition!"

Jeff had, in fact, a certain sympathy for the older man's present emotional dilemma; yet how on earth Perky could make such an ass of himself over a white woman Jeff couldn't imagine. Now all the man's rancor and jealousy was focused in rage at Sherl's latest piece of extravagance (and duplicity), which he proceeded angrily to report.

Blumstein's store, leading a revolutionary change in retailing policy in Harlem, had recently opened its charge (credit) accounts to Negro customers; and Perky, a staunch believer in deferred payments, had opened one for Sherl. But she had bought a fox piece without telling him. Not only did he have to pay for it, but the girl had the brass to wear it to the Shalimar escorted by Satin Cosey, whose red turban, goatee, and weird trumpet playing had brought him local renown.

Jeff wiped his mouth with a napkin. He wanted to say, "Let's face it—the woman's dead wrong for you!" But instead he kept quiet in deference to the older man's feelings.

Perky bowed his head and considered his situation unhappily. He mumbled something about always being "misused by ofays," his face quivered with self-pity, and after a few minutes he left.

The proprietor was normally a generous man, as most young musicians would testify. His helping hand was legendary. Whenever they were unemployed he frequently fed them and, equally important, allowed them afterward to sit in with the band (a practice that outraged the business agent of the Musicians' Union). These young men's moods often carried them into vague, untried areas which were the beginnings of new ideas, techniques, harmonic structures, and melodic phrasings. Jeff once suggested to Perky that these sessions might give him a place in jazz history, but the proprietor had said, "The stuff don't sell."

Perky may not have been able to predict the place he might achieve in the history of jazz; but he saw grief ahead for somebody, because these wild, uninhibited guys who often sexualized their instruments were unduly attractive to Sherl. But he hadn't noticed their seizures of hysterical paralysis, periods when they were unable to play a note, periods when they were unable to perform the sexual act. By this he might have been consoled.

Instead, he had reached deeply into his fund of loosely gathered knowledge to rationalize Sherl's conduct. He suspected that in some mysterious way she was "teched" by what he believed was the phallic symbolism of the jazz instruments; for, as a "Geechee" from coastal South Carolina, he had inherited the superstitious beliefs of his sorcery-ridden forebears who held totem concepts. The truth was, however, that Sherl was a potential camp-follower, ready to join that unorganized band of amiable whores who trailed the army of jazzmen and catered to their outlandish appetites.

Harlem had no two opinions about her. The mere mention of her name made people look from one to the other with speculative smirks. Many, no doubt including the sensitive editors of The Penguin Club's *Weekly Bulletin*, mouthpiece of an organization of Negroes married to white people, believed that ". . . a good stomping was the only thing that would bring her to her senses." These were mostly female opinions.

Maybe, then, there was some sort of inverted sense of justice in everyone hoping Sherl would get hers. Under the stings of needling even Perky mused, "May hafta beat this bitch yet!" And with that thought he was seized by one of those queer shiverings which warned him there were footsteps on his grave. He was indeed capable of running amok, if very juiced-up; but he was firmly restrained by thoughts of being dragged off to jail, asked harassing questions by the police, and afterward the prospect of having to suffer the endless, loud-mouthed nagging of his wife, Tempie.

Short of actually beating his mistress, Perky had noisily promised to knock her on her "fat, sassy ass" and let the situation rest there; but lately he had taken to brooding, and sometimes he turned bitterly on the world in a vain effort to relieve the pressure he felt. He often had fits of blackest depression; another turn of the screw and even Jeff wouldn't vouch for Perky—a fact that worried everybody, and many were fearful that some untoward incident might touch off anti-Negro riots or in some manner bring down the wrath of the white community of Harlem, at least that segment that hung around The Back Door.

–6–

By now there was an air of contagious conviviality in The Back Door and Jeff felt it. Tired of the brown nudes in the mural behind the bar, he watched Floyd nimbly twirl the tray aloft, balance it dexterously on one finger as he circulated between the tables; then he casually looked over the bumptious crowd. He tried to pigeonhole the variety of types crushed three-deep at the bar. They were, in the language of the Negro press, clabber-whites, kinky-haired blacks, yellow-skinned redheads, ebony-skinned blonds, coffee-and-cream browns, and many types between that defied description at all; yet he realized that in their kinship they formed a miniature portrait of Harlem.

Perky came back to his seat opposite Jeff and ordered another drink. They didn't talk much. The older man eyed his young companion and sighed. He felt keenly that Jeff was not making the most of his abilities, and an old saying came to his mind: *Dog that got bone, ain't got no teeth; and dog that got teeth, ain't got no bone!* "The boy's born in New York, has a college education, old man's no pauper, and he got a lot on the ball—yet nothin' happens! Maybe if he'd stay tight with a smart broad like Zabee he'd be in clover . . . well, somethin' oughta be done—and tonight could be the night!"

He said, "How 'bout doin' a number, Jeff?"

"Sing?"

"Yeah."

"For kicks, maybe, but don't try palming me off as a singer."

"No singer!" he exclaimed. "Man, I ain't heard no better."

[13]

Perky, trying to keep the discussion in this groove in spite of a note of impatience in Jeff's shrug, added, "You know, you could make yourself some real loot singin', and settle down in a nice crib with Zabee."

He pronounced the girl's name as if it rhymed with Abie; this always nettled Jeff. "Perky, her name is *Zah*-bee, like a French word."

"Aaah, Zaah-beee," Perky repeated dutifully, as if the word were a juicy delicacy he was rolling around on his tongue.

"Let's not bring her into this, anyway."

Perky wagged his head like a man in the know. "Well, she's got some mileage on her, but she's got big, big eyes for you, as everybody knows—and *she* thinks—" He broke off meaningfully.

Jeff was silent, and Perky saw now that he would have to handle the boy differently. But his conspiratorial air made Jeff suspect he might have something up his sleeve.

Suddenly a draft that caused Perky to shiver slightly drew the proprietor's eyes in the direction of the open door. "Well, well, here comes your 'boon coons,'" he said.

Jeff's eyes lit up.

Three men about his own age ambled up to the table, and one swung his arm around Jeff's shoulders. After much noisy greeting, they seated themselves and ordered drinks.

This was his crowd and they had gotten into the habit of meeting at The Back Door, where they talked about their vague projects and the problems of being Negro. They laughed together, often teased each other unmercifully; but they looked upon the world with audacious eyes.

"And where's Zabee?" they asked in unison. Tonight they had planned the get together, for the first time in several weeks.

"Yeah!" said Perky, "ain't your girl friend comin' tonight?"

Jeff was forced to say, "I honestly don't know."

"What's with you two?" asked Benn, a banjo-eyed, pock-marked, ginger-colored fellow whose consumptive look made the crowds call him "Spongy Boy." Daytime he worked as a bellhop at the Times Square Hotel. He wore a skimpy jacket, but this bore no relation to the fact that he was also a candidate for the ministry.

"Nothing, really."

Jeff's defensive tone of voice brought a cynical snort from Dave, a mahogany-skinned painter who worked the WPA.

"The guy's being cagey."

"Well, stop pushing," admonished Fess half crankily and gave them the forbidding look he usually reserved for the pupils he taught at Public School No. 89.

Fess had taken a seat where his long legs made it difficult for anyone to pass him. He looked at anyone who did pass with mock resentment; but every once in a while his brown skin crinkled in humor around his intelligent eyes. He turned to Jeff.

"Hear you're headed for the big time!"

"Hope so; who told you?"

"Your sister, Priscilla—she says she got it from you."

Fess looked at him thoughtfully, and across Jeff's hand-somely candid young face there came the intent, anxious expression his companions knew so well. He had all at once remembered, with a sensation of excitement and foreboding, that a symphonic work he had composed was scheduled for a performance. As any Negro might be, he was supersti-tiously cautious, fearful talk might put "bad mouth" on the project. He said uneasily, "I'm not sure, yet."

"You? a guy who's already won prizes—" Fess shrugged. "Of course, you'll do your stuff!"

"Yeah—if the ofays give him a chance," Dave added.

There was a chorused "Amen."

Jeff felt deep gratitude at their inverted applause. He knew if he succeeded, they would share his emotion. Then he heard the rustle of a dress very near to him, turned around—and there was Zabee. The dress of Haitian fabric fitted her trimly. Her fluid exciting movements betrayed her occupation as a dancer.

Jeff got up, and pushing a chair up to her, said warmly, "What about a drink, stranger?"

Zabelle Desvigny smiled her acceptance, and her emerald-green eyes, partly hidden by long lashes, swept the faces of the assembled young men who had stood and greeted her with mock homage.

The sudden sight of her struck Jeff oddly, and he had to revamp his feelings.

They had quarreled two months ago. He had hardly seen anything of her since. Now, at his invitation, here she was in the chair next to his. Her hands were clasped in her lap. The light caught her so that he could see her features clearly, as he remembered them, excitingly provocative. But now her faint, meaningful smile momentarily disturbed him.

—7—

Zabee, a chummy version of Zabelle, which she had come by in her tomboy girlhood in New Orleans, was a Creole, tall and shapely, with a waist, between her well-developed breasts and hips, as slender as the leaves of Guiana grass. Her blue-black hair was set in a neat bun at the nape of her neck. She had long tapering legs, silky light brown skin, and a profile as regal as the sculptured head of the Egyptian Queen Nefertiti, whose slanted eyes and elegantly long neck she faintly echoed.

By design, her clothes were made of African and Haitian fabrics, her long jangling earrings and her rich tan make-up all emphasized the exotic aspects of her Negro ancestry. She often carried this theme to dramatic proportions in the costumes she created for her dance routines. For, as a colored creole with Caucasian-looking features, she felt she was too frequently mistaken for a white girl—but, as Jeff once said in response to her complaint, being a Negro is an idea that becomes real only when your skin is black and you look or smell or sound as people think a Negro should, and thus set in motion those subtle reactions which make such people reach down and dredge up muck from a secret well of prejudice.

Zabee was a sensible sort, and hardly flattered by the mistakes about her racial identity. But the combination of softly delineated features and creamy, sepia-tinted skin was one of the things that always gave Jeff a peculiar satisfaction of the senses when he was with her, and particularly when he slept with her. He remembered Ma Henry's topfloor bedroom. He could see again the broad brass bed with the two towels always neatly folded across each pillow, the unused birdcage in the corner, and the venetian blinds, like the eyelids of the dead, shutting out the tumult beyond.

"You haven't changed," he said.

"No? We had a ghastly time in Miami, that is, the troup and I. Miami has a curfew for Negroes. We had to have special transportation after hours, special accommodations, special bathrooms, special everything. To cross the bridge back from the white sections of town to the colored—separated by chains incidentally—we had to show passes. Imagine that!"

"Wow!" exclaimed Benn, while Jeff eyed her with new admiration.

The conversation was slow at first but was livened up by Dave, who was chewing on a warmed-over topic: Perky ought to use the club's wasted wall space to exhibit the work of Negro painters. The proprietor, as if in haste to escape him, suddenly scrambled to his feet and rushed to the entrance. There he greeted a white couple who had a triumphant appearance of well-being. His obsequious bows focused extravagant attention on their arrival: dark faces eyed them as they gingerly threaded their way through an aisle of tables, and ripples of comment followed like those provoked by the entry of a celebrity.

—8—

Jeff looked up just as the girl was coming down the aisle. She had a distinctively delicate skin and a well-bred manner. Her smile was open, and what he could hear of her well-modulated voice was cool, gentle, exciting . . .

Dave, who was saying that the cluttered mural behind the bar was a "monstrosity," lost his audience in a deep silence. They all could hear Perky's surprisingly cordial tones as he led the way to a table and busily brushed imaginary crumbs from the tablecloth, while his gold tooth gleamed happily.

"Did you see that?" Benn asked at large, and like the others was taken aback by the congeniality of Perky's welcome.

"Now that's a *real* ofay!" Dave exclaimed.

"For painting?" asked Fess, and had visions of standing before Dave's creation—which undoubtedly would be brightly colored, frightening, but strident and symbolic.

"Yeah, for painting—and for loving, too."

" 'White is Right!' don't they say?" said Benn, laughing.

"Yeah, but what a woman!"

And Benn joined Dave in a low whistle of admiration. But they were quieted by a look from Jeff.

He had detected the undercurrent of racial hostility and thought: "As a people will we ever really like white people?"

He himself had always liked individual whites, feeling at home with their humor, their tastes, their cooking; but he could sometimes look at them with an objectivity that made race missionaries declare him poor material for their brand of crusades.

Jeff seemed aloof now, taking no part in the ribaldry of his friends; but his musings were suddenly invaded by Dave, who asked him somewhat deferentially for his opinion of the white girl.

Jeff didn't answer, his mind a million miles away.

Fess, whose disenchantment at being dropped from the faculty of a Southern state college for racial radicalism had caused him to pause and wonder—until he had untracked himself and had started writing a book to reconstruct the Negro's historical past, was halfway wondering whether what his companions were saying ought to find a place in his book.

Then Benn, an imp dancing in his big, round eyes, turned to Zabee. "Good-looking, isn't she?"

They all watched Zabee curiously.

She stared for a moment at Spongy Boy. Then she smiled. It seemed to Jeff that she was mocking them.

But Zabee sat there, resenting the girl's delicate white skin, translated into her creole French, a skin *blanc,* without blemish. It was seductive in a way not to be overlooked. Moreover, Zabee, now nearing thirty-seven, fiercely resented the difference in their ages. She judged the white girl to be in her early twenties, and it did not console her that she herself looked much younger than her age.

Finally, she said quietly, "Oh, yes, indeed, she's quite, quite lovely."

But she was thinking: "She's cold, some people'd say she looks like a statue, like Venus or somebody; me, I'd say she looks like a great white cat, who maybe hasn't learned to velvet her claws."

Jeff listened vaguely to his companions, and what he said now was mostly obtuse and pointless, for he could not keep his eyes off the girl who had just come in. Suddenly he wanted very much to talk to her. He was normally not an intriguer. But this disquieting sensation prompted him to start scheming a way to meet her. Her glacial exterior soon discouraged daydreaming—and everything seemed wild, impossible, futile. . . .

He lit a cigarette, determinedly keeping his restless fingers from shaking.

Zabee, who thought she knew Jeff so well, watched him almost maliciously—and jealous suspicions stung her when she saw him look at the ofay with what seemed a strange longing.

II

Deborah Comstock and Knox Gilbert sat opposite the long, polished bar. The girl had a feeling she was being stared at by a young man at an adjoining table, and she was alarmed. What was she supposed to do? ("Colored people can be so terribly sensitive!") Smile? Or turn away?

She looked at Gil. He was bent over, absorbed, studying a list of drinks. So she calmly tried to concentrate on the naked brown girls dancing behind the bar in what she afterward described as one of the most unlikely forests in night club art.

Deborah was hot and perspiring. Her dress clung to her like wet paper. Her damp shoes pinched at the toes. She felt conspicuous and a trifle uneasy among so many Negroes, and was annoyed, too, for having succumbed to Gil's persuasion to join him in this fruitless tour of the Harlem circuit.

She again turned to her companion. "I'm bushed, Gil—how about you?"

"We won't be too long now," he said. "Give me a few minutes to finish up a little business with the proprietor."

Her eyes wandered in a casual survey of the narrow, low-

[21]

ceilinged cellar whose precise dimensions were lost in the jumbled mass of people, and involuntarily she looked in the direction of the young man sitting next to her. He was joking with his friends. His laugh, deep and infectious, was attractive. It somewhat dispelled her fears and quickened her curiosity about him. When their eyes finally met, she quickly averted hers and watched the men and women who formed an irresistible dance tableau of lively figures and provocative postures—a sight Breugel might have relished, she thought.

Deborah felt the amiable atmosphere of The Back Door without gratitude. But she admitted to herself that it was different from any of the other places they had visited during the evening—all so alien to her own bland but well-upholstered environment. For the moment she only knew she wanted to escape the noise and smoke. She sucked in a lungful which almost made her yawn, and was about to plead again to leave, when the man who had been introduced to her as the proprietor pulled up a chair, and, without invitation, sat down alongside Gil. His manner was wheedling, and he pitched his voice accordingly, like someone about to make a proposal to a superior. Even with the eyes of an amateur, Deborah could see that her escort had prestige with the fat man.

"How's business?" Gil asked, sparring until the proprietor showed his cards.

"Good! I can say without blowin' my own horn that I make it, 'cause I only shows top talent!"

"Is that so?" Gil said, neatly blending belief with skepticism.

Knox Gilbert was an old hand at appraising selling techniques, and particularly shockproof to Sparhawk's propositions, especially his enthusiasms involving new talent. For years Perky had trotted out big-eyed, wistful aspirants for

celebrity, whose performance, at least to the agent's satisfaction, interred the popular legend that all Negroes can
sing, dance, or toot a horn. Of course there was always the
chance that he might come up with a real find. It was, actually, this prospect that had brought Knox Gilbert to The
Back Door tonight.

Perky leaned toward Gil, whom he judged to be about his
own age ("fifty if he's a day old!"), and half smiled as though
he held a secret all his own. The proprietor had turned his
back to Deborah, and she noticed with distaste that he oozed
perspiration which smelled faintly of a lavender-like toilet
water. He had several layers of flesh back of his bulging
neck that looked like webs on a squat screw. He rubbed his
sweaty hands as prelude to speaking, and then she heard him
address her companion with repressed excitement.

"I've really got somethin' terrific tonight, Mr. Gilbert—
somethin' a manager like you could parlay into big dough!"

The agent, whose sharp and finely chiseled head with its
long nose and narrow mouth sometimes caused him to be
mistaken for a Jew, shrugged. He said at last: "Who the
devil did you corral?"

"Wait. Lemme show you."

"Not one of your turkeys?"

Perky raised his eyes heavenward, as if to call in God's
supporting testimony. "Me! show you a turkey? You got me
wrong." He put his finger to his lips to signify silence. "Shhh,"
he said. "Jes wait."

Perky was saturated with all the prejudice and legends of
his race, and believed that elaborate flattery was the essence
of every transaction with a white man. He was playing this
little farce now.

He coughed lightly, and turning to the girl, said, "And
you'll really like this too, Miss Deborah, though, as a top

manager, I think Mr. Gilbert would hafta be the judge—no offense meant, miss."

Without direct connection, he elaborated on the esteem in which he held the agent and fulsomely described to her the quality of Knox Gilbert's "stable of performers," which, he reported, was the basis of her escort's reputation, perhaps a basis of envy. (An equal asset in Gilbert's own view of himself was the enduring belief along Broadway and Madison Avenue that he knew when to dangle bait, when to simulate diffidence, when to play hard to get, and, at a profit, how to pace a singer, actor, dancer or musician to stardom.)

But Perky's extravagant opinion only brought a crooked smile to Gil's thin lips. The agent was keenly aware that Madison Avenue's advertising executives, with whom he dealt in providing talent for their clients' radio shows, regarded him as "only a hack of the trade." He was, in fact, a victim of snobbery because he represented so many Negro performers, a not altogether altruistic enterprise. The Rialto called his office "Uncle Tom's Cabin." But he hoped one day to achieve the chrome and glass, the titular power of the impressario. This drove him on his endless searches in places like The Back Door for someone with the potential of a great artist, perhaps of Carnegie Hall stature.

Gil was silent for a while. He flicked an ash from his dark gray Brooks suit, well-tailored to the current Ivy League costume, and thought of all the 'fly chippies' Sparkhawk had tried to unload on him. He looked sadly at Perky and said, "No—not again. Not a white girl!"

This remark had an explosive effect he had not intended, but both Perky and Deborah were shocked. The violence of his candor seemed obscene.

"Oh, dear," thought the girl, and her confusion increased when she felt the young man's eyes resting on her again with a strange, searching look.

[24]

Perky straightened up, and a half smile slowly curled his thick lips. He wet them uneasily and clearly managed to show that he was offended by the manager's remark; but he also recognized that he now had him at a disadvantage because race had been introduced into the discussion.

The smell of Perky's cigar, on which he had begun to draw heavily, suddenly assailed Gil's nostrils, and Gil heard himself challenged aggressively.

"What's wrong 'bout a white girl—if you're not prejudiced." There was a kind of stern self-righteousness in Perky's voice; and behind his outburst seemed to sound the rumbling violence of angry generations before him. His kinky hair, his spade-black skin, his bulging eyes, gave him at this moment the tragic look of Porgy.

Perky was frightened by the effect he had produced, yet he plunged on with his slantwise approach. Leaning back in his chair, he spoke out with malice. "Well, if what I hear is gospel, you gave the Shannon kid the bum's rush 'cause of me."

The tone of his voice brought color to Gil's face, and to Deborah's as well.

"Whaddya mean, bum's rush?" Under stress Gil's language frequently echoed the gutter.

"You know 'zactly what I mean," Perky replied cryptically, trying to justify himself by bullying.

He was not so deeply offended as he pretended by what the manager had said; but in maintaining a posture of racial injury, although it was wholly fraudulent, he was able to employ an old ruse he used to maneuver white people into a defensive position. He was so convincing that even he himself mistook it for the genuine article.

Deborah, innocent of Harlem, was embarrassed both by Gil's bluntness and Perky's hurt look. Her ideas about the different races, complicated already by her abolitionist ancestors and her snobbish up-bringing, became somewhat confused, and she couldn't think of anything to say, and she wondered how the young man would have acted in a similar situation.

Finally, assuming that her escort had, like herself, no hostility to Negroes, she said, "Surely Mr. Gilbert doesn't mean quite what you're thinking, Mr. Sparhawk."

Then she was annoyed by the ineptness of her little speech.

Neither of the two men spoke. They had almost simultaneously cast meaningful glances at a fleshy, auburn-haired young woman who had come in quietly and was now seated at the bar sipping a cocktail. A spotlight played on a rotating mirrored chandelier, hanging in the room's center, which cast myriad reflections across her rose-colored features. She had a cigarette poised in her hand. She smoked with elaborate casualness, and as Perky suddenly left his seat next to Gil and joined her at the bar, she took the cigarette from her lips in a long, swooping motion.

"Sherri Shannon," Gil said. "They call her Sherl—that one sings for her supper."

"Oh!" Deborah said. That was all, but there was a feline quality in her voice.

"Love's a queer thing, a damned crazy thing sometimes," Gil said speculatively and stopped. What the inspiration was for this sudden piece of philosophy he did not say, but an impulse to unbosom himself had almost overcome him—but not quite.

"The Greeks made love a goddess," Deborah said.

"Yeah, but did the Greeks have a word for dames like Sherl?" He jerked a thumb in Perky's direction. "She's that fathead's girl friend. How about that!"

"I fancied she might be," said Deborah dryly, but she was

startled as she watched the pink-skinned female and the sweaty black man.

At first she had only casually looked at the girl; but now, observing her more carefully, she was somewhat surprised to discover that the girl was actually white. Indeed, she might have been lifted from a painting by a Flemish master. Her shoulders were fairly broad for a girl's. But she had fine breasts and she flaunted them proudly. The glaring green chiffon dress she wore flared widely at the bottom, and was cut low to the fold of her breasts—obvious, but fitted by somebody who knew the tricks of feminine appeal. Deborah was unaccustomed to such aggressive sex.

Knox Gilbert served as Sherl's manager; but although physically involved with her, he frowned on her loose goings-on and her uproarious way of living. He was convinced that she was fated for a tawdry end. Sherl was addicted to the frivolities of the bed, and Gil on more than one occasion had had to extricate her from scrapes that ended with stabbings in hotel corridors between midnight and dawn.

Whenever he attempted to criticize her, she scolded him with snarling vulgarity, and once had even slapped him across the mouth. But as her manager, Gil had the upper hand. Lately, though, there had been a suppressed humility about her that puzzled him—it was an ill wind that bore no good; indeed, a new facet of her personality: silent, intro-verted, perhaps explosive. Even so, his lusty dislike had not declined. He long ago decided not to represent another female like her; but his exasperation held a certain jealousy he was not prepared to admit to himself.

He had written her off as a tramp and troublemaker; no good even for Perky.

Thinking of Perky Sparhawk almost made him want the woman, and this revelation of his relationship to her was somewhat startling to him now. He was actually no more impervious to Sherl's sensuality than other men had been; and his mind went back to the night he had violated her drunken, unresponsive body. The thought of her sleeping with a Negro filled him with revulsion—indeed, he even hated to see white tramps mixing with Negroes at The Back Door's bar, as they were doing tonight. He felt restless and depressed.

The proprietor had come back to his seat next to Gil, and both men were now hunched over the table as if the glasses before them were documents they were studying. Both had, during this mute encounter, the feeling that they had torn open an old wound; and anyway, Perky decided, this was not the moment to stand on principles.

A wheezy note from the saxophone, unnoticed by Gil, suddenly intruded upon Perky's thoughts, and he found himself drumming his fingers on the table impatiently. He had lately supplemented the piano, bass fiddle, and guitar at considerable expense by hiring a fellow who played the saxophone and called himself Linton Brokenburr. There was a lot of music in the instrument if the boy would only put some guts into it, he thought irritably, and sighed wearily. These musicians!

Deborah, her head slightly cocked to grasp any nuances of meaning, soon sensed that the two men shared a common frame of reference involving the sexy, auburn-haired young woman they called Sherl; and, without a word had carried through their struggle, and now had come to a mutual, if wordless, understanding. A fraternal glance exchanged between them made it clear that Deborah was not to be admitted to the intimacies of their thoughts, which had raged now and subsided.

Deborah studied the sulky, melancholy face of the young woman.

Sherl crushed out her cigarette, and a quick resolve in-

stantly transformed her face into a smile. Then she stepped
down from the bar stool, and gliding, aloof yet personal,
moved from table to table, patting a cheek here, squeezing
a hand there, as she toured the room and throatily greeted
her admirers.

"Dahlings!" she said expansively as she reached Gil's table
and paused. Her voice was low-pitched and pleasant.

Both men nodded, but there was a second of suspense
before she moved on. Gil had not introduced her to Deborah,
nor had Perky. Sherl's self-possession never deserted her,
though, and a strange smile came to her lips; but as she
swished imperiously past them, a subtle antagonism came
alive in her.

Deborah noticed that in her wake trailed an odor of perfume that demanded attention: it was musky, nocturnal, full
of erotic suggestions—and Deborah realized that the smell
served the young woman's feminine motives perfectly.

She said to Gil, "She does belong, doesn't she?"

"Yeah, she cottons to the type!"

–2–

Perky had indulged himself in his race's talent for indirection at the expense of Gil's discomfort, and he had fulfilled
the inscrutable law of his people to confound the white man.
He of course well understood that the agent had expedient
reasons for rejecting a type like Sherl. But as he saw he
could not keep up pretenses with Knox Gilbert, he burst into
laughter, and explained somewhat elaborately that he had
been talking about a colored fellow, who had been the subject of the note that had brought the manager to The Back
Door tonight.

"Now, that's a horse of another color!" Gil said curtly.

"The kid's big money, if I ever saw a dollar!" Perky enthused lamely. He hoped to whet the manager's appetite, but there was no conviction in his voice.

Gil was silent. "Don't give a good goddamn," he thought, and hardly listened to the proprietor's voluble effusions, annoyed as he was.

After a while he turned back toward the proprietor and grunted, "Okay, let me see what you got."

Deborah watched as slow, sulky anger burned brighter in Gil's eyes.

Perky lifted himself from his chair, stepped out on the floor, and, with a vast display of his gold tooth, introduced Jeff Kirby.

The ceiling chandelier dimmed and blinked out, conversation declined and died, a spotlight picked up the tall figure in a dark blue suit; and much to Deborah's surprise, it was the young man seated at the table next to hers, who stood, smiled, and walked to the piano.

From her seat in the dark beyond the spotlight's rim, she watched him intently. He was supple and brawny and brown; his close-cropped hair was jet-black, a trifle crinkly, with wisps of premature gray about the temples. He had an attractive face, clean-cut, boyish, the dark eyes large and intense, the lips full and sensuously expressive, and she smiled to herself when she thought that he might have been one of those gangling youngsters, with braces on his teeth and bizarre pets, whom aunts, sisters, and female cousins tried to spoil; yet he had character in his face, and seemingly had stored in himself considerable manly strength, maybe erotic power.

He set his own stage—with a husky, resonant baritone voice and an exotic, taut body. There was an involuntary gasp from the women in the audience. ("There's a man— Mister Jesus!!") He was nervous and awkward, but what he lacked in showmanship he made up for in real appeal and

a voice charged with explosive feelings. Afterward Deborah
found it difficult to remember precisely what she had felt—
she did not even remember the songs; but she was always
to recall the voice with deep tones from the bottomless sadness of his race, and again and again she was to wonder
what grief racked a young man like him.

"Wow!" someone yelled, and was roundly echoed as Jeff
finished, softly and without flourish.

The lights went up and a dozen or more people rushed to
the piano. They pumped his hand, slapped his back, and
noisily shouted their applause—indeed, everyone gave vent
to their feelings, releasing a paroxysm of loud comments,
whistles, yells and rhythmic hand-clapping.

Jeff accepted the tributes with a grin.

Deborah liked what she saw, and smiled.

Gil, his features unmoved, saw a look on her face that was
new to him; and he wondered what the hell she was thinking about.

"He's a talented sort—don't you think so?" she said.

The manager indulged his habit of looking at people with
a slight slant of the head, and did not reply for quite a while.
He had assumed a posture of objectivity. Finally he gave her
a sidelong glance and said, "Think so?"

Perky, who once had ambitions of becoming an Irish
tenor, if the species would have been accepted in black, was
vastly unhappy: he had expected Jeff to end with a noisy
crescendo, which would have better served the ends of his
salesmanship.

Jeff, still idling at the piano, allowed his gaze to drift
briefly toward Deborah. She instantly retreated behind an
impenetrable dignity, so he could hardly have surmised that
she could not help feeling disturbed whenever she saw his
eyes rest on her now. He shifted his search and caught the
eyes of Perky, who had returned to his seat beside Gil. Jeff

nodded meaningfully in Deborah's direction, which in the idiom of The Back Door meant he had declared himself and had staked a claim to exclusive pursuit of the girl—Knox Gilbert notwithstanding.

Perky subscribed to the customary idea that a white man had few rights in Harlem which the Negro was bound to respect, and almost coldly evaluated this feminine parcel brought into The Back Door by Knox Gilbert: she had class, was modishly dressed, and beautiful—a little too pale, a little too skinny, a little too short, but her eyes, her mouth, her bosom, her hips! He would have whistled in a different situation. "Too good to waste on a white man!" he mused.

His feelings toward white women were simple: he loved and hated them, which perhaps was not very unlike what Jeff Kirby felt. But to Perky possession of them was equated with righteous revolt against the white man's unwritten laws.

Now only practical considerations made him hesitate to encourage Jeff: he could not see the young man running the risk of antagonizing Knox Gilbert for the sake of a flirtation. But a sudden impulse made him feel reckless, and anyway the agent had annoyed him, the building inspector investigating The Back Door's electrical violations had irritated him, and Sherl had gotten in his hair—indeed, tonight, he felt like the "peckerwoods" were arrayed against him. "To hell with them," he thought viciously.

He nodded back to Jeff understandingly, raised his eyebrows slyly in appreciation of the girl's good looks, then to divert Gil's attention unobtrusively engaged him in elaborate conversation to give Jeff a chance.

Jeff's dark eyes returned to the girl.

Deborah's hands were folded on a large, black suede pocketbook with a big gold catch. They were small, shapely hands. Her eyes were bluish gray; her hair appeared genuinely dark blonde—seemingly with dark strands—and it was parted in the middle and clasped at the back like a ballet dancer's with a neatly tied black velvet bow. Her dress was plain black with a frilly white collar and cuffs, cut to fit her slender figure, forming background for a green, lobe-shaped brooch which helped to dramatize her delicate skin. From the V-point of her frock, her neck swept upward gracefully, making her rather sharp nose come as a surprise.

The spotlight touched the black dress and translucent skin of the girl, and Jeff saw her classical profile. Her head turned over so slightly, and she looked at him. Her eyes, large and liquid, seemed to contain faint echoes of his own tumultuous feelings, and his pulse pounded furiously. . . .

–3–

The Back Door was emptying rapidly, so Deborah was somewhat surprised at the sudden gathering of an unclassified assortment of white females—known variously in Harlem's rich jargon as "ofay," "gray," or "pink-meat" chicks —whom Perky had left his seat to greet in performing his duties as host. Besides herself and Sherl, she counted ten seated at the bar. The women were heavily made up, well dressed and glossy, and seemed constrained. They were waiting the arrival of escorts—lovers, husbands, pimps, or "sponsors." One of the girls, known as "Memphis," Gil had told Deborah, was very, very radical, a Columbia graduate student who believed ardently in the Negro's rights. She lived in a small apartment in Greenwich Village, with a large abstract painting of a Negro nude on the wall above her living room couch, and it was there that she liked to be flogged with a wet towel before being made love to.

Deborah thought her presence might embarrass the white women, in some way make them self-conscious; instead, she found herself suspect—their wary eyes betraying hostility.

She soon laughed to herself, and her eyes sought out Jeff Kirby, who had left the piano and with his friends who had been with him at the next table was headed toward a door marked PRIVATE. She saw them trying to persuade one of their group to come with them, and then she shifted her gaze incuriously to two men who appeared to be hangers-on. Perky had identified them as Junkie Joe, a man of explosive and unpredictable violence, thick-bodied and dark; and Spongy Boy, ginger-colored, pockmarked, and tall, whom she recognized as the big-eyed boy who had been seated at Jeff Kirby's table. They were walking about with half-filled glasses, intently observing the white women at the bar as if they were so many head of cattle, so many possessions—especially Junkie Joe.

Deborah looked at her watch and started to say she thought it was time to leave. Then she looked up and saw that all eyes were turned toward a spot between the bar and the juke box. Old Jake, the bartender, looked terrified. Complete silence came over the place.

She looked at Gil. His face was gray but he squeezed her hand reassuringly. Spongy Boy was playfully flirting with one of the white women.

"Her name is Trudie, she's Junkie Joe's girl," Gil whispered.

The quiet and the suspense appalled Deborah. She trembled and she could hear her own breathing. Trudie sat sedately on her bar stool, sipping a drink. She half smiled and shrugged her shoulders. Then, as if she didn't know what to do with her hands, she self-consciously smoothed her reddish-tinted bobbed hair and her blue, too-tight taffeta dress.

Junkie Joe's squat body swayed, his heavy-lidded eyes were bloodshot with rage. He made an ugly snarling sound as he jerked Spongy Boy around, spinning him like a top,

[34]

and shouted, "You goddamn fairy bastard, whatd'ya mean insulting my dame!"

The bellboy-preacher laughed at him.

"You sneaking creep, I'll call the cops and tell 'em you're a no-good shit of a junk peddler!" he screamed in a hysterical soprano voice.

Junkie Joe turned away and bent his head as if he had decided to stop the quarrel. There was a click, and he came up again, flashing something shiny—

"A switchblade!" old Jake screamed.

Spongy Boy stood quiet in fright, his big eyes rolling.

Junkie Joe's arm sneaked up in a violent arc, then stayed there as he sparred for position with small mincing steps like an expert fencer.

Those nearby scattered and the two men were left in a neon-bright arena.

"No! No! No!" Trudie cried as she beat her forehead with her palms.

Deborah grabbed Gil by the sleeve.

"Don't just sit there!"

"There's nothing anybody can do; it's Perky's unwritten law: "Every pot stands on its own bottom."

Deborah bit her lips. She felt as if she were at the top of the downward plunge of a roller coaster. She was horrified and revolted, but she was fascinated and could not turn her head away.

Benn tried to run, but was paralyzed. His prominent Adam's apple moved up and down in his long skinny throat. His lips opened, but his voice was strangled and he could not make a sound.

Junkie Joe's smooth black arm, like a graceful piece of ebony sculpture, did not hint at his tremendous strength. His wrist, too, was smooth and rounded. He wore a bracelet of silver links that gave a perverse touch of vanity to his spectacular capacity for violence.

Now his arm, reversing the arc, flashed down and the blade struck into Spongy Boy's back. The skimpy coat flapped, and there was an audible groan, then the eyes bulged, his yellow pockmarked face grimaced, he staggered a few steps jerkily, and pitched forward. Like a baby crawling, he tried to move on all fours, a dark flow of blood making a line from lips to chin.

Deborah's stomach twisted with nausea. Her own fists were clenched as if she were fighting someone or something. She thought it unbelievable that no one even tried to stop the man from killing the boy.

As Spongy Boy, still crawling on the floor, suddenly managed to attempt to escape, Junkie Joe leaped on him and started to stab him again, then stopped. Instead he kicked him again and again in the face and shouted, "Take him, you whimpering bastards! He won't be having much stink of a woman on him soon."

His face still shapeless with rage, he ran through the door.

Trudie was screaming, "Joe! Joe!" But someone hushed her, and several of the men picked up Spongy Boy, bloody and sobbing, and helped him stagger out.

"Okay, okay—no stampedin', folks!" Perky shouted, using the practical tone that he always used to calm and reassure excited customers. "Act like you ain't never seen a little scuffle! Everythin' groovy, no need for uproar now."

Slowly the tavern came alive again. Jake cleared and washed the floor. The remaining patrons began to talk and order drinks.

Perky came and sat down next to Gil, and put on his most sympathetic expression. He was sorry such things happened, but assured Deborah and Gil that Spongy Boy was only a "blow top." Then, at Gil's suggestion, he had Floyd fetch a cup of black coffee to settle Deborah's stomach.

Astonished, Deborah observed that Perky's basement, like life itself, hardly missed a beat in the rhythm of its ebullient existence. Jeff Kirby and his friends had returned. They were obviously disturbed, but now they sat down again and slowly accepted the renewed liveliness of the room.

–4–

Negroes can be ugly and dangerous when things inside pain them, Gil had told Deborah. But the unexpected character of the attack on Spongy Boy, like an inexplicable dream, was sickening, and she still felt it deep down in her stomach; yet one day she would learn that Negroes are rarely on the side of heroic folly, or desperate savagery, with no hope for final victory. But Junkie Joe's blind urge toward destruction gave her a frightening glimpse of what lies in the dark of many Negroes' hearts and what violence has lurked for centuries beneath their patient endurance—what contrary ideas she had had about her mother's maid, Sarah, and handyman Poe!

Deborah had watched the Trudie woman curiously, and was conscious that she had been unnaturally intimate in a public place. How could she cling to and fondle an ugly, brutal man like Junkie Joe. She had said so to Gil.

"Lots of females, like lots of males, are just naturally perverse. She probably likes her men tough and elemental. Maybe she's tough and elemental, too. Likely they're emotional kinfolk."

But Deborah wasn't satisfied by Gil's cynically glib reply. Was this the role played by white women who frequented Harlem? She found herself wondering about her own undoubted interest in Jeff Kirby. It frightened her. Deborah, in

spite of her daring and apparent poise, was not truly coura-
geous. Was Trudie a warning to an outwardly calm Bos-
tonian? She wanted violently to know more about Trudie.
She demanded Gil tell her all he knew.

"You want to understand too much too fast!" he said and
laughed, but he complied.

–5–

Trudie, a Slavic peasant type who chewed her fingernails,
was a social waif. She had first come to Harlem shy and
stammering, with the unvarnished look of a sweat shop
worker. At forty-three, unmarried, she had felt useless, old,
finished—and just when she was on the verge of losing her
mind in her cold isolation, a porter in the factory where she
worked slipped her a note inviting her to visit The Back
Door. She had emerged from her tenement room, abandoned
the frowzy pink bunny that had slept in her bed since childhood, and in an otherwise drab, routinized existence filled
with fearful boredom she found adventure. She soon grasped
the fact that a white skin and dyed hair, even if it was
matched by a plain face, snub nose, and freckles, gave her
an advantage in competition with Negro girls. ("Man, it
ain't the beauty—it's the booty!" explained the curbstone
philosophers.)

Trudie was very ready to love and be loved and she soon
abandoned her porter for Junkie Joe—uncritical, flattered,
easily amused, and lonely like herself; but under compulsions
of warily side-stepping disaster, implicit in her every trip to
the Negro neighborhood, she was kept in a constant state
of anxiety. If she had not had a peasant's superb instinct for
survival or, perhaps, tact enough not to ignite to blazing
anger the smoldering jealousies of the Negro women, who
firmly believed white women came to Harlem only to

swindle or whore, in all likelihood she would have been driven from the section. ("Those white women," said Negro women, in a definitely virtuous tone, "must have certain ways of doing things which they use on these silly men.") This was all Gil knew or cared to tell.

—6—

Tonight as Trudie had come in to The Back Door, she had looked over the male contingent, had deliberately flirted with Spongy Boy, and he had responded. She merely wanted to prove to herself that she had not sunk to such depths as to be unworthy of attention by men other than Junkie Joe—and her man had misunderstood, even though she had tried hard to be loved by him. "I started out makin' a woman outa you and I'm gonna finish the job," Junkie Joe had once told her triumphantly.

For her part, it had given her intense pleasure to contemplate initiating this black peasant, so wonderfully ignorant, into the ways and manners of her knowledge. ("What I'd like," she frequently said, "is to see him develop a taste for the finer things.") But Trudie reached for something which all her life had eluded her. And she, in violently sexual embraces, clinging desperately, pleading silently, had sought from Junkie Joe something he could not give her.

If some perversity within her loved to be loved as she was, she nevertheless was left unsatiated—her haunted eyes betrayed this around their gay edges. In the long run, the shabby interludes to which she was a party demolished her dignity and reinforced her isolation from the white community; and now, like a drug addict, she had to feed her habit of intimacies with blacks, however clumsily, to give her life a shabby meaning. If her tragedy dismayed the few who knew her intimately, Trudie had the triumphant status of being an ofay in Harlem—a separate breed of woman, exciting, wanted, and somebody quite special.

—7—

If Deborah could have seen her own self clearly, she might have suspected that she had attempted in her own way a similar rebellion against the boredom of her patrician background, an almost ruthless unconscious determination to be "somebody quite special."

But she could not have known, and did not sense from her brief encounter, that this too was Jeff Kirby's weakness, and that, like Trudie, she was being drawn toward a part of her fantasy.

III

Deborah had had enough of The Back Door. She looked at her watch and at Gil.

"Leave?" He had forgotten the time. "Only two."

"Really, we must go," she said. She found herself looking again at Jeff Kirby.

"How exasperating can she get?" Gil thought, but he said, "Let's hang on a bit. Perky wants a word with me about this young singer. I don't want to rush away and have him making a racial production out of my leaving."

"All right—but please . . ."

"Another drink?"

"No, thanks, Gil," she said.

Gil had a disagreeable feeling that she might become difficult if he was too long in settling his business with Perky.

It was stiflingly hot. The door had been opened to allow a draft into the place, and with the swirl of fresh air his imagination soared, and across his mind flashed the word "impressario." For the first time since he became a manager he felt he had perhaps reached below the topsoil of mediocrity, and in his long search had finally discovered a dazzlingly bright talent. He decided the young musician must be persuaded to sign a contract. He didn't allow his expression to betray any excitement.

"Wasn't he terrific, Miss Deborah?" asked Perky.

"Oh, yes—yes indeed," she managed to say, preoccupied with her own thoughts.

"Well, I only had him tabbed for Harlem," Perky said.

"What's wrong with Broadway," Gil asked, not confiding his thoughts of all Jeff Kirby's possibilities. "If I can build him into an attraction, he'll make the grade with whites, and can always play the colored houses for more money."

Perky enthusiastically shared the manager's psychology of selling to Negroes, but he pursed his thick lips thoughtfully. "He ain't black enough," he pronounced soberly. Then he added with the rhythm of a familiar nursery rhyme his own view of Caucasian psychology:

"Never seen a white man who didn't like his colored men black and crude, and his colored women yaller and smooth."

Gil tugged thoughtfully at his sharp nose. "Yeah, maybee— But the boy's a cinch; he's got personality, talent—"

"And can pass as a Hindu, Cuban, or somethin'," Perky said, and licked his lips in anticipation of perpetrating a hoax.

Gil laughed and sang "That's why darkies are born?"— Nope. The newspaper boys would tear him apart."

Deborah, thoughtfully silent while the two men talked, looked carefully about her and listened only with one ear. She was somehow being drawn toward Jeff Kirby, who now sat lazily exploring chords while he talked to a clump of people gathered around the piano. She got up and started in the direction of the alcove.

Perky, sensing her destination, bounded to his feet and, with courtesy that had something obsequious about it, offered her the comfort of privacy, while Gil watched her with bemused pride. The proprietor led her to the small black door marked PRIVATE, a cubbyhole he pretentiously referred to as his study. It contained a cracked mirror, a file case, two chairs, a desk, and a washroom clean of the foul doggerel scribbled across the walls of his public toilets.

He swung open the door and switched on the lights. It was a gesture calculated to impress Gil; and while Deborah sensed this, she felt that politeness demanded she show some appreciation. However, she was only able to muster a wan smile.

Perky closed the door. Without a backward glance she pushed unsteadily into the washroom—and vomited.

—2—

Deborah rinsed her face in cool water, applied new make-up, and came out almost gay.

She nearly collided with two or three drinkers, who, glasses in hand, were headed toward the piano where Jeff was playing softly and telling a story or explaining something that apparently delighted his hearers. His voice was deep, warmly accented, and had a familiar and haunting ring that made her feel she had heard it before, perhaps in her dreams as a little girl. She felt impelled to stop, and did so somewhat nervously.

Everyone turned and watched her, particularly the women. Their glances were wary, curious, suspicious. They scented danger and were on their guard against the stranger, who might poach on their property rights in Negro men. A few coarse remarks were made about the ofay "lady" which she did not hear.

Deborah did notice one wide-mouthed fellow ogling her, his eyes riveted on her bosom. She pulled her frilly collar together and felt a sense of frightened embarrassment. For the first time in her life Deborah felt like a "white woman" —in a defensive sense.

Jeff had not immediately realized what was happening, but when he saw her coming toward him somewhat hesitantly, he smiled.

"I'm Deborah Comstock," she said.

"And I'm Jefferson Kirby. Call me Jeff—everybody does!"

He got up from the piano, his tall figure hovering over her like a dark shadow, and invited her to the bar for a drink. She felt herself being gently led and she had a feeling she dared not refuse. He might be offended. After all, he was perfectly polite and reserved; indeed, he had been quite careful not to show any familiarity.

What she had first noticed about him were his brown eyes that sparkled, eyes that caressed her.

"May I?" Jeff asked as he pulled out another bar stool for himself. He took a package of cigarettes from his pocket. "Smoke?"

The light he offered fell on her neck and arms. The full, soft pallor of her neck above the black frock gave her an alluring strangeness.

There was now some faint applause, and across the room in a shaft of spotlight Sherl, leaning against the piano voluptuously, had begun to sing, and the buzzing sounds of talk and laughter stopped. Deborah and Jeff turned to listen. Jake shuffled toward them with a smile.

"Martini as usual, suh?"

Jeff nodded. "And coffee—black—for the lady."

"How did you know?"

"Simple—after what's happened, I felt you might want coffee."

Before she could collect herself, Jake was pushing the coffee and a delicately-stemmed glass before them. He poured Jeff's drink from an ice-cluttered shaker. The trickle tinkled musically. With a final ceremonial flourish he expertly twisted a fresh lemon peel and carefully dropped it into the glass, while he brooded over its contents as though searching for something.

Deborah, watching the barman, was unable to tell whether his studied concern was about the drink or about many things which must be rummaging around in his ancient head; and she wondered, too, about his overly solicitous manner toward the young man.

The lemon peel with white side up had floated lazily to the bottom of the glass and left an oily swirl on top. Jeff waited expectantly for the usual titillating aftertaste as the drink tickled his palate, smoothly cascaded down his throat, and reached the pit of his stomach with an astringent effect. It was precisely the stimulant he needed. He was grateful for the lift, and he said so to the beaming old man. Then he lifted his glass to him in a salute of appreciation and asked that he join them in a drink.

Jake smiled uneasily, and reached within easy distance for a rag, slowly wrung it dry, and started to wipe the bar in jerky, dilatory motions. Then he paused. "Son," he said, "if you doan mine my sayin' so, ah believes in stayin' under my own vine and fig tree."

Jeff laughed and looked at Deborah, who, while she idled with her coffee, mulled over the old man's meaning.

Jeff climbed down from his stool and stood close to her, trying to guess what sort of perfume she was wearing.

"Let's talk about you—hope you weren't too upset by that fracas," he said. "We don't have things like that happening often."

"Well, I must admit—I still feel a bit queasy."

"Please don't judge us too harshly."

"Why, of course not," she said quickly, thinking of her own experiences with obnoxious, badly behaved whites. She felt

[45]

strangely drawn to him because of his love and worry about his people. She was impressed by his words and emotion, for she sensed how desperately serious he was.

"Do you always feel personally responsible for your people?"

Her words started a turmoil in him. In the past he had stood up for his people, even if their behavior or beliefs were sometimes crude and indeed repulsive to him; now, suddenly, it was as if he were caged up with them, caged up with that something revealed by Junkie Joe, which was revolting, inexplicable, and embarrassing to him.

"I have no choice," he said. "Every Negro is his brother's keeper."

Deborah wanted to say, "What a cross to bear!" Instead, she nodded in Zabee's direction. "The girl at your table—she's rather attractive."

"Yes—isn't she? She's a dancer, and a very good one, too."

"I'm sure she is."

Zabelle Desvigny, he went on to explain, had studied ballet and specialized in Afro-Haitian rhythms. But nothing in her look gave any hint of her demonic energy in search of material, of her almost passionate devotion to the origins and impulses of her people; yet to improve her work as a choreographer she had studied anthropology at Columbia University under Boas. Jeff said people were often misled, too, by her chic and charming appearance; when, in fact, her circumstances were such that she performed at colleges and concert halls and also in the rowdiest night clubs, jockeying back and forth to keep open the doors of the Desvigny School of Dancing.

"Quite a remarkable person," Deborah said, and found that she was slightly jealous.

"And what do you do? Write or paint, perhaps?" Jeff asked.

There was warmth but little color in Deborah's cheeks

now; her large, bluish-gray eyes were soft and liquid. But it was her lips—asking a question, giving an answer, with a shadowy smile—that made his pulse leap: they were sensuous, sensitive lips. . . .

"I do social work, at the Adams Street Settlement House."

"Your accent—you're not a New Yorker?"

"Boston."

"Which probably means a boatload of ancestors."

His tone was unaccountably harsh, but she laughed. "Well, to start with Mother—she's still in Boston; and my father—he died just about two years ago."

"Sorry about your father."

"And yours?"

"Mine? All I seem to do is give him trouble."

"He doesn't want you to be a musician, is that it?"

He trifled with the glass before him. "Not only does he not like the idea, but he stays salty nowadays." And Jeff told her about his scholarship to Julliard, his intention of becoming a serious composer.

"But if your father's against your becoming a composer, what does he want you to be?"

"An undertaker, like himself."

"Oh!" she said with genuine surprise. "And you feel you can't?"

"Right." And he told her of his composition scheduled for a concert hall performance.

"How wonderful!" she said.

But if he failed, Jeff explained, he would have to eat crow, and according to a rather loose bargain with his father, more implied than sealed, he would have to buckle down to the undertaking business. Success would mean a chance to live and work exclusively with music—which he loved.

Jeff's mood silenced Deborah. In a changed voice, he said

emphatically, "I don't want to do anything phony—insincere." He paused, then added, "Do I sound stuffy?"

"Not at all," she quickly reassured him. But she had detected the undertone of revolt against the highly publicized Tin Pan Alley tunesmiths. So she said, "It must be wonderful to have something to attach oneself to like that—to do something meaningful, to feel that sense of belonging."

A brooding look darkened his face.

"Not really enough—not without someone who shares and understands," Jeff said soberly, his dark brown eyes meeting hers.

He was about to offer to take her home, when he remembered her escort.

He stole a glance at the man seated with Perky.

"Mr. Gilbert is an awfully good manager," she said, "and I think he's very much impressed with your talent."

"You do?"

"I do. He just might be the person to help you."

"Yeah?"

Gravity transformed his face, and lines of bitterness deepened at the corners of his mouth. He felt anger mounting in him: she had probably used him, she had used him as all white people use Negroes. She had indulged in her little flirtation for some proposition the manager must have in mind. There was such a note of complicity in her voice that he was forced to believe this. They had a name for broads like her! What a damned clown he'd made of himself!

"You seem upset," she said. "Did I by any chance . . ."

Jeff pushed back the bar stool and reached for his wallet. "Jake! The bill," he said.

His face was angry, frightening. He paid in silence. Was he going to give her some kind of reply?

"Forgive me," he said, "I misjudged you." His tone was

edged with undisguised vindictiveness. "Shall I take you back to your table now?"

As she looked up at him she saw an unbearable look of rage in his eyes.

—3—

Knox Gilbert was blithely taking the liberty of settling Jeff Kirby's future. He had now reached the nub of his discussion with Perky. In a moody silence he shuffled the pros and cons. The proprietor emptied his glass and eyed him anxiously. Then Perky's wary eyes narrowed shrewdly.

"What's the pitch, Mr. Gilbert?"

The manager shrugged. "The boy's raw," he said. "He's not even ready to walk on a stage yet. He needs training and a build-up. Takes lots of money—publicity, orchestrations, wardrobe, coaches—and I always got to grease a hand here and there. Lucky if I break even." He stopped talking awhile, then said: "Could sign him up to a tight, long-term contract —with an option, of course—and cut you in for, say, two per cent, net. How's that?"

Perky squealed.

"Say, man, the way you figure figures, that means a fat eighteen per cent for you if you take your usual commission!"

"What's your squawk; your cut's gravy."

Perky was unconvinced and looked at the white man crankily. "Five, at least, man! The kid foots the bill anyway —not you!"

"Nope."

Here Perky's tone changed. "Well, more dough—or else!"

"Else what?"

"Else I'll manage him myself."

Knox Gilbert laughed. "Like hell," he exploded viciously. "Now, I don't mean to be unkind, but you know as well as I do, you can't deal downtown—don't I have to handle Shannon's bookings? Now, how in hell can *you* manage anybody?"

Perky shifted slowly in his seat.

"Could try," he offered lamely. "Well, you got me cornered."

The manager had to cup a hand over his ear to hear Perky's reply. He felt sorry for him.

Born a Negro, there was little he could choose to do or aspire to be. The man had so much savvy, and no place to use his abilities except in exploiting his own kind; yet, the agent reflected realistically, Perky had a crapshooter's outlook. "Okay. Three."

"Okay, and no funny business, either."

"You got my word, haven't you?"

"Your mouth ain't no prayerbook," Perky said, and flicked his cigar ashes viciously. Without connection, and as if talking to himself, he added, "Now, I gotta sell Jeff."

"Well, it's a damned good deal, if you ask me. After all, he'll make more money than he ever saw."

"Still, twenty per cent is a tough bite in anybody's language." Perky shook his head and wet his lips uneasily.

Gil, observing him closely, had an impulse to laugh. "And when did you become so richly sentimental?"

Perky laughed ruefully.

–4–

It was Perky who first saw Jeff coming toward them now. He had Deborah in tow. Jeff nodded acknowledgment in the agent's direction and put an arm on Perky's shoulder.

Gil, already taken aback by her drink at the bar with the young musician, watched now to see whether Deborah would seem embarrassed.

"Mr. Kirby was very kind," she said and her face became unusually pale.

Both Gil and Jeff were instantly conscious of the contrast in their colors. Neither of the two was going to acknowledge the superiority, or indeed the equality, of the other; when, in fact, they were in unspoken conflict about a white woman.

Perky was sorry he had encouraged the young man's flirtation, especially since Jeff had now developed a moody silence. But to divert him he greeted Jeff with hearty familiarity.

"Say, man," he enthused, "you were real groovy tonight. Now, let me introduce you to the greatest personal manager in show business, and a right guy, too. Shake hands with Mr. Knox Gilbert." And he added blandly, "And of course you've met Miss Deborah."

The manager smiled affably and swiftly appraised the young musician: he looks bright, but he has the air of a person who doesn't know on which side his bread is buttered! Gil concluded that the "boy" should be easy to deal with in money matters.

"Jeff," he began, with the first-name superficial intimacy characteristic of his occupation, "you've got a first-rate voice."

"Thanks," Jeff said as he measured the manager carefully. "Actually, I'm no singer—I compose. Tonight was for kicks, a lark—"

"I don't know what kind of a composer you are," Gil interrupted, "but as a singer, you got it made."

"You see, sir—"

"Call me Gil—no formalities, please."

"Well, you see, Gil, I'm studying piano and composition at Juilliard—"

"Quit."

Perky chimmed in with, "Sure, quit. No percentage in that—man, you could have chicks eatin' outa your hand!"

[51]

The manager said: "I'll stake you. Now, that's what *I* think of your ability."

"I really don't know," he said, fencing. He stole a look at Deborah. She was silent, her lips were parted, and he wondered whether he had been hasty or unfair, and ought he to offer her an apology—but *how?*

Perky saw his cue to say, "Listen, kid, Mr. Gilbert is talkin' sense. If I was in your shoes, The Man wouldn't have to twist my arm."

"I appreciate his attitude, but I don't want to give up composing and tie myself up—"

"They all do," Perky said firmly, lying.

"They may," Jeff replied sharply, and turning to the manager he detailed the experiences of the Negro theater folk he knew who rarely could procure year-round employment; some indeed had not worked in five and six years and were driven to accept employment as porters and domestics to eke out a living. Between sparse engagements, those who stayed in the theater were thrown deeply in debt. If they sought advances from their managers, they were forced to make all sorts of ridiculous deals: offer to undercut their earnings, tie themselves up with agents in incredible contracts, and sometimes end up working for sums fixed arbitrarily by their managers and agents.

And Jeff finally quoted Duke Ellington's remark about the Negro theater people being little more than sharecroppers.

Knox Gilbert was intelligently aware of the economic realities; but he was discovering that the poverty in Harlem was grimmer than he had imagined and he silently admired the young man's grasp of his people's plight—and indeed his honesty about it. He was, however, surprised by Jeff's cautiousness, and found him a good deal more astute than he expected.

Perky, characteristically obtuse, thought this the moment

to step into the breach and advance some economic folklore
which the harsh facts of the period had thrown into discard—
at least, temporarily.

"Cuz," he began, "I knows 'zactly what's eatin' you. But
it ain't like that—anyway, you can always put aside somethin' for a rainy day, specially with the kinda loot you'd
make." (His use of the intimate "Cuz" was meant to soften
up Jeff and draw them together into a racial bond of trust
and understanding.) Perky jerked his thumb in the manager's direction. "Now, listen Cuz, Mr. Gilbert ain't no fly
cat—he'll take care of you, and no flim-flam, either."

Leaning back in his chair, Gil underscored Perky's remarks. "Jeff, these are hard times and you're a bright fellow.
Now, you don't want to go through life always sorry you
didn't take your big chance—do you? A young man must
think of his future, and, believe me, you're a shoo-in as a
singer."

After this speech, Gil and Perky were silent, and Jeff felt
that after so momentous an offer he too was entitled to a
pause; but his whole body was tense. He was annoyed, too.
Perky had put him in this dilemma. Now, as things turned
out, the price of the proprietor's little intrigue had been his
abortive meeting with this girl. He did not feel compensated
—indeed, he felt bilked.

He said, "Maybe I'd better think this over."

The two businessmen shook their heads in disbelief.

Deborah was embarrassed for them both. She saw that Jeff
was bitter and hostile again; and suspicion seemed to under-
score his conduct. This fact made her feel guilty for the
collapse of the negotiations. She could not see why Jeff
would throw away this opportunity for possible fame. This
was certainly not being an undertaker! Composer? Certainly,
but why not on the side, in his spare time. She felt it was a
pity not to use that electrifying voice and the sensitive ap-

pealing personality that went with it. Didn't the Lord expect us to use our natural gifts?

Knox Gilbert looked tired, like someone who had tried with all his reasoning powers for a solution to a problem, long and in vain, and a blotchy, middle-aged pallor came over his face. He wondered how sincere Jeff was about being a composer, and he speculated to himself on the boy's future as a serious musician. No, he wouldn't say anything to him about this now. The kid wouldn't understand anyway—race always muddies the issue. Maybe they should all just have a drink—there wasn't any way now to see inside this youngster, find out what kind of person he was, whether, indeed, he really wanted to be a composer.

"Drink?" he offered finally, and expansively ordered for everybody as Floyd suddenly arrived from nowhere.

Jeff made a movement toward his wallet.

"This one's on me," said Gil matter-of-factly.

"No, no, I insist," Jeff said. It was clear he would accept no gratuities from this white man.

Gil tugged in characteristic fashion at his nose and eyed the proprietor dubiously.

"Jes wait," Perky whispered, "we'll bring that stud to terms yet . . ."

IV

There was a hum of distant traffic and neighbor-talk floating down from the tenement windows above The Back Door as Deborah and Gil settled back in a taxi. The street was deserted except for a frightened cat scurrying underfoot; but the beat, beat of Perky's basement, like a haunting fugue, echoed in their ears as the cab pulled away.

For some time they sat, not talking.

Gil had a long ride ahead—to Deborah's place in Greenwich Village and then back to his own in midtown Manhattan. He felt restless and discouraged. He was not often thwarted, as he had been in his attempt to deal with Jeff Kirby. He thought gloomily of the young Negro's attentions to Deborah, which must have inspired coarse jokes about the white lady with an irresistible liking for "spooks."

Until tonight, Gil had written her off as a girl who had no intention of yielding herself to anyone, at least emotionally. He had tried to be on good terms with her, as one naturally would with any attractive girl. But he experienced a sense of exasperation when he remembered how he had looked forward to this evening with delight, and had planned for her to see a bizarre but entertaining side of Harlem. Instead he had seen her make a spectacle of herself—and, in effect, spit in his eye!

He felt he knew women; they weren't made with soft eyes and attractive figures like Deborah's for nothing, as that spade might find out, if there was any truth in what people said about the passion of those guys for white women.

He'd be damned if he'd let a nigger possess her like some jazzy strumpet . . .

–2–

Gil had mostly known mature women, maybe a few young floozies who had stretched sex across the barrelhead in exchange for night club employment. He had taken them, enjoyed them, and then abandoned and forgotten them. He lived without formal female attachments. Marriage always had added up to harness and gait, and he'd feared losing his liberty, maybe sharing his money. Periodically he was frightened by seizures of a kind of satyriasis, when his tastes turned sadistic. Perhaps this had discouraged the less hardy, perhaps less neurotic women.

He looked at Deborah and at her slender thoroughbred neck. She was ravishing, he decided. Not like Sherl's glossy look, but beautiful in the Newport style. He had never seen so clearly before how desirable she was, and he had a sudden urge to embrace her; the driver's presence restrained him, and he felt defeated. She had always been remote, and he thought of all the evenings he had seen her: always soft and passive, but unreadable. What had he to give her? Money, leisure, admiration—but was this enough? He couldn't plead with her like a love-sick oaf; he had his dignity.

He was overcome by the feeling that he had more than an itch for this woman, a feeling instinctively unpleasant to him; but he had not as yet recognized that a subtle transformation had taken place in his attitude toward her. If he could not have her as a mistress, which he ardently preferred, he was now prepared to take her as a wife.

He had to face the fact, however, that the girl could have been his daughter. He morbidly thought of Faust, bartering his soul for youth, but he soon dismissed age as inconsequential. Her family's social status didn't bother him either —after all, he could buy and sell them. And he wondered whether anything would be gained by telling her all this bluntly. He thought not. But he was convinced that as a woman Deborah was capable of facing every anguish life could bring her.

−3−

The taxi had reached the point where one leaves Harlem and enters white New York, traveling the paved lanes that curve like ribbons around Central Park, leading to downtown Manhattan. The greenery was fresh and fragrant. The branches of the trees drooped motionless across the road without the slightest stir of their new foliage. It was still dark, but few stars shone.

A slight pulsating of the evening's heat rose through the open windows and Deborah, musing over her tumultuous experiences in Perky's basement, put a hand through the window and let the wind, churned up by the moving vehicle, swirl through her fingers.

It was really nice of Gil to have planned this evening for her. How warm it was! How good it smelled! What an extraordinary adventure—to have been in Harlem, to have met Jeff Kirby!

Gil's voice interrupted her thoughts.

"Well, you saw Harlem tonight," he said, elaborately casual, and watched her with his shrewd, watery blue eyes.

"Yes, Harlem was fun—but frightening too."

"What got into you tonight?"

Her eyes looked up. She studied him earnestly.

"Me?"

"Yes, you."

"Nothing."

"Half the time you acted like I wasn't even around."

She looked at him again while he waited, uncomfortable, and growing angry.

"I don't know, Gil . . ."

"Weren't you kind of familiar with that colored fellow?" The lines around his mouth were sarcastic. He wanted to yell at her, but caught himself.

"You're teasing, Gil," she said.

"Oh, no I'm not—I couldn't be more serious—and further-more," he warned, "when white girls act like that uptown they're asking for trouble."

"Why?"

Startled, Gil looked at Deborah. That "Why" had been direct—almost sharp. A purple vein bulged in his temple. "Oh, I see," he said.

"I'm sorry." Deborah said.

"I should think so," Gil said, feeling that he again had the advantage. But Deborah smiled.

"Does it really matter now, Gil?" she said quietly.

"Yes, of course."

Deborah detected a note of reproof in his voice, but she was surprised by his having referred to the young musician.

"Oh?" she said at last.

The situation seemed out of joint now. She had known Gil nearly a year, and they had never exchanged any in-timate words. They had been happy in each other's company, and since her arrival in the city he had frequently taken her to dinner, the theater, and the opera, but he had never revealed any deep feelings—except to shield her from what he called the "scum" of the variety theater. Gil had always been nice, just like an old friend, and now unexpectedly he was giving a new face to an old coin.

"Well?" he asked impatiently, his tone almost accusatory. Before she could answer his question, he had asked a second.

"I mean—that singer, Jeff."

She burst into laughter—not loud or scornful, but kindly.

"One can't tell too much about most colored people at first glance, anyway," she said, playing with the gold clasp of her handbag. "But I thought he had a voice—and a lot of personality."

Gil was determined to corner her. "Think him attractive?"

Deborah was embarrassed by what he left unsaid.

"Yes—very."

Her answer was so low as to be almost inaudible. They had now reached the noise, the hurry and blaze of Broadway. She looked through the window at the countless night-pale faces.

"Then, maybe, *I'm* not quite your type—"

Now that he had spoken like this, he was surprised at himself. Fierce jealousy, which, with a peculiar neurotic twist, turned into fierce desire.

"Type?" she repeated sharply and she was bewildered. "Really," she said, "I don't know what you're talking about."

Gil took refuge in bluster.

"Then, you mean it's my background." He said this with artificial objectivity. "Maybe you don't like my language when I forget The Ivy League polish." But Deborah answered firmly, "I don't care a bit about anyone's background, but I must say, Gil, this does seem like an odd position for you to take after all these months. I naturally assumed you took

[59]

my attitude for granted. I certainly did not expect to have to explain myself at this late date."

Deborah spoke so sharply that he believed her now. He knew he had angered her, even perhaps challenged her basic philosophy of human relations. But if he were to accomplish the act of courtship, even love, he felt he first had to cause her mental or physical pain; indeed, it was a compulsion over which he had little control. But he gave her his most disarmingly engaging smile now.

"Forgiven?" he pleaded half jokingly.

"Oh, Gil—" She sighed, somewhat perplexed and annoyed.

Now, suddenly, the half dark shadows of the taxi, the cigarette smoke mingled with Deborah's perfume, stole into his consciousness.

"Well, you can't always tell what's in people's minds." His voice sounded pathetic.

For a long time Deborah sat in the shadows, her eyes centered on the broad tapering back of the cab driver, and tried in her mind to reconstruct the incidents at The Back Door.

There was no doubt she had been drawn toward the young musician. It wasn't because she had been so powerfully attracted to him, either; she hadn't been, she thought. It had been merely because he was talented, and she had always been curious about anyone who was gifted. That was all the motivation she admitted even now.

—4—

Deborah at twenty-two had already side-stepped marriage—the ordinary and conventional kind—and brushed off any number of less respectable proposals. She was working diligently at the Adams Street Settlement House; her superiors, observing her sympathy for the underdog, had said she had a bright future in social work. But she was not sure what she wanted to do. Back in Boston there was Paul Inge, whom she had known since her school days and to whom she was now supposed to be engaged. He was honest and plodding—but a monument of everything she rejected in her parochial social background, and thoughts of him started no fires of excitement.

She often wondered if she was perhaps cold—"icy," Paul called it. She asked herself this question often, though she suspected she was so far from being frigid that she didn't dare experiment. Deborah Comstock was a disciplined girl who had no idea of throwing herself away. Then what had gotten into her tonight? What had pushed her on at Perky's place, and now what had created this tempest in Gil?

Deborah was truly bewildered, though she saw clearly the reason for the crisis between herself and Gil: had the young musician been a white man, her companion would certainly not have been so upset, so apprehensive, so quick to judge harshly. He had been unfair, illogical, racial. Annoyed, she thought now of her Uncle Ellery, who had introduced her to Gil by letter. Before she left Boston, her uncle had said to her, "He just might be helpful," but he had not said Knox Gilbert might be trying, even difficult. Uncle Ellery had felt she needed more friends, needed to see some of the variety and liveliness of New York.

A curious smile settled on Gil's thin lips. He, too, was thinking of Ellery—at least, what Ellery symbolized in her "good family" background. They had been at Yale together and though Gil did not belong to his set, Ellery Comstock had taken him to Mory's for dinner, had introduced him to fraternity friends. As a young man from the streets of New York, Gil had felt self-conscious; but he had wangled advantages whenever possible, and earned the reputation of being a decent fellow with an unfortunate touch of the hustler, and a curious mixture of stilted phrases and street argot in his talk.

He now felt he had pushed Deborah too far. He was prepared to offer excuses.

"You seem upset?" he said. "Anything I might have—"

"No, not really," she answered. But she wanted to escape, to change the trend of the conversation. "Gil, you've never told me how you became a manager."

Her manner was again warm and vivacious. Gil was relieved. He started thinking of his early days in the theater: how to tell her all that he had done, seen and knew, felt and said, in the three decades he had managed stage folk through the maze of angles, intrigues, and barters that clutter the road to stardom, even cluttered the way to a livelihood on the stage.

"Bread I could earn in any business—but my dish was stars and caviar," he said, hoping to give sweep to his accomplishments. He wanted desperately to justify himself in her eyes; subconsciously perhaps he was trying to do more.

"You studied at the Baker Workshop, Uncle Ellery says. Had you planned to be an actor, a director?"

He shrugged. "Yes, I had a fling at the Yale School of Drama, but not having any parents to support me, I was forced to drop out early. So you could say I'm a manager by default."

"What a clever way of putting it, Gil."

Encouraged by her compliments, he said, "You probably didn't know it, but my folks were immigrants."

"Really?"

"Yes. They died when I was small. I was brought up by my old man's sour-puss brother, my Uncle Herman. He had a beat little hardware store in Brooklyn—couldn't even keep me in small change when I was in high school—and, well, there's no point to dragging that in now!

"Even then I knew I wanted to be in the theater, and I became an errand boy for a Broadway producer. After I graduated I worked as a stagehand in Hoboken stock. Then I talked a director into letting me stage-manage his road show—*boy,* was that a turkey!

"I tried song-plugging for music publishers, carried a spear in a play, took a fling at publicity, and had a brief spell as an advance man for a booking agency.

"Along the way I made friends and contacts. No one gets places without connections—I mean, you've got to have important people in your corner to say the right word in the right places. . . . And something slowly jells. . . . For myself, I was on the run.

"I went back to slaving in my Uncle Herman's store, and became an agent evenings, Sundays and holidays, and during lunch hours. But after a while I saw I needed a front— an address, a certain look in the theater district—so, with some money I'd saved and a few dollars I borrowed, I got an office in Broadway's Gaiety Building—and first thing you know, I'm wheeling and dealing!"

His vernacular seemed to Deborah to sum up his whole philosophy, and indeed the rapacious philosophy of Broadway agents.

"And colored people—how did you come to manage them?"

"Negroes?" he chuckled. "I'll never forget the first one I met—and the beating my Uncle Herman laid on me just for shaking hands and saying 'sir' to him! He was a barber who had cut my hair."

Shocked, Deborah thought: "Immigrants! Not a generation away from Europe, and already prejudiced against colored people—native Americans!" She almost asked, "Do all immigrants absorb American race prejudice that swiftly, or are they prejudiced before they arrive here?"

Knox Gilbert went on: "And would you believe it, they've brought me luck ever since. In that colored fellow's shop, I met the producer who gave me my first job on Broadway. Yeah," he recalled nostagically, "those were the pork-and-bean days—but I wrote to Roland Hayes, a great Negro singer, asking him to let me manage his bookings." He smiled at the recollection. "'Some day,' I used to say then, 'I'm going to manage people like Roland Hayes, maybe even the concert star himself.' He didn't answer, and I haven't managed a Negro concert star yet; but, as you know, I'm still partial to them as performers."

"How wonderful to be on intimate terms with such attractive people." Deborah said.

"Yes, I suppose, but you'd be surprised how those *intimate* terms can get you snarled up."

"Snarled? How, Gil?"

"We managers are called a lot of things—and worse; but any performer needs a manager who'll believe in him till hell freezes over, who'll fight for him, who'll help him creatively and guide him commercially. We do all these things—and besides, we pay bills, give the brush to hungry broads, fend off creditors, save money, remember wives' birthdays, choose schools for the kids and psychiatrists for their folks, and even blow noses."

Why, then, Deborah wondered aloud, the wide circulation of unkind insinuations about Broadway managers and agents? Suddenly she thought of Gil's harsh dealings with Perky.

"My dear," he said, "I wouldn't be honest if I didn't admit there is some truth to the rumors. I mean—there are managers and managers!"

—5—

Gil leaned back in his seat, crossed his legs, and while he thought, slowly drew on his cigarette. He said somewhat bitterly, "If I'd been born on the right side of the street, I might not now be dealing with some of the lice I—"

Deborah interrupted. "Well, don't you think people find a level no matter where they're born?"

"Not if a lid is dropped over your cradle."

A day four years ago came back to him. He had gone abroad to see for himself what sort of place his people had come from.

He had found two old, decayed farms in a sleepy, deserted hamlet in old Slovakia, with cart tracks rutted into the worn earth leading to a mill; and a small gray crumbling church, where his people had worshiped their God. The stream that worked the mill came down in a pitiful trickle, and pigs and dogs foraged about. The feet of the Golinkos—this was the family name before Gil Anglicized his to Knox Gilbert—had been deep in mud, poverty, and ignorance for generations.

He had recoiled from the realities of his birthright, and never afterward had mentioned this unhappy pilgrimage, nor did he mention it now. It was, however, this tarnished memory that now made him throw out words he probably had long held back. "So from the start," he said, "my goal was to own talent, because I learned the hard way that by controlling the key people someone like me could pull strings. But don't you forget, I also rowed in the theater's galleys."

Deborah marveled at the ability of people like Gil not only to survive but prosper; and yet, she thought, they seemed to feel the need to flog themselves for any success they achieved, like thieves who pick pockets for pennies and

[65]

find dollars. They seemed to feel they did not deserve what they got.

"Well, you certainly earned success."

Gil pursed his lips and raised his shoulders.

As he did so, a sudden familiar curve jostled them both as the driver turned the cab sharply. They were nearing her apartment and she said so to Gil. But still he kept talking, as if to work out some secret punishment, perhaps give vent to some jealous rankling of his instincts—though of course in admitting things, he half excused himself. Deborah had her first insight into what having been an orphan of poor immigrant parents had done to warp his outlook; and how, to compensate for what he felt he had been denied in his childhood and youth, he had used management as a lever to give him superiority over other men. And when she thought that perhaps as a little boy he was not kissed before he went to bed at night her sense of compassion was touched.

"And that, I suppose, is the story in a nutshell," Gil said, rousing Deborah from her reverie.

"I think that's fine!" she said with sincere admiration.

"Maybe," he said, "I ought to qualify my views in light of my own experience. I guess everybody to some extent creates his own inferno."

They both laughed, for at the word inferno a shaft of blazing light suddenly flashed through the windows of the taxi.

They had reached the tall lamp post before Deborah's door.

The taxi shrieked to a stop, and she suddenly remembered to remind Gil of his promise to get her tickets for a play.

"Yeah, yeah," he said hurriedly, remembering. "Sorry I can't go. Maybe you can take somebody—your roommate, Tina, perhaps. Let's see—this is Saturday night—rather, Sunday morning. Why don't you drop by the office Thursday—

say, about fiveish, and pick 'em up. I'll buy you a drink, and maybe we can sandwich in dinner."

Deborah smiled warmly.

"Well then—Thursday," she agreed.

Gil jumped out of the taxi, paid the driver and gave her his hand.

Unconsciously he held himself straighter, walked with a more elastic step. The vestibule door was open, and he stepped in behind her and followed to the locked inner door. There was a faint flush in his cheeks.

"Deborah," he said softly, and his voice was a touch maudlin.

Why he had dismissed the cab, why he had followed her up the stairs, and what he intended to do, he really did not know; but her nearness had suddenly affected him; and he grabbed her shoulders and bent forward to kiss her. Her body grew rigid in his grasp, and as he touched her lips, he met two hard lines. His face was pressed away by her hand, and he heard her say, "Oh, no, no, no—Gil, don't spoil everything, please."

Deborah evidently had her key in her hand. She disappeared at once.

He walked away, embarrassed and conscious of his own awareness of inferiority.

V

The stream of brilliant sunlight had opened a new day for Jeff Kirby. He clutched a manuscript under his arm as he came out from the subway station and walked east to Carnegie Hall. His step was lively but he felt uneasy. He had dreaded and anticipated this hour for many weeks. He stopped to check his watch to make sure he was on schedule for his three o'clock appointment, and he nearly bumped into a man coming out of the venerable concert hall.

"Pardon me, sir," Jeff said as he recognized the bulky figure.

"Yes. What is it?"

"Mr. Weisgold?"

The man had a ruddy complexion, a short nose with glasses perched on it, and a thick lower lip which somehow blurred his speech. His moonbeam face screwed into a squint in the gloomy corridor.

"Oh, yes, yes—I remember now. You're Kirby."

He didn't, Jeff thought, say "Mr. Kirby"; just shortly, familiarly, and patronizingly, "Kirby"; but Jeff didn't resent it much. He'd been through this often enough to blunt his sensitivity. Now he merely noticed again, a fact he would pigeonhole in the racial section of his memory. Like most Negroes, he was inclined to believe a day of reckoning was inevitable for white people because of their discourtesies, insults, and humiliating condescension, a belief which probably had its inspiration in the Bible's prophecies.

"I'm afraid there's nothing doing now, Kirby."

"But you wrote and—"

"Yes, yes. It was all arranged. But there was a slipup somewhere."

The young musician's face fell, and noticing this the man quickly added, "Well, it's just possible I can do something— wait a second, will you?"

He turned to retrace his steps, and stomped up a flight of steps off the spacious, high-ceilinged lobby. Jeff stood looking after him.

Fifteen minutes went by, and Weisgold came back accompanied by a short, bald man who spoke with a foreign accent.

Jeff recognized the Czech conductor, Youry Schurck, and his heart started pounding. His excitement faded, however, when he saw that the two men were involved in animated conversation and he had apparently been quite forgotten.

He stopped Weisgold anyway.

"Oh, yes, yes," Weisgold said in a preoccupied manner, "I have to go somewhere with the maestro, now. I'll see you when I come back. Why don't you have a seat in my office and make yourself comfortable. I won't be gone ten minutes."

And he was off again, leaving a faint scent of garlic behind him as the maestro trailed at his heels.

Jeff took the elevator to the third floor and walked to the familiar glazed glass door which he had opened so often in the last few months. Black letters: JEROME WEISGOLD, ARTISTS' REPRESENTATIVE.

He pushed into a lonely little paneled cubicle which served as a waiting room. There was a backless bench, an ashtray standing on thin, iron stilts, and an old out-of-focus picture of Beethoven—severe, august, cold.

Jeff lit a cigarette nervously.

He was too excited to sit down and too excited to stand. But he stood—and when he had chain-smoked a half dozen cigarettes, he asked the freckled girl at the reception desk behind a glass partition where the agent was.

She peeped through a round hole in the glass.

"No one tells me anything," she said somewhat plaintively; "but maybe he's still at lunch. If not, he's probably somewhere in the building, or at a rehearsal in the main auditorium."

Jeff, now desperate, started out in search of the elusive agent. The gray, feeble man who operated the elevator thought he might be next door in the Russian Tea Room. Jeff bolted down the steps of Carnegie Hall, turned to his right, and pushed through a green-painted door.

He felt a hundred eyes look up as he stopped to look the place over.

Weisgold was there—eating borsch hungrily.

Jeff caught the agent's eye finally as he lifted his head from the bowl he had corralled and was stuffing a piece of black bread into his mouth.

"Oh, yes, Kirby!" he exclaimed in a muffled voice, not looking directly at the young man approaching his table.

"Did you—" Jeff began and broke off anxiously.

"Yes, of course. But there are wheels within wheels, you understand, my boy. Nothing now—I'm sorry. I'll send your stuff back in the mail. But keep in touch."

And as he spoke he gave the air a final stab with his bread.

"Thanks, anyway," Jeff mumbled and headed back toward the door between a long aisle of occupied booths.

He felt as if he were being driven through a gauntlet of cold blue stares.

–2–

Jeff Kirby had made his assault on the ramparts of the white world and had been driven back. He felt routed.

He rolled the manuscript he was carrying and shoved it into his pocket, and aimlessly faced the street filled with evening shadows. He looked back wryly at the venerable structure which symbolized the Mecca of his hopes, and thought, "Well, that's settled!"

He toyed with the idea of going back to Harlem, back to Perky's basement to talk with the old bartender, Jake. No, maybe he ought to see a movie. He turned at the next corner and started in the direction of the Radio City Music Hall.

The theater's marquee blazed at him and then he remembered Knox Gilbert whose office was somewhere in this rock pile of stark gray modern architecture. Perky had kept on badgering him lately: "You don't hafta go whole hog—but at least you can drop in and say 'howdy-do.' Maybe, one of these days he might do you some good. Remember, Cuz," he had warned sagely, "if a Jackson is gonna make the grade, he's gotta have Mister Charlie's arm round him."

Before long, Jeff found himself before the double doors of Knox Gilbert & Associates. He hesitated, then turned the knob and pushed his way into the plush-looking, glass-partitioned offices. A blonde, stylishly dressed receptionist, sitting at a broad bleached mahogany desk, asked if he had an appointment, and warned that if he didn't, he would have a long wait to see Mr. Gilbert. Would Mr. Forsyte do? No. Well, Mr. Gilbert had several important appointments, and she nodded meaningfully at a motley group of people who had the look of pale, tired welfare clients. They were, in fact, actors and actresses between shows, seated in a semicircle facing a huge oriental urn half filled with white sand, which they were filling with chewing gum wrappers and cigarette butts.

He paused indecisively, then he heard Deborah's voice. "And thanks so much, Gil!"

Jeff felt his heart leap as the man ushering her to the door nearly bumped into him.

Both Deborah and Gil stopped in some amazement when they recognized the young musician standing there. He had been in their minds but their thoughts of him had been very different.

When Deborah had arrived a half hour or so before, she looked about, intrigued by the modern, elaborately stylized private office.

"This, my dear, is the most comfortable," Gil said, pushing a slouchy, upholstered chair up to her, adding, "I call it the 'conditioning couch'—use it to soften up difficult clients."

Deborah sat, thought of Gil's unsatisfying encounter with Jeff Kirby, and colored slightly.

Gil looked at her approvingly. She was wearing an emerald-green smartly tailored suit, a black beret, and carried a black handbag and white gloves. A single string of pearls laced her neck and emphasized her pale skin. Perhaps these careful touches are meant for me, Gil thought; and he remembered that this was, in fact, Thursday and he had said he might be able to arrange cocktails and dinner. He was sorry the pressure of work made him forego this pleasure. He could not have known she had dressed so cleverly hoping to meet someone else.

How could anyone have known her precise motives?

Even Deborah did not admit anything to herself, but she hoped somehow in Gil's theatrical environment to discover something more tangible about the young musician. She firmly believed she had come merely to pick up two tickets for a play. But now when she saw Jeff, she wasn't sure even at this moment whether she had come this far for the tickets to a play or for the long chance that she might run into him.

For Jeff, too, meeting Deborah Comstock was both un-expected and disconcerting, and he was momentarily lost for words; and in his mind the busy click-clacking of the office typewriters began to sound like hammer blows on his nerves. He had not thought there was the faintest chance of seeing her again. He felt he had to apologize to her for his conduct the other night. He found himself devoured by a hundred anxieties as he vainly walked the streets searching and scru-tinizing faces, hoping he would run into her accidentally. His lack of success had caused a curious sadness to settle on his spirit. Now suddenly she stood there, and the over-whelming fact made him instinctively avoid Gil's eyes for fear his face might betray his complex thoughts about this girl.

Gil was the first to speak.

"Well, Mr. Kirby," he said heartily, "you of course remem-ber Miss Comstock!"

Jeff nodded, and he and Deborah looked at one another intently. Then he walked straight up to her and, in his con-fusion, griped her hand; somehow he caught himself, and relaxed it almost tenderly. With some embarrassment Deborah slowly withdrew her hand.

Gil, watching them curiously, saw the look in her eyes, the long clasp of their hands. In spite of their outward calm, he sensed the tension in their gestures and was suspicious. Just as soon as Jeff had come into his office, he had perceived to his annoyance a return of her old absorbed and aloof manner toward him; and he smiled cynically.

"Oh, I was just leaving, Mr. Kirby," Deborah said, trying to appear casual by ceremoniously pulling on her gloves.

"Yes, yes, leaving . . ." said Jeff, and listened with irritation to his stumbling and meaningless words. Then turning hesitantly to Gil, he said, "I came to talk with you but I suppose—"

"Yeah, yeah," said Gil. "I've been looking forward to a long talk with you. Can we arrange a date now?"

Somebody tapped Gil on the back and spoke to him; and in the exchange over his shoulder, he missed Jeff's answer, which now seemed to ease the tension.

Deborah mumbled something about the late hour, said she had to leave, and smiling, offered her gloved hand to Gil.

Jeff immediately opened the door and indicated with a swift, offhand goodby to the agent that he was going to go along with her, not just to the elevator but wherever she went. And he left without looking directly at Gil, so that Gil did not see his confident eyes.

—3—

Deborah's heart beat furiously as they went down in the elevator. Throughout a descent of forty-three floors they said very little, though as her eyes wandered she noticed the operator's face had a vulgar grin.

It seemed like an endless journey down, and when they arrived in the main lobby there was no question about his going with her. As they walked through the doorway, he suddenly halted before her, pointed towards Fifth Avenue, and said, "Come for a moment. Over there is a good view of the plaza and the sweep of buildings behind it. Somebody has called them 'springboards to oblivion for misfits,' but someone like Utrillo could have made a masterpiece of that stone pile."

She felt his bitterness creeping back, but she was more surprised by his reference to the French painter, and why she should be surprised, she couldn't quite fathom; but she said nothing.

[74]

He pointed to the massive buildings in the background like so many long thin shafts stuck in the sky; then, leaning against a railing, they peered down into the sunken dining pavilion which in winter served as an ice-skating pond, and she began to share his unspoken emotion about the sweep of grandeur.

Deborah looked at it bemused. How could it be real that she was walking the streets of fashionable midtown New York City with this young Negro? She could see the look of superior horror that would spread across her mother's face. She felt queasy, a little guilty, but had she been asked, she would have denied it; actually she felt guilty about feeling guilty.

"There you get a real view—no, a bit more to this side," Jeff was saying, as he pointed towards the set of tall, irregular buildings, that now seemed like a grotesquely-angled pile, aflame in the sunset. He was careful as he spoke to keep his distance from her; and she noticed how far he kept to her right—"a mile," she thought.

Abruptly, caught by his feeling for the scene, her mood expanded and she smiled in a way Jeff was to remember for years afterward. Its radiance encouraged him to edge closer to her. Then he moved away again, as if he had approached dangerous ground, though he was beginning to feel some warmth and intimacy in her manner.

"This is one of my favorite places in New York," he said almost with a sigh.

The promenade, gay with flowers, the sunken plaza, with umbrella-shaded tables, the attractive small shops, all cooled by the fountain, gave the place a foreign, Old World feeling that always transported him to what he imagined the boulevards of Europe were like. He frequently prowled here to escape the tawdriness of his own parochial Harlem. He felt especially thoughtful whenever he walked here, for the edge of his feelings sharpened, and life seemed to take on a subtle, purposeful meaning.

"I mean, the place has a special glamor," he said, and felt a pleasurable shiver of the nerves.

He found an unoccupied bench, and they sat, facing the cafe on the opposite side. Behind the window they both saw a couple who rarely moved. But suddenly the woman's neck was encircled by the man's arms—they became a single form, like a sculptured statue of passion, open and unashamed. The watchers quickly turned their glances away, not to pry into the intimacy of these enlaced lovers; but Jeff noticed that a faint flush had come to Deborah's cheeks.

She said nothing for a while, and then asked, "As a boy, did you explore the streets?"

"I've always found them exciting—particularly the sounds. How about you?"

She laughed. "Well, as a very young girl, I naturally wasn't allowed the freedom of Boston streets—had I been, I might have become a tomboy."

"You a tomboy?" he repeated, and he laughed at the incredible idea.

"Well, not quite, I suppose."

"Boston always your home?"

"I was born in Haverhill, Massachusetts. The family moved to Boston when I was a baby. Something about my father having offices in Boston and getting tired of commuting, I guess. It was good for Mother, too. She was an invalid for many years."

"Any brothers?"

"No. But I have a sister—older—Sybil."

"So have I. Your sister—what's she like?"

"Beautiful, I suppose—and I'm terribly fond of her—but when we were teenagers I was always jealous of her. I was skinny, quiet, and had this funny nose. She was vivacious and all the boys ran after her. She's married now."

"How about the rest of your family—I mean, uncles, aunts, and cousins?"

"My relations? I don't know most of them."

"Many?"

"Scads. And you?"

"Mine's a tribe!" But he did not add that the Kirbys, like the majority of Negro families, had been dispersed early by mob violence in the South and the economic depression.

"My people are awful, most of them," Deborah said. One's relations always are, aren't they?"

"I expect they think us awful, too. But tell me more about Deborah Comstock!"

"Well, as for school, I went to college in South Hadley. Mt. Holyoke—"

"So, now," Jeff interrupted, chuckling. "Only ten miles apart and we never met. I was at Amherst!"

"Now, that's a genuine coincidence," she said, laughing. "Then *you're* the Kirby that played football at Amherst."

"Halfback—'30, '31 and '32," he said proudly.

"Why, I think I saw you play in my freshman year—yes, I'm quite sure now."

"Those were mighty exciting days for me."

"For us, too. After the games we used to look forward to the hops at Wilbur's."

They became abruptly silent and somber, as if conversation had been shut off by a switch, and they looked at one another in desolation. They had both recognized a brutal fact: as a Negro, Jeff was of course not admitted to the dances attended by the girls of Mt. Holyoke, and therefore a social meeting between them in the ivy atmosphere of these two venerable New England institutions would have been almost impossible. They might as well have lived on different planets.

Deborah tactfully moved on to talk of the days following her graduation, and Jeff was relieved to stop reminiscing of this period of his school days. But the old violence could still shake him, the desire for revenge. Occasionally it had overcome him on the football field, when he felt the lunging body—contact with a white opponent. The coach had talked to him quietly several times and cautioned him to harness a temper that when unleashed gave him the impulse to maim or even, to his own horror, to kill.

"After graduation," she was saying, "I fiddled around awhile with routine things—Junior League and Red Cross, and Bar Harbor in the summers."

Jeff frowned.

"They don't sound so routine to me."

"Not if you believe in suburban distinctions," she retorted. Then a peculiar expression came over her face. "Believe me, it *was* routine. And I'm not too grateful for it. I've just realized how ill-equipped I was to deal with anything outside the pattern." Her voice trailed off unhappily. But then she brightened again and said, "At last I tossed over all that to do something with meaning, I hope, and so I came to New York."

—4—

Jeff found himself trying to seem calm to Deborah despite the compulsive and violent thoughts troubling him. He attempted a quick and confused examination of conscience and motive. The unhappy coincidence of Deborah's Boston background both tempted and angered him. Was she truly determined to break with her past, or was his attraction for her a mixing of rebellion and sex that she herself did not recognize. He wanted her and his desire went beyond a fantasy of seduction. He realized that he would possibly dare all the hazards and torments of a marriage to get her and hold her. But was he enough of a humorist or a realist to marry her and prosper in his own soul? When she discovered what her own urges were, would she be able to face them if they were as complicated and deep-seated as he suspected they might be. She might eat him away, or eat away years of him, or eat away his ambition, even perhaps destroy him. When he, on the other hand, found himself out (that he might not be able to accept himself with her), it might be too late. He did know that he was stubborn and proud. His father would hate Deborah even more than he hated Jeff's musical career. And then he thought of his grandfather. Much of his own violence must be a throwback to Ditcher Kirby. And his father had tried hard to forget Ditcher.

Jeff remembered a day when he and his sister had had one of their almost bitter arguments with their father, who had turned on Jeff and said, "The more I look at you, the more I feel you're the spit image of your grandfather."

"And where would the Negro be today if men like Grandpa hadn't had the guts to fight for our rights?" Jeff had challenged, in effect attempting to challenge his father's whole theory of human relations.

"And people called him 'Crazy' Ditcher, too," Mr. Kirby submitted contemptuously. "And, like him you're bringing unhappiness to your mother and me. A damned fool radical, that's what he was. Maybe that's the way you're headin', too. Away from decent, conservative, honest business folks."

—5—

Mr. Kirby had tried to bury his past forever. Ditcher had died long before Jeff and Priscilla were born. Indeed they had no knowledge of their grandfather until Jeff was in college; and then, quite accidentally, he unearthed the skeleton Mr. Kirby had hoped to keep buried. Jeff had been assigned the preparation of a history term paper on slavery, and while browsing through the old newspapers of the period, he saw an advertisement in the Richmond *Compiler* headed, WANTED FOR MURDER—DITCHER KIRBY, NEGRO. The ad contained a description of the man and offered a reward of $500 for his capture, dead or alive. Jeff was so startled by the discovery that for the next several days he did nothing else but hunt down the facts of why the old man was sought as a fugitive. When he confronted his father with the information, Mr. Kirby had reluctantly admitted the details were true, and even added a few unpleasant facts of his own. He forbade further discussions, but as youngsters, Jeff and Priscilla were elated by the secret knowledge they possessed and proud of the old man's exploits.

Ditcher Kirby, it seems, was a slave on the plantation of Richard Birch, near the Old Brook Swamp about six miles south of Richmond. It was here he became involved with the law. He was perhaps a gifted man of sorts—black and calm, with a hairless bullet head set on broad shoulders. He was once considered the strongest man in Virginia. He bore a nasty scar across one temple, another back of his head, and a big knot on the bone of his wrist—all produced by blows. Ditcher's mother had tried to kill him as a child to save the boy from the fate of a slave, and his father had made countless attempts to escape. As a youngster Ditcher was precocious; indeed, he had learned to read early, experimented in making gunpowder, sculptured in clay, and industriously studied the Bible. He developed mystical inclinations. He was twenty-five when he came to feel himself a man of destiny and decided to lead his people out of bondage. While everyone else danced at celebrations and toiled in the fields, Ditcher brooded—and preached freedom.

One summer morning the sun rose without its usual brilliant golden hue—instead a pale, greenish tinge covered its surface. That afternoon there was a solar eclipse.

"The time has come!" Ditcher announced. He declared he had seen visions of white and black angels locked in combat. And he quoted from his Bible: "From that time began Jesus to show unto his disciples, that he must go unto Jerusalem, and suffer many things of the elders and chief priests, and scribes, and be killed." Ditcher drew about him a handful of friends, who had daily listened to his talk of revolt, and persuaded them to march on Jerusalem—in this instance, the plantations of their masters. He set the time for the last Sunday in August, 1860, midnight. So as not to arouse suspicion, he planned a barbecue. While the slaves ate he quietly outlined his plans to them; they called for the slaughter of all white people—extermination.

Six men, led by Ditcher, took up crude weapons, and set out at the appointed hour. The first stop was at Ditcher's own master's big house. He himself stealthily climbed a ladder to the upper story, climbed in an open window, crept back down the stairs, and let in his co-conspirators. They insisted that he should have the honor of striking the first blow for freedom. Ditcher stole up to the bedside of his sleeping master and struck him with a hatchet. The white man jumped from the bed screaming for help. He was silenced by a confederate of Ditcher, who split his skull with an ax. As the mistress of the house came in the doorway, she was struck a fatal blow on the head. When the Birch baby smiled sweetly at Ditcher, he lifted the child, kissed her affectionately, and gently laid her in the cradle. Two men forthwith snatched the child by the heels, and dashed her brains against a brick fireplace.

And so it went, as Ditcher and his men swept across the countryside dealing quick death.

The terrible news spread quickly, and panic-stricken white people fled their houses. The slaves, left to their own devices, joined Ditcher's rampaging crowd. Hysterical masters gathered in Richmond. Messengers were hastily dispatched to beg the governor to send troops.

Two miles from town, the insurrectionist Negroes attacked the Cornish estate. While Ditcher stood guard at the gates, his men searched the house, and finding everyone had fled, loitered about sampling the Cornish rum. Ditcher had to drag them away, silence their loud talk, and retreat with his drink-sodden men to the swamps. There, while they slept off hangovers, the militia surprised them. Nearly the whole band was killed. Ditcher escaped and went into hiding, only venturing out at night for food and water, believing Negroes would rally for a final blow.

Within a week a thousand white people were hunting him. People couldn't sleep easily while Ditcher still eluded the hounds and hard-riding hunters. Every dark night was a threat. Every rustle of a leaf, creak of a door, and crunch of a stone underfoot, was the sound of approaching death. By night every house was securely locked. Masters, with pistols in hand, unlocked the doors only in the mornings to admit trusted slaves to light the fires. People soon concluded that if they were to be safe and keep Negroes in their place, drastic measures would be necessary. They knew that Ditcher could read. Henceforth no slave should be allowed to preach. Ditcher met no opposition along the roads. Patrols must be increased, every cabin kept under watch, and every assembly of slaves guarded.

The brutality that accompanied this surveillance eventually brought a reaction, and Ditcher Kirby became a hated man among the very Negroes he sought to free. He had eluded his pursuers for weeks, and in the hold of a schooner that sailed out of Norfolk had escaped to Boston. Actually, he hoped to obtain arms and financial aid from the New England abolitionists, but they rejected so wild a scheme. Nevertheless he lived in daily hope of persuading them to take up arms and forcibly free the slaves. Since there was no communication, his purposes were unknown to his confederates in Richmond. So Negroes concluded that Ditcher had run away to save his own skin, and, having instigated a bloody uprising, had left them to the mercies of their enraged masters.

Even when he returned to Richmond following the Civil War, married, and established himself, his repeated explanations were of no avail. Hatred had turned to contempt, and the name of Ditcher Kirby became the butt of cruel jokes. Jeff's father, as a boy, was often forced to defend himself with his fists. Schoolboy playmates, reflecting the opinions of their elders, taunted him and gleefully corrupted "Ditcher" into "Slicker." Whatever the deep psychic reasons, Ditcher deserted his wife and five children—Jeff's father was then seven years old—disappeared in the fleshpots of Norfolk, and wasn't heard from for many years afterward. His abandoned wife, Cora, was left destitute, and was forced to parcel out her children to relatives in the country while she supported herself as a laundress. Jeff's father had been put to work as a field hand, pulling tobacco "suckers." He accepted the situation obediently. But as "Ditcher's boy" he never knew a moment's peace until he escaped to Harlem.

—6—

As Jeff and Deborah sat in Rockefeller Plaza the sky, brilliant blue all day, had deepened after the sunset to a red-orange. The branches of the few birch and cherry trees spaced methodically about the plaza drooped motionless across the walks, and were wrapped in velvety shadows. It was growing dark and the tall buildings now slowly became darker shapes in the dusk, reminding Deborah that it was growing late.

"I really must be going," she said at last, her studied lightness concealing her inner turmoil.

Jeff looked anxiously at his watch. "Only six!" he said as he led her out past the statue of the huge, bronze Atlas, whose bulging muscles seemed to have been burnished by the sunlight. On Fifth Avenue they were greeted by the inexorable roar of the city. New York had begun to disgorge its workers and shoppers, and the streets were crowded with bustling, homeward-bound people.

It was a happy, good-humored crowd that felt the stir of spring. But when they saw Deborah and Jeff their eyes, so inquisitive and direct, swept the faces of the two young people, and their smiles turned to what the Negro felt were stares of malicious curiosity. Deborah's striking good looks ordinarily invited attention; but Jeff's instincts were instantly alerted. He feared there might be overt racial insults, especially when he saw white men treating her as fair game for offensive ogling, and he scrutinized every face with double watchfulness as they walked through the dense crowds.

His figure had become tense, eloquent of his feelings, and triggered into anger. His shepherding of the girl became strongly protective.

Deborah was not entirely oblivious to the crowds; but because of her secure position among her own people she was not so sensitive as he. When he unexpectedly suggested hailing a taxicab, she, perhaps hoping to make a show of defiance to the hostile crowds, offered the alternative of a crowded bus where they could face them down.

But he had halted a cab, was helping her in, and without

asking permission had stepped in behind her. The driver, regarding her with the contempt he reserved for tramps, and ignoring her escort to the point of denying him the dignity of his presence, looked at her quizzically. Jeff urged her to join him for cocktails, his voice urgent, and directed the driver to Harlem and The Back Door.

Deborah didn't refuse, telling herself that she must not again offend him. She had noticed the censure in the cab-man's face, and wondered idly if all the people who gave service in New York had a dark conspiracy against her. Nettled as she was by Jeff's highhanded manner, the driver's attitude doubled her annoyance. She had enough intuition, however, to recognize that something had deeply disturbed Jeff. He had lit a cigarette and was nervously exhaling clouds of smoke. She felt alarmed for him.

After he had been down into a whirlpool of doubts and misgivings, he sat upright and did not move an inch closer to Deborah, nor did he lean back in the seat; he was indeed unconscious of the cab's sways and jerks or the suffocating smell of gasoline. Then quickly his gaze was full upon her, and his eyes traced her outline from the wisps of hair escaping from under her black beret down to her shapely hands, which trifled with the handbag resting on her lap. He now thought of her again as a woman whom he was hungry to possess.

The taxi sped on and passed in mechanical procession trees, houses, shops, vehicles, and people; but all this had no significance for either of them. This was the first time they had really been alone. Neither of them spoke now. They were too tense.

Jeff had many times rehearsed this meeting in fancy. Re-hearsal was no help now. He simply could not speak with articulate sureness. He had never thought that the sight of this young woman, whom he had not seen for nearly a week, could affect him so decisively. He had imagined himself speaking and acting with poised authority, and his inadequacy, now made a kind of defensive irony, welled up in him.

Her musing had been troubled, and now a brooding look darkened Deborah's face.

"What horrible manners some creatures have," Deborah said after a while, as she remembered the malevolent stares of the crowds.

Jeff's mood was broken by this completely feminine remark. Her understanding was a new experience for him; and it seemed to him that he had been looking for just this in all the girls he had known. He convinced himself that she was spiritually responsive, with feelings which seemed to go hand in hand with his own, conditioned more by emotion than reason.

She was, after all, as Perky had said, "a fine frail!"

"I must seem like an awful oaf, but today . . ." He hesitated.

Deborah was instantly alert and sympathetic.

"What's the matter, Jeff?"

She saw a troubled line come between his thick eyebrows. Then he burst out with the details of what had happened earlier; his arrival at Carnegie Hall for a rehearsal in preparation for a public performance of his music; his discovery to his dismay that none was scheduled; nor did the agent who had written him saying it was, seem entirely candid about what had happened. Someone would laughingly say a practical joke had been played on him.

"Incredible!" she said, and bit her lip.

Her sympathy was a delicious antidote for his feelings, and he plunged on. "Now, I'm sort of up a tree," he said miserably. "So much hung on that one performance."

"Why not try someone else?"

"I've done the rounds: agents, radio stations, publishers, and even a music critic I once met."

"You'll have a performance; if not today—tomorrow."

He retwisted the rolled manuscript and shoved it under his arm.

"Well, I can't make believe the grapes are sour; they look awfully sweet to me, and my mouth's watering."

"You must believe in yourself—and your work!" And looking full in Jeff's face, she added earnestly, "I'm sure your friends do."

He was pleased at the concern in her large eyes and felt more than ever determined. "Deborah, thanks," he said.

It was the first time he had used her first name. His tone of voice was soft and meaningful, and he spoke her name as if it were some mysterious formula. Her strength left her completely. She abandoned herself to his protection. She felt a sensual pleasure in his weakness; and she leaned back in her seat and looked at him.

"Yes, I'm sure you'll make it, Jeff."

This time the girl had spoken without raising her eyes; but when she did look up, those bluish-gray eyes clinging to his were more expressive than any words.

He felt queerly disturbed, shaken to the foundations of his lanky frame. For he had never experienced anything of such emotional intensity, and the words "Deborah, I adore you!" almost escaped his lips.

Maybe there was something in the driver's surly manner that brought him back to reality. In any case, with a clearness of which he would not have believed himself capable, he vividly saw the maze of paths, the clouds of possibilities ahead. And he lapsed into the gloomy meditation that had reawakened in him the ancient memories of his race. Momentarily cold fear settled in the pit of his stomach.

Deborah was a symbol of the racial prohibitions dictated

[87]

by society's unwritten laws, and he thought of the brutality and hypocritical censoriousness of the racial commandment: "Thou shalt not touch a white woman!"

Tradition had spoken, but Jeff's instincts rebelled, and he became more and more determined not to allow himself to be chained. He was damned if he'd conform to a past that denied him his humanity. And his manner gradually assumed a decisive character, and the possessive instinct triumphed!

Jeff caught the scent of her perfume, saw the rise and fall of her bosom, the languor in her eyes, her parted lips, and a look on her face which intoxicated him, and whatever vestige of his racial fears and his conscience that lingered seemed to evaporate.

She sat very still now; and he saw on her brow, her hair, her lips, and in her eyes, all the beautiful white women he had seen in the movies and magazines. His hand searched and found hers. Their passionate longing to possess one another overwhelmed them.

"Deborah," he whispered.

There was a compulsive drive in his movement and speech, and the girl swayed a little under his masculine touch; but mostly was she fascinated by the brownness of his skin, smooth, hairless and muscled, which might explore her body, explore the very intimacies of her secrets; and she shivered as though her clothes had been torn away.

"Oh, Jeff!" she breathed.

He thought of the perversity of a society that had thrown them together and now forbade them to embrace. Her surrender had heightened rather than allayed his fears that as a Negro he was a social cripple and handicapped in carrying out the manly role of the lover and protector of this girl.

"What if the man you loved was a cripple?" he asked and watched her carefully.

[88]

Deborah perceived the quaint indirection of his question and flushed.

"I should love him," she said after a pause. Then she slipped her arm through his, and her eyes rose to his.

Jeff's whole body shook. In her look and simple answer he found more, he found a sort of racial emancipation, he found her. There was something about her, in the taxi's shadowy corner, that contained warmth and hidden fervor, as though some quiet change had taken place deep within her. As he looked at her, he felt a strange, slow satisfaction. He had scored a victory over the whole white world; and since, in unspoken words, she had consented to all that might happen to her, the racial hurts and humiliations of the past were temporarily assuaged for him.

Silently, almost reverently, they sat now before this revelation of their secret; and though they were blissfully unaware, they had begun the inexorable journey into a racial inferno.

VI

Deborah's hair hung loosely over both shoulders. She was brushing it in long strokes as she considered her situation. She felt disturbingly shaken. An old resolve had been shattered. Her aim had always been to avoid errors and complications. Yet she had been idiot enough to become involved with a Negro. In self-justification she thought; after all, she had only drifted with the stream. But she really knew she had acted as though she were under the compulsion of an insatiable drive.

She walked slowly up and down the length of the spacious, slant-ceilinged, skylighted living room. It had a fireplace, a few pieces of modern furniture in it, several attractive lamps, a radio, and some books and pictures she valued. This third-floor studio apartment was one of four made in the remodeling of an old brownstone house. It had two bedrooms that hardly gave elbow space to dress, and a discreet alcove that had been made into an efficient Pullman kitchen.

She shared the place with an amiable co-worker, Tina Viviera, whom she now ardently wished was with her to help resolve her dilemma.

There was no doubt, none whatever, that she had passively

allowed the relationship to develop between herself and Jeff Kirby. She felt it was she who had seduced him, and that in doing so, she had seduced herself. Now she could not escape twinges of her conscience. What was to be done? Keep still and wait to see what happened, or confide in Tina? Tina, however, was so unpredictable, sometimes so excitable. Do nothing and trust to luck? After all, what guarantee did she have that the melody lingered on and she would see him again! She had been dragged into a maze of paths, a cloud of negations.

She lit a cigarette and gave a long sigh as she inhaled.

She walked into her bedroom restlessly and flung herself down before the mirror at her small dressing table. Her chin was slightly raised, her eyelids half closed as she let her hair ripple through her fingers. She was wearing black velvet slacks and white silk shirt open at the neck. The shimmering reflections from the swaying trees before her windows, the slight pulsation of the evening's heat, and her recollections —above all, the reality of her recollections, which had held her captive ever since last night—increased her distress and anxiety.

It had begun to grow dark while she sat there staring at herself in the mirror, and through the long windows deeper dark slowly crept in with the dusk. In a kind of lightning radiance she lived over again the scene of last night, when Jeff had made love to her. It was agony, then, but also bright joy. She was sophisticated enough to know that some passions are felt differently after a night's sleep, and she drew away from what this might mean for her. But Jeff's boldness, his passion, his tenderness, had carried her headlong into something she had never quite anticipated, or so she told herself.

The sun had set as Jeff and Deborah climbed hand in hand to the top of a cliff, high in the seclusion of the Palisades of

New Jersey, majestically overlooking the Hudson River, the skyline of Manhattan, and the jungles of Harlem. The car Jeff had borrowed for the ride there stood beside the road in the valley below like a black, inert ant. The scraggy sweep of hillside lay before them.

Deborah walked to the restraining rail along the cliff and looked at the dazzling sight, while Jeff watched her from a distance. Her eyes were sparkling and she idly kicked a stone over the cliff, then silently watched its crazy descent, as though she herself were tumbling into an abyss. She stood without moving, her body statuelike against the sundown, and felt Jeff melt into her mood. Afterward she only remembered fragments of what he said, but she had a feeling that his point was never made. She could see he was enraptured by the vision of her, a look of wonder and intoxication on his face.

As if to avoid disaster she instinctively looked at her watch and said, "Shall we go now, Jeff?" he nodded, silent. But his whole body was tense, demanding, and she half doubted what she saw, and felt. She would have been shocked if she could have known that at this very moment he was wondering whimsically whether what they said about white girls was true. . . .

They started down the hill, down a path where thick ferns grew under high pine trees, where in June lady-slippers blossomed, and where in the fall berries stretched endless strings of red beads. Jeff beat back the briar and bushes to clear the way, then, with quick force, he turned and seized her roughly, possessively. Her slender body was responsive and aroused, an invitation to violence. He brought her face close to his. She saw that his full lips were opened slightly.

"How lovely you are!" he said gently, but he was thinking, "How white you are!"

And she was thinking, "How brown you are!"

His mouth slowly met hers. Holding her close to him, he kissed her. She was sure his lips had been trembling. She lay motionless in his arms. Then he gently let her down into a natural enclosure of ferns and bushes, where she looked at the sky through a shaft of trees, and where the green mossy scents were like a subtle aphrodisiac. Her cool slim body shook as if under the restraint of misgiving; but then with wild trembling she yielded, surrendering passively, and physical communion engulfed them.

Jeff crouched on the mossy grass beside her. Transported as he was, his voice was low, whispering huskily, as he felt the luxurious exhaustion of victory. He looked and looked, as if he might never see her again: the excitingly unmarred white translucent skin tinted with pink nipples, and the blond hair spread like a spill of champagne, the crystals of sweat on her forehead, and her heavy, scented breathing.

—2—

There was no question last night of who wanted whom; they were together in desire, but now as she looked at her reflection in her dressing table mirror, again anxiety and even panic gripped her, and she wondered uneasily what thoughts were now drifting through Jeff's mind.

The familiar creak of the loose floorboards in front of the door of her apartment interrupted her thinking and her pulse started to beat rapidly. For a moment she did not move. Then she heard keys rattle, and relieved, hurried into the hall, she recognized the voice of her roommate and quickly helped her to open the door.

"Tina!" she said and hugged her with such force that the other girl cried, "Hey, look out—my hat!" With arms linked, they went into the living room.

Tina Viviera, five years older than Deborah, had olive

coloring and black hair, and was perhaps a bit fuller in the hips, but otherwise she was slender and of the same delicate complexion as her friend.

"You're so pale—is something wrong?" she asked as she put her hat and luggage aside. Her dark curved brows raised.

"Nothing, really," Deborah said as she reached into a box on a table, picked up a match, and lit a cigarette.

"Well, what trouble have you gotten into these three long weeks I've been away?" Tina asked, quietly observing a nervous quality in her roommate's manner of moving and speaking.

"I met an unusual man," Deborah answered with a matter-of-factness she didn't feel.

Her friend relished a nice bit of gossip; but she looked up quizzically, silently. Then after a pause she urged: "Tell me all, tell me every last bit!"

"Only—I picked up a man."

"Who made the first pass at whom?"

"Well, he wasn't quite a pick-up. I was introduced to him. While you were in Boston, Gil took me up to Harlem. But—brace yourself—he is a colored man!"

"A *Negro!*" Tina stared straight ahead without a change of expression. She was sure her roommate's words had an undertone of tenderness. Then, in a low voice, she intoned: "Holy Mary, Mother of God, pray for us!" Finally she said: "Go on, please, spill the gruesome details. Don't leave me in suspense. Out with it all, girl!"

"That's all there is."

"Just wait till your ould mather catches wind of this!" Tina said, throwing her hands up in mock despair.

"Well, he seemed awfully nice."

" 'Seemed awfully nice'! What's got into you lately? Tell me, Comstock, are you going to see him again?"

The questions shot stinging darts of doubt into Deborah's heart. She tried to be casual.

"Oh, I don't know—perhaps, sometime soon."

"What's he like? What does he do? What does he look like —one of those silky black ones?"

"Tina, please!" Deborah said sharply. "You know we agreed; no remarks like that about colored people."

"But I only wanted to know what he looks like, and what he looks like to you."

"Well, you know how I detest that sort of thing, even when you're joking."

The color had deepened in Deborah's face, and Tina watched her suspiciously.

Deborah lit another cigarette, threw herself across a large pillow-filled couch, their apartment's one real luxury, and stopped to think. She looked across the room at a bad Orozco reproduction Tina had picked up in a Third Avenue junk shop, "for a song," she had said. Deborah's mind was churning more than ever under her friend's probing questions.

"I hardly know what to say about him," she said slowly. "You'll probably think I'm an idiot. Well, to begin with, his name is Jeff Kirby. He plays the piano, and is, well, he's nice, *really* nice."

"There you are, talking like a woman half in love already!" Tina exploded. "If you had to pick up a colored man, why didn't you pick one of those dancing fellows like Bojangles. He makes a thousand dollars a week, they say!"

"Don't be vulgar, Tina!"

Both girls were silent for a while, each mulling over the ideas they batted back and forth like a badminton cock. Deborah looked with affection at Tina's wide eyes, preposterously plain, round face, with its heavily rouged lips. This outspoken girl, half Irish and half Portuguese, with her flippant manners, was one of the most successful social workers on New York's Lower East Side. Her manner and looks seemed to condone human weakness, and she had a persuasive way of suggesting remedies or courses of action to people who were contentious and dissatisfied with the dole society offered them. She could overcome the most obstinate resistance without creating suspicion and distrust. Deborah knew all this and envied her, but Deborah's mother was upset to learn that her daughter lived with such a flibbertigibbet. She had often dwelled at length on Tina's "shanty-Irish-Catholic" background, and Deborah had stoutly defended her friend.

Although Tina knew Deborah well, was perhaps closer to her than anyone else, their camaraderie was still detached. In fact, Tina had never called her anything but Deborah, or of late, Comstock. She had quickly learned that no chummy brevity was possible with a girl like her. Her aloof, preoccupied manner kept everyone at arm's length. Tina had learned in Boston that Deborah hadn't even acquired any sort of nickname, even as a child, not even a pet name that would indicate some familiarity between her family and herself. Maybe her well-bred and self-contained mother had early dismissed any attempt to call her "Debbie" or "Debs" or some other corruption she would have considered vulgar.

As for thoughts of money being truly vulgar to Deborah, Tina was somewhat skeptical. It was true that she worked with the poor and unfortunate, but this did not entirely conceal her love of various types of luxury. Her clothes were simple-seeming but always costly. She sought out more and more off-beat people of various racial backgrounds. Her reason for this, she told Tina, was that she felt she needed such contacts in order to broaden her knowledge of human beings. She was undoubtedly sincere enough in this, but might this not unconsciously be to give her a sense of superiority and power?

"And now what?" Tina finally asked.

Deborah left her own doubts unspoken.

—3—

The doorbell rang indecisively.

"It might be a 'special' from mother," Deborah said as she got up from the couch, walked to the hall, and pressed the buzzer to release the lock of the vestibule door. Then she opened the apartment door, walked to the balustrade, and leaned over. Even in the shadows she instantly recognized the figure coming up the stairs as that of Jeff. She felt a faint giddiness. His unannounced arrival had surprised her; yet somehow subconsciously she had been marking time, waiting for him.

He looked up from the landing below and smiled. Under his arm he carried a long box of what were obviously flowers, looking for all the world like an earnest suitor. He was dressed differently from the evening before, now in a neatly pressed dark blue suit, and it crossed Deborah's mind that he might be wearing his best. As he reached the head of the stairs, he took off his hat and his tall, lanky figure stood before her.

"Well!" she said at last, because she could think of nothing else. "Well!"

He did not know what to answer. His dark brown eyes met hers with frank affection. For a moment they stood face to face, silent. Then he put his arm around her waist. Yet he did not attempt to pull her close, and she, feeling his hesitency, turned toward him and kissed him lightly. Then she gently pulled away.

"I hope you don't mind," he said apologetically. "I had to come, just to bring these flowers. I hoped you'd be in because I wanted you to have them for—for very special reasons."

Deborah smiled warmly and held the door open for him. As he started to come in the floorboards creaked. "That's our built-in burglar alarm," she said. They both laughed, and the tension receded. He took her arm and walked her through the door, stooping instinctively as very tall men do when they approach unfamiliar doorways. Then he handed her the box and followed her into the living room. The place had the pleasurable odor of mingled tobacco fumes and perfume. It smelled as he had presumed her home would smell—and he liked it.

"Jeff, this is Tina," Deborah said, opening the box; she peeked in then hurried toward the kitchen.

He nodded politely in the other girl's direction, and Tina smiled broadly, mischievously, as they talked about the weather.

"I must find something to put these in," Deborah was saying, her voice sounding from the distance as if she were in an echo chamber. She came back with two vases filled with water, and set them on the coffee table. With obvious pleasure she pushed back the green tissue in the long box containing long-stemmed red roses. "Oh, Jeff, how perfectly lovely! Thank you!" she exclaimed, as she carefully lifted them out of the box, and started arranging them in the vases.

"I'm glad you like them."

Tina echoed Deborah's sentiments. But she could hardly have known that her roommate's delight was for vastly different reasons. Deborah understood the intimate reason for this gift, and inside she exulted. Both she and Jeff recognized it as a symbol of their secret, and she understood that after all the overwhelming impressions of their first meetings, this was the first moment of real love.

Jeff smiled and chose a seat facing Tina. He looked at her and something about the merry-whimsicality of her face made him feel that she was a person without color bias. He liked her instantly. But it was obvious that she was most curious about him, and Jeff did not know what precisely to make of her easy informality.

"Tina," Deborah began, as if she sensed his bewilderment, "is my roommate and works at the settlement house with me. I think I told you about her."

Jeff did no more than smile.

Deborah returned to the couch, and made herself comfortable by propping her elbows on a pile of pillows, her fingers interlaced and supporting her chin. Her eyes were lifted to Jeff. Tina noticed there was warmth but little color in Deborah's cheeks, and an understanding smile came to her lips. Jeff meantime had seen an easel standing in a corner cluttered with stacked canvases. He caught his breath. "Are *you* the artist?" he said to Deborah with surprise edging his question.

"Not really, but I try on weekends."

"If I were in her shoes," Tina said admiringly, "I'd quit the settlement house and just paint—that girl's got real stuff in her! She's already had a show of her own."

"Jeff's really *the* artist, Tina. He composes music."

"So—you're both artists!" Tina watched Deborah's eyes cling to Jeff's.

He caught Tina's meaningful glance at her roommate. "She knows of my feelings for her, then," he thought. "Of course. How can one hide the fact from such a girl!"

He said, "I've had nothing published, and things look none too promising right now. Sometimes I wonder if I can honestly call myself a composer."

"Even to be a composer and fail is something!" Deborah said as she got up from the couch and headed in the direction of the kitchen.

Tina nodded.

"What sort of things do you compose?" she asked, thinking to herself that she liked his honesty.

"I write serious things, if that answers your question. But I'm afraid I'm stereotyped as a Negro composer."

"How do you mean that?"

He looked gloomily at the floor. "Well, every time a Negro concert singer opens his mouth people somehow expect him to sing spirituals!" There was a puzzled frown on her face so he added, "For example, to ask a Negro to sing spirituals only—and people often do—is like asking Paderewski to play mazurkas only." He explained further, and when Deborah returned she quickly caught the drift of their conversation.

"I agree—to a point," Deborah said. She brought a tray of martinis and a plate of canapés, and put them on the coffee table before them. Seating herself on the couch, and plumping up the pillows to form a rest for her back, she declared: "Jeff, it seems to me that's no reason not to identify oneself with Negro music—especially for a Negro."

"No?"

"Why, you're denying yourself a rich heritage. Dvořák in his *New World Symphony* certainly had no inhibitions about using the spirituals!"

"Now, there's an idea for you, Mr. Kirby," Tina offered, and lifted her glass to toast him.

Jeff was silent now, a look of complete absorption on his face. He trifled absent-mindedly with his drink then ate a canapé. Deborah did not take her eyes from him. She noted how correctly he ate; he managed to take the canapés into his mouth without the crumbs settling on his lips, he barely moistened his lips while eating and drinking, yet there was nothing finicky or dandified in his gestures.

"Why, of course," he began, continuing his thoughts aloud. "You're right—so right!"

Deborah was elated that her ideas had impressed him. The

excitement of a new discovery showed in his eyes. He realized that a whole field of music he had ignored in fear of being typed as a Negro composer was open to him, and the possibilities seemed limitless. He was skilled enough as a musician to know that many spirituals were large enough in form to permit further development, even symphonic development. And he suddenly remembered what Gershwin had done with the Negro syncope in his *Porgy and Bess*.

"Well," he said, "this begins a new approach to composition for me, and a battle for acceptance." Then he added with a laugh, "Be my guests at the barricades!"

He had quickly made a far-reaching decision, but he did not feel the anxiety that often accompanies the exploration of the new. He was not to be a lonely occupant of this position toward his work. Deborah had made this clear. He looked at her intently, and he loved her more, in a lyric sort of way. They exchanged looks of understanding, and Deborah felt personally triumphant. Her lips softened. She felt as though she would cry, and she carefully cleared a lump from her throat.

–4–

Tina saw their tenderness as she sat silently watching them both; and in her mind they were emotionally linked in spite of their outward discretion. Then her eyes concentrated on Jeff. The wistful candor in his brown eyes gave her a sudden feeling that she must protect him. She was now eager to take up his cause, whatever it might be, since she saw clearly that both he and Deborah were in love.

She got up from her chair heavily, and with a few parting words of apology headed in the direction of her bedroom. They soon heard the door slammed to, and Deborah drew a long breath.

[101]

"Tina had a tiring day traveling," Deborah said as she switched on the radio. "She'll be dead to the world in five minutes!" Dance music came softly into the room. Jeff got up, took her in his arms, and to the slow tempo they danced, then stopped and clung to each other.

When he attempted to lead her to her bedroom, she resisted nervously, but after a long while his kisses and whispered persuasions met less and less resistance. Then he lifted her off her feet and carried her into the room, and put her down on the bed. He crept alongside her, slipped one arm under her, and pulled her close to him. They crushed each other in a wildly passionate embrace.

It was not only the martinis they had drunk, it was something else that gave their desires such volcanic eruption—a contact between the different races which they could both now acknowledge frankly; for her, skin to skin with a Negro; for him, skin to skin with a white girl. Jeff, who until now had treated Deborah with deferential tenderness, suddenly ripped open her blouse, unzippered her slacks, and locked her white body fiercely within his thighs. His passion rose as her white arms clutched his shoulders; and all rational thought left her when he took her naked breasts into his brown hands. They made love. He had to put his hand over her mouth to stifle her cries, for fear Tina might overhear them, until finally they both collapsed, exhausted . . .

While they rested she took his hand and pressed it to her cheek, and kissed each finger one by one; and he kissed each pink nipple of her breasts lightly. Then they heard a noise in Tina's room, followed perhaps by the rustle of a dress and the squeak of a door.

At least they thought they heard these noises. For a moment neither of them moved. He twisted around suddenly and looked at her in the dimly lit room. She said in a whisper, "That might be Tina getting up." They quickly dressed and composed themselves as best they could, then discovered in alarm that her door had been left ajar, and returned to the living room. There were crackers still uneaten on the tray, and the empty glasses. She sat in a chair, and he put a glass in her hand. Light fell on her there, so that he could see her face, eyes, and hair, as he remembered her during their love-making—a strangely beautiful young woman from another, perhaps preferable world. He sat on the edge of a chair.

"Suppose she heard us," Jeff said.

"She wouldn't have known what was happening—but I don't want her to suspect anything." Then she explained candidly: "Poor Tina. I've had plenty of callers but this has never happened, not in the whole time we've lived together, which is almost a year." Jeff felt reassured on several counts. But all the same they were both not so sure of their privacy that they could return to Deborah's bedroom now; so they sat there silently listening.

The floorboards before the apartment door creaked. Then the bell rang loudly, followed by a peremptory pounding at the door. Jeff was instantly alarmed. He looked at her questioningly. Deborah, carefully smoothing her hair, opened the door. On the threshold stood the superintendent's wife, a wide-hipped woman who had a habit of prowling about the halls at night. She was, as Tina said, a "dilly." Tonight she had a worn expression, and dark, markedly undercircled eyes. Her face was clabber white, and she was breathing with an audible wheezing sound. The arteries on her temples were distended, and when she spoke her hard, metallic voice shook.

"This is a pretty goings-on," she said as she pushed her way into the living room and saw Jeff. "Entertaining Negroes, eh! This ain't that sort of place, and I won't have it." She turned to Jeff. "I'll trouble you to leave—and now!"

They stood motionless, staring at the woman.

[103]

"Mrs. Ellerton!" Deborah shouted indignantly as she struggled to keep her composure.

"Hey, lady," Jeff exclaimed, greatly distressed, "what's eating you? I haven't—"

"Out! Out, I say!" the woman interrupted imperiously. Her lips were drawn back from her yellowish teeth, and her breath came in short hisses.

He hesitated, and his eyes appealed to Deborah. He was dismayed by the woman's venomous manner; and stunned, too, by the stern self-righteousness of her absurd posture.

"Leave! or, I'll call the police," she insisted loudly. "This is a respectable house, and I won't have this sort of thing."

"You ignorant, evil woman!" Deborah gasped, steadying herself by the mantlepiece. "You better go," she added to Jeff, "and let me handle this."

"The woman's drunk," he shouted as he reached for his hat and started toward the door.

"Drunk am I!" the woman screamed, her eyes wide and red-rimmed. "Well, your kind ought to be horse-whipped."

Deborah turned, her face was deadly white, her eyes burning dark. "Please, Jeff," she managed to say. "Please go— and call me later."

"Aha!" cried Mrs. Ellerton. "So, you go with him. Shame, you huzzy!"

Jeff wheeled around sharply, the doorway framing his great shoulders, and glared at the woman as if he was about to strike her, but Deborah's muted appeal softened him. In that moment she herself could have spit and kicked, and happily pounded the woman's ugly face, as the indignation she felt twisted angrily within her. And to his dismay, Jeff saw that she could not help the tears rolling down her cheeks.

"I'll ask you to move, young lady—and in short order!"

Tina disturbed finally by the commotion, dashed into the

room. She was wrapped in a pale green robe, and her head was bound in a yellow scarf—she had washed her hair. She immediately recognized the crisis for what it was. She faced the landlady belligerently. "'I'll ask you to move,'" she mimicked. "What do you mean *move*—we've got a lease!" Then turning to her agitated roommate, she said," "Why, the old biddy is insane."

Anger had swelled the veins in Jeff's forehead. He opened his mouth to vent his rage but could not. Tina's voice had gone up an octave.

"We'll move when we get right good and ready, and we'll have anybody we choose visit us!"

The uproar continued as Jeff made his way down the stairs in wordless protest. The neighbors of the two girls were gathered in the hall. They eyed him suspiciously, and he suddenly felt beaten, depressed, and alien; but he was mostly concerned for Deborah, who he decided, was helpless in the face of the noisy prejudice the woman had exhibited. The street was quiet and bleak as he finally extricated himself from the emotional debris, still outraged and feeling weak and impotent.

VII

From the wet of the day's slowly ending fall afternoon, it became one of those damp, misty Boston evenings with occasional thunder showers. The red cobblestones and cement sidewalks shone under drizzling rain as Deborah's taxi stopped in front of 23 Arlington Hill, a two-story, red brick house. The windows were lighted, shining through the thin, slanting boughs of sturdy elm trees that stood in trimly measured distances along the street. Three shallow steps led to a white-painted door with a brass knocker and a small brass plate with engraved letters: COMSTOCK.

It was six o'clock. Deborah fumbled for her key and opened the door.

"Mother," she called from the hallway as she took off her white beret, raincoat, and the jacket of her navy blue suit. She hung them in the closet and put her overnight bag aside. "It's me—Deborah."

"I'm here, dear, in the living room."

Deborah stopped to look at herself in the long, hallway mirror above the triangular table against the wall, and there saw a special delivery letter addressed in familiar handwriting, a letter from Jeff. How thoughtful of him! She started to open it, decided instead to see her mother first, and stuffed it into the pocket of her skirt.

The house, warm and bright, was shining with cleanliness and smelling its own house smell, characteristic but indefinable. Abbie Comstock was standing in front of the fireplace when her daughter came in, apparently preoccupied by a painting hanging above it. Deborah always thought the painting rather too large for the room, and always had to squelch an urge to say so.

Tonight she had arrived to spend her monthly weekend with her mother—"tours of duty," she called them. Mrs. Comstock approvingly saw the pearls, white turtleneck sweater, and slim-line skirt she wore, and kissed her daughter hungrily. With small mincing steps, Mrs. Comstock found a chair. And as always, her daughter was solicitous about her health. To Deborah's and everybody's astonishment, Mrs. Comstock had on the day of her husband's death miraculously abandoned her wheelchair, in which she had taken refuge some years before.

–2–

Abbie Comstock was in her early sixties, tall and fleshy, with a magnificent head of blue-white hair that made the rest of her features come as a surprise, when she turned around in her blue, shapeless print dress with splashes of big flowers. She wore spectacles, and there was a suggestion of a double chin. Her lightly rouged mouth was prim and innocent.

"I'm expecting the family tonight," she said.

"Oh!" said Deborah tentatively, but she realized that her mother's tone carried special emphasis.

Abbie Comstock had reared her two daughter in this venerable house, so neat that it was anonymous. It had, in fact,

a forthright solidity that suggested her complacent character. You could no more imagine Mrs. Comstock stuffing her
possessions into suitcases and trotting off for a weekend then
you would expect her to fly to Tibet. She belonged in these
faded green surroundings, as much as the stiff-back chairs,
the grasscloth wallpaper, the begonia plants in the window
alcove, and the pieces of old porcelain bric-a-brac.

If the room had any distinction at all, it came from two
gilt-framed, well-executed paintings done in somber colors.
Each was neatly spotlighted by a shaded electric bulb
attached to the top of the frame, perhaps to dramatize their
importance in this household: one was a portrait of Abbie's
dead father, Simon Heath, whose gaunt features bore a
startling resemblance to the pictures of Christ, and occupied
the place of honor above the fireplace. On the wall opposite
was a portrait of her father-in-law, Levi Comstock, who had
the fierce look of the bearded John Brown. She had moved
her own father's picture to the place of prominence above
the fireplace after the death of her husband.

"You must be tired, Mother. Maybe a cup of hot tea will
help," Deborah offered as Mrs. Comstock settled heavily
into her chair, sighed, and for a moment wearily closed her
eyes. It was a posture that had lately become usual.

"Yes, a little tired," she said. "But really, you know, I'd
almost rather do the work myself than have Sarah around."

She spoke with her eyes averted, so that she did not see her
daughter stiffen. Sarah, as so often happened, had not come
to work that morning and Deborah knew what her mother
meant. She suspected it was because of newly developed
feelings toward Negroes. She turned away to go to the
kitchen to make the tea.

"Here's your tea, Mother," she said when she came back,
after waiting patiently for Mrs. Comstock to rouse from her
reverie and take the cup and saucer.

Mrs. Comstock straightened herself to a position of greater comfort in her chair, took the tea and smiled.

No one could say that Mrs. Comstock's Negro maid, Sarah, was a really pleasant woman. Even Deborah felt a sense of strain, often exasperation, in her presence; but lately her mother had taken a kind of passionate notice of Sarah. Her mother's tendency to be angry with the colored help was increasingly disquieting to Deborah. Lately, too, she had been full of stories about the nasty habits and ill temper that was being exhibited by "these people." Only yesterday, she told Deborah, the colored handy man had made a point of sweeping and puttering about the yard and basement, avoiding Mrs. Comstock's orders.

When her daughter pointed out how frequently she had told such stories, Mrs. Comstock simply stared at her and said, "Why, they're insufferable since—" and broke off.

When Deborah quietly rebuked her about her attitude toward the maid, her mother said in the most matter-of-fact way, "Why, she just hates us."

Deborah finally became really annoyed when her mother reported a list of all the precious things she suspected Sarah had stolen and of others that "that woman broke out of sheer meanness. Mind you," Mrs. Comstock added, "never once has she broken anything cheap or ordinary; only things I've treasured."

Mrs. Comstock, of course, would have denied any prejudice against Negroes. She was the sort of woman who denied all prejudice, sure that her enlightened, Christian mind was immune to pedestrian aberrations. It was proof enough that, as a hobby, she wrote liberal children's plays for the distinguished Lowell Day School, where she had taught briefly before her marriage to Park Comstock, and where her children had begun their education. Her plays, if haphazardly constructed, nevertheless were full of noble sentiments. In them she asked all children to be friends and good neighbors regardless of race or religion or nationality, and some of these sentiments, as had been true with her own children, did rub off on them. Moreover, she was not only a friend of the school's lady principal, but was friendly as well to the office secretary and the porter.

If Mrs. Comstock seemed unbalanced these days on the subject of Negroes, the truth was she had, as Tina predicted, "caught wind" of Jeff Kirby and, to make it worse, in a rather roundabout way. Not that Deborah had dishonestly hidden the facts from her mother. She had been waiting for a propitious moment to break the news to her. Unfortunately she had been anticipated by nosy Charlie Stowe, who, in one of his periodic trips to New York, met Deborah at the theater accompanied by this colored fellow, Jeff Kirby. With bizarre elaborations he had reported the incident to his Aunt Emily, who had posthaste relayed the details to Mrs. Comstock.

Deborah's mother was sufficiently alarmed to summon her daughter to Boston. Deborah's forthright explanation gave Mrs. Comstock little satisfaction, since she was unable to dismiss the incident as a vagary, perhaps a mere harmless flirtation. She wisely did not become angry, hoping not to close the door to discussion. The days passed, and Mrs. Comstock, drawing herself up to her full dignity, was forced to say to Aunt Emily's insistent inquiries: "My dear, it's a subject we do not talk about!"

—3—

These had become days of tension between Mrs. Comstock and her daughter. Each trip Deborah made to Boston was another reprieve for her parent, as Mrs. Comstock did not yet know exactly what Deborah intended to do about her Mr. Kirby. Outwardly she acted as though the girl would come around and she therefore refused to become seriously disturbed; at least she maintained appearances. She talked cheerfully and immersed herself in plans for the scheduled Christmas play in Christ Congregational Church. Yet for days she had been more and more overcome by a sense of despair. She felt as though Deborah were packing to go away forever.

Mrs. Comstock's heart and mind were indeed heavily burdened during the months after she had learned about Jeff Kirby. After all, love of her two girls was now the prime motive of her existence. But Abbie Comstock must have been completely unaware of what her daughter actually felt and thought. She had forgotten the child's championing of the colored servants and friends of her childhood.

—4—

Abbie Comstock had become a mother late in life. Deborah was born when she was in her forties. Even so, her children had early made her feel unworldly, with their breezy manners, slang, and sophisticated talk. Tonight when Deborah finally told her mother that she planned to marry Jeff Kirby, Mrs. Comstock's startled reactions were a piece of the same fabric. As always, she grappled futilely with something beyond her powers of logic and understanding.

"I suppose you mean you don't think I ought to marry him," Deborah said. Her voice was as light as she could make it sound.

Mrs. Comstock gestured helplessly. "As I say. I hesitate to tell you what I think. After all, we've never agreed about anything. You've always been a headstrong girl. But it does seem to me a rash step. You've the right to expect a husband of distinction. Your looks, such as they are, and your family all give you the right. If you wait, there is no doubt you would marry well. Why, only yesterday—"

"I know, mother. You saw Paul Inge's mother."

[111]

"Well, in choosing a young man, a colored man, in an exceptionally precarious calling, you seem to me to be throwing yourself away. But this is *my* opinion. It's perhaps not worth much to you, but to me—it's painful to say—but I do think this is the outcome of your extraordinary ideas, and selfishness."

"But I love him, Mother, and he needs me!"

"Two years ago, when your father was living, the starving Chinese needed you. Now it's the Negroes who need you."

"Isn't love important?"

Deborah had yet to realize that though love was praised everywhere as pure, noble, and beautiful, love involving a white girl and a Negro became a physical thing of dirty jokes, dirty thoughts, dirty practices, was denounced as something evil, impure, and alien to respectability. No wonder Mrs. Comstock looked at her daughter with irritated reproof.

"Please Deborah! No cheap histrionics. We're not talking about the plot of a dime novel."

"But you'd have me marry a drip like Paul."

"Well, you'd be a secure woman, at least. Now, if you marry that Mr. Kirby you'll be handicapping yourself. Instead of marriage helping you forward, it will drag you down."

As she spoke, Mrs. Comstock had visions of her daughter holed up in a tenement in Harlem, a place as distant and incomprehensible to her as the jungles of Africa, and perhaps, in her mind, as hazardous. Inwardly she recoiled and perspiration broke out on her forehead beneath the powder.

"How can you think such a thing, Mother," said Deborah as she watched Mrs. Comstock shudder. "I've heard you express your own views of *dull* marriage often enough. Why have you changed all of a sudden?"

"I haven't changed at all! I think your marrying Jeff Kirby

is in perfect accord with everything I've always said and believed about you.

"And further," Mrs. Comstock went on, "I am sorry for Mr. Kirby. For him, too, it's a mistake, a terrible mistake."

Deborah's lips quivered. "I don't think he would agree to that or even think it. I know he wouldn't."

"My dear young lady, the best woman becomes a burden to a poor man, much more to a poor colored man. No, my dear child, since you really want to know what I think, I think you're behaving like a selfish child. You've forgotten everyone but yourself and your appetites. What about me and my position—and my friends? How can I face people? What about your poor sister and her children? They'll have a *colored* uncle—heaven forbid! No, Deborah, this sort of thing isn't done. You must think of the family."

"I don't mean to be unkind, Mother, but isn't it better to have a decent and honest colored uncle than an uncle who absconded with other people's money, a thief!"

Abbie Comstock ignored the attack on Sybil's wayward brother-in-law. Indeed, if she had been pushed to a decision, in all likelihood she would have chosen without hesitation the white knave to the black saint.

"There's a difference in your position and his," she said, "not to mention the differences in race and culture and up-bringing. You will, to say nothing of him, regret this absurd step if you don't change your course. Yes. You'll regret it."

"Oh, Mother, don't be angry with me. Please—try to understand."

—5—

The sound of the door knocker startled them both.

It was nearly nine o'clock. The storm was moving away. The rumble of thunder was dull, so that the knocking at the door was heard clearly in the living room.

[113]

Deborah, relieved to escape her mother's vast unhappiness, hurried from the room to open the door, and was surprised to see the family lawyer, old Philip Channing. He was, as she remembered him, in character: erect, his folded raincoat and umbrella hung on his arm, he carried his crushed felt hat gingerly; his glasses perched perilously on his big nose, and his long face had a lugubrious expression. His voice, a little tart, betrayed his human irritation at having to be in the streets on a sloppy night.

"Well, Deborah," he said.

The girl hugged him affectionately, her lips touching his cheek. His wrinkled, yellow, starched face screwed up in pleasure.

Her tired eyes had a strained look, which somehow added to her loveliness tonight. Mr. Channing, privy to the family's secrets, wondered if she suspected he had already been told about her Mr. Kirby. It had saddened and exasperated him. What was the world coming to! Suddenly he thought of her cousin, young John, who went abroad to study and had married a foreign girl. What a sad blow to his Aunt Abbie, and to all the Comstocks—and such a promising fellow! He simply could no longer grasp the reasons for people taking risks for the sake of passion. But he gave Deborah a furtive look of admiration. As he thought back wistfully, a longing to escape into fantasies beset him.

"Mother," Deborah announced as she led the way to the living room, "It's Mr. Channing."

Abbie Comstock came forward to greet him, and they shook hands cordially. Her face, he thought, had a quelled expression.

It was immediately apparent that Mr. Channing was expected, as her mother chose a conversational grouping of chairs, and offered one to him, all of which implied a long visit.

"Well, Abbie," he said, and detected an apprehensive quality in her smile.

There was a long silence before Deborah tactfully slipped out of the room to her own room upstairs to allow her mother to talk alone with the lawyer. As soon as she was in her room, she immediately ripped open her letter from Jeff.

DEBORAH, LOVE:

I've been working like a dog these last few days. Even though this will be only a note I believe you'll understand. Just today I finished my term's work at Juilliard—and as you predicted, everyone likes the Negro syncope in my work. One professor said it distinguished mine from the work of the other students.

We had to submit a string quartet, a double fugue, a thesis consisting of two songs (I wrote the words to one myself. You must wait to hear them until they're actually sung in public), and a work for full symphony orchestra. I've already received three requests for the first performance rights on the quartet and it will probably be done sometime this coming season. I was going to submit the "orchestra set" to Dimitri Metropolous, and/or George Szell, as I told you—but Gil has asked me to let him handle it. He says he can get it performed by Birnbaum because they're old pals.

I've missed you very much these last hectic, lonely days. I shall call you Monday night, as soon as you get back! I love you much more than you even suspect, and more again,

JEFF

P.S. Regards to your mother! ! ! !

Deborah reread the letter with a feeling of elation, but she could not help remembering how crestfallen and dispirited he had been when his work was rejected before. And now she hoped anxiously for him. Even so, his letter had given her a soaring lift and fortified her against her mother's objections.

—6—

Mr. Channing, like Deborah, was quite unaware that he had been summoned to a gathering of the Comstock clan to deal with Deborah's intransigence about a Negro. Most of the time when he saw Abbie nowadays it was to answer whether this or that innocuous business plan was a good idea. The last time he had told her bluntly that old ladies have no business using their principal to speculate in any stocks, especially those not even listed on the Exchange.

Mrs. Comstock sighed deeply. She looked unhappily up at the Gothic features of old Levi Comstock, who returned her glance from the square frame with a determined glint in his eye. She hesitated before she spoke, and when she did so her voice was urgent.

"Philip, what I wanted to ask, I know I'm asking a great deal, well, could you, would you talk to Deborah?"

"Yes, I'll talk to her," he said, frowning. "I suppose something should be done. I still don't know quite what, nor, I think, does anybody else." The answer was the necessary one; but he could not help adding, "Only I'm afraid there's little anyone can say unless she should suddenly come to her senses, and in that case, there would be nothing to say."

He made a curious gesture of distress.

"Well," Mrs. Comstock said, "she's making quite a spectacle of herself being seen about with a—a colored person. And now she says she wants to marry him!"

He said coolly, "Maybe she's fallen in love."

"Absurd, but she says so."

"Then it's probably true, which makes the situation all the more difficult."

He watched her face change and worry deepen on it.

"I suppose"—she lowered her voice—"my daughter comes by her extraordinary ideas naturally; in her blood, so to speak. On her father's side, you remember, they were all freethinkers. Her grandfather, Levi, was an abolitionist, always doing something for colored people. Nowadays he'd be called a Communist!"

"You might say it's a Comstock tradition," Mr. Channing said. His type of legal mind never wasted time on causes; he weighed consequences.

Thoughtful, Mrs. Comstock said, "Yes, but it's a terrible burden to carry."

"Well, maybe old Levi outlived his times," he said. "But take a man like your husband. Anyone who knew him would agree that if there ever was a fair and just man, a man absolutely unbigoted and unprejudiced, it was he. Yet I honestly think he would have opposed Deborah's colored associations."

"Probably. He himself at least had the good sense to forget that obsession about colored people. It ruined many lives, and is now ruining my daughter's."

Mr. Channing understood the tears that came into Mrs. Comstock's eyes, yet some strange perversity suddenly seized the old gentlemen. "Why not let the old goose stew in her own juice!" The thought immediately upset his honest soul. He was not enough of a scoundrel, or sadist, to turn his back on the agitated, helpless Abbie; perhaps a vague sense of loyalty to Deborah and his old friend Park Comstock stirred in him. His own inclinations to chivalry settled the question finally, and forced him back in the groove.

Abbie Comstock was silent now, disturbed as she had never been in her life. Worry creased, lined, and tightened the features of her face. It was clear that her recollections now concerned her husband. Mr. Channing calculated that it was almost two years now since he had served as a pallbearer at Park's funeral. His eyes wandered to the portrait of Levi Comstock and back to prim Abbie Comstock.

She caught his roving glance. "Yes," she said. "There is a bit of Park Comstock in her, I'm sorry to say, a total disregard of the feelings of others. There's his brother, Gregory, too; well, I won't bring that up now. Much of it you've never heard, but because of my husband's people, I *knew* that something like this would eventually happen to Deborah . . ." Mr. Channing bristled at her hint of fault in his old friend.

–7–

What Abbie Comstock saw, looking back over her life with Park Comstock, could not be known to Mr. Channing, but he had been aware of certain selected particulars along the way. As a boy, Park Comstock was never allowed to forget his father's exalted passion for the rights of Negroes, and indeed the family's responsibility for them. His mother, Esther, her bony face shaded by an old-fashioned bonnet, her Bible in one hand and the strong fingers of the other clasping those of her small son, would frequently take him to his father's study kept intact for many years after Levi's death and remind him of the family's abolitionist tradition and what naturally was expected of him.

Before his marriage he showed Abbie the place, cluttered with old furniture and faded grey-brown tapestry. It was a veritable museum of antislavery memorabilia: old, dusty, and yellowing copies of newspapers, crudely written slave narratives, pamphlets, books, letters and photographs, one signed by the great Frederick Douglass, ex-slave and statesman. Stacked in corners were leather bull-whips, handcuffs, iron

[118]

tongs, shackles and coffle chains—briefly, the Old South's
paraphernalia for keeping the Negro enslaved. These his
father had industriously collected in gathering firsthand information about the slavery system, and he often used them
as exhibits during his public orations denouncing the institu-
tion of Negro slavery.

Park Comstock lived daily with these things, poignant and
tragic in their meanings, as the selected heir to his father's
mission. In fact, he was the one of her six sons that his
mother had high hopes would enter the ministry, as a distinguished way of carrying the Word abroad; but inwardly,
as he grew to manhood, he rejected everything. Only when
his mother died did he abandon the cause, finally and irre-
vocably, and like Lincoln's son, Robert, develop a hearty distaste for the subject of Negroes.

Mr. Channing was quite aware, however, that Abbie Comstock had waged a vigorous campaign to keep Park from
backsliding and returning to his inherited responsibilities,
and had won, even to the point of persuading him to dis-
mantle old Levi's study, drop his membership in the Boston
Urban League, give up his inherited place on the board of
Attucks Institute for Negroes, and resign his trusteeship of
the National Negro Scholarship Fund. But she was not quite
so successful with Deborah. Her daughter wrapped herself
in the mantle of the missionary, so Mrs. Comstock explained
to Mr. Channing, and in her relationship with Mr. Kirby was
assuming the fanatic nonsense about Negroes that Park Comstock had abandoned.

"My husband must be turning in his grave," she said
miserably. "I'm glad the good man was spared the knowledge of his daughter's—ah—misalliance."

Mr. Channing nodded and pursed his lips.

Mrs. Comstock sighed wearily, as if collecting her
thoughts.

"I have sometimes wondered if it was wise to have sent Deborah to college," she said. "But she was bent upon going, and of course her father always backed her up in everything. That's why I never was very good with her. She had only to go above my authority whenever she pleased."

The expression on her face when she talked about Park Comstock was revealing of the many human characteristics she was unable to comprehend. Her husband was not the cocksure extrovert she portrayed him to be. Philip Channing had gathered quite a contrary view of him as his attorney. He was, no doubt, a good man, a successful man, as she had said, and had, in fact, accumulated a good deal of money as an investment broker. But Park Comstock had doubts, deep lingering doubts, doubts specifically about whether he had dissipated his best years in a sterile occupation; and doubts, even guilt, about having abandoned his liberal responsibilities.

He had tried, then, to share these doubts with his wife, but she had failed to add anything but frustration. He had confided diffidently to Mr. Channing. As Park reminisced with his friend he alluded to his brief, unromantic courtship with Abbie and the years since then, which had come to mean little to him. He described her extraordinary interest in the settlement houses before they were married; then the time he walked into his study in the house in Haverhill and found her, flushed and breathless, reading his will. He had later talked of divorce, but hesitated to make a move when she suddenly became ill and finally a chairborne invalid.

Mr. Channing suspected that Simon Heath was the reason for the warped relationship between Park and Abbie Comstock. Her father, who had lived amiably off the proceeds of his sharp-trading Yankee forebears, was a sweet, temperate man if contrasted with the turbulent Levi. He had been a poet and friend to such great men of his day as Emerson,

Thoreau, Whitman, and Henry Ward Beecher—but he had lacked Emerson's gifts, Thoreau's self-discipline, Whitman's sense of values, and Beecher's dedication to a cause. He was a man of pacific inclinations and turned his head aside at the fanaticism of the abolitionists, whom he called "impassioned illiterates."

As a young man he stood apart from all the issues churning men's minds, as he stood apart from life itself. He had done nothing noteworthy until in the twilight of his pointless existence he quite by accident became a model for the painters, one of whom had discovered that he bore an extraordinary resemblance to pictures of Christ. He afterward made an ego-stimulating career of this fact. Not only did he sit for the prominent painters of his time, but he was much in demand for church plays of the New Testament. And he did indeed come to feel himself anointed.

Abbie Comstock, whose mother died when she was an infant, admired him extravagantly, and because of her husband's lack of understanding (maybe virility), clung to this pale, ineffectual man with a desperate passion. As he more and more walked the earth with the air of a messiah, she more and more developed the worshipful pose of the acolyte. Her domestic debacle started, when, in Simon Heath's declining years, and maybe because of his declining income, she brought her father to live with them over her husband's objections. Soon afterward she rejected the offensive masculinity of her husband, forbade him access to her bed, and sought instead the kindly attentions of her senile father.

"Mother acts strangely around Grandpa," Deborah had innocently said to her father as a child. "She kisses him too much; she scares me. And her hands are always hot when she touches me afterward. Maybe Mother has a fever or something, Father."

Park Comstock had listened and merely pursed his lips.

He of course had observed his wife's emotional dependence on the old man, whom he seemed unable to displace in her affections. But even Simon Heath's death at ninety-three made no material alteration in her conduct toward her husband. Abbie shifted her selfishness to indulging outrageous whims, and Park indulged her; yet all this, increased by the steady decline of his children's interest in him, struck Park Comstock cruelly.

The final blow came for him when Deborah, whom he loved more than his wife and daughter Sybil, assumed a posture that was a constant rebuke. He soon recognized that her respect for him was vanishing. She had a basic honesty like his own, and the discovery that he had repudiated everything for which Levi Comstock stood shocked her, and strained the relationship between them. He struggled to explain the overwhelming upholstery of his life that had made him choose the course he had—and failed. Deborah had tried to illuminate a new path for him, and he had grasped futilely in the blinding light, but was lost in the shadows of indecision when he died, and Deborah had understood, if belatedly. How was she to know he had long since been castrated?

Mr. Channing sighed to himself. He doubted, even at Abbie Comstock's insistence, that he could change the leopard's spots. Deborah was a product of her upbringing—Mrs. Comstock's upbringing. She had been frilled and embroidered, fashioned and packaged, by her, and he marveled now that the girl had the gumption to revolt against her own kind.

"My sister's good looks, my father's success, even my mother's small talk," Deborah once confided to him, "depreciates my ego terribly."

He did not quite understand then, but he suspected that with dubious talent and inclination it had something to do with her taking up such things as dramatics in college, perhaps as a way to express her inner feelings and still have the stage as a shield against the Philistines.

The doors that Deborah tried to open, Mr. Channing concluded in a sudden burst of insight, were not so much rebellion against parental authority as a stuggle for survival, survival as a person, when she instinctively discovered decay in the Comstock veins. Now, perhaps, her deep yearning for a young man of Jeff Kirby's racial vitality was as instinctive as a desire to revivify her own breed.

VIII

By half past eight, the Comstocks had solemnly gathered in Abbie's living room, and as they entered she stood stage center directly under the chandelier. Tonight's family gathering, resembling a bleak Gothic tableau, was a great rarity; no such meeting had been held for two years, not, indeed, since Park Comstock died. As everyone knew, when a Comstock became engaged, married, died, or was born, the Comstocks were on hand; but no Comstock had yet become romantically involved with a Negro, as Deborah had waywardly done. Naturally anything so bizarre set the family's soul to vibrating, and started alarms that could be quieted only in the intimacy of the family bosom.

Until now Abbie had veiled and wrapped away the naked truth about Deborah. How the rumor had started, then, that "something dreadful, my dear, involving Deborah and a colored man," no one could tell exactly, since Abbie had tried to keep everything quiet, even pledging Charlie Stowe and Aunt Emily to secrecy. The family nevertheless was buzzing with the incredible rumor: it was being whispered among the elders and frankly discussed among the young (who were not allowed to be present tonight), and already it

[124]

sounded like an old established legend, labeled "Miss Deborah and Her Colored Gentleman."

All of the adult Comstocks had responded to Abbie's insistent invitation to deal with this common peril. As she was the wife of the eldest Comstock, they quailed before her seniority and incorruptible figure, and ordinarily avoided her if they possibly could. There were, of course, to be no fire-works, no angry scenes or loud recriminations. Indeed they had never as a group had the plebeian pleasure of an explosively violent scene. Mr. Channing, who absent-mindedly offered his condolences to Sybil, distinctly felt the atmosphere of a wake.

They had come, no doubt, expecting to hear a doleful report of Deborah's conduct, and to leave with some notion of what position they were to take publicly. In spite of their differences, and these were monumental, they had a tenacious unity when anything threatened their respectability. They were now on guard. After all, they represented a family of some social consequence in Boston.

There was plainly a crisis, and though they were mostly Park Comstock's people, as always, they all looked to Abbie —her inflexible posture a symbol of the Comstock rigidity. There was her brother-in-law, literate Uncle Ellery, and his foppishly ineffectual twin brothers, Gerrit and Smith, named after the famous abolitionist Gerrit Smith; and her husband's sisters, gossipy Aunt Emily and calm Aunt Julia, who had knitted through more than one family crisis and were preparing to do so now. Abbie's own maiden sister, Aunt Grace, who kept to her room these days, was absent. (If only all this could be kept from her!)

They had a groomed, assured look; and all of them, including her husband's sobby Cousin Agatha and feeble Aunt Kate, were behaving admirably, maintaining an air of quiet self-possession as disaster threatened to rage and break about their well-bred heads. Only Uncle James particularly relished this session. As always he loved a bit of scandal. Licking his lips when he arrived, he said of his brother, the family's black sheep: "Yes, yes, that woman and Gregory; they tell me they left the Riveria and are now living in Mexico— Acapulco."

A hush had fallen on the room, as if all present were thinking secrets too precious, or too voluptuous, to be spoken. The six women and four men, and Mr. Channing as well, seemingly waited for something or someone to whip them into action. Perhaps as Levi Comstock looked down on them from his square frame he stirred the family soul uneasily, reawakening memories of his activist soul which had produced a family tragedy. Only a pale water color by Bonnard, a master at depicting ladies of exquisite refinement, would have caught the mood and feeling of that scene accurately. Not until Mr. Channing looked at his watch anxiously did they realize that it was time to come to grips with Deborah's problem.

The approach was naturally by cicumlocution: there was a discussion of New England's unpredictable weather by Uncle Ellery, some innocuous remarks about Sybil's lovely children by Cousin Agatha, and a few thoughtful inquiries all around about friends and absent relatives. But they had reached the point where they all felt it late in the day to be reticent, even delicate, about Deborah's "misalliance."

—2—

Deborah was in the kitchen preparing sandwiches and coffee, and level-headed Sybil took advantage of her absence to report what she had attempted in her sister's behalf.

Sybil had done really well for herself, and she had not had a care in the world since she married Reade Tait, who was in real estate. They lived in a large, rambling house near Old Lyme, Connecticut, and she had invited her sister to spend the summer weekends with them. Then, when Abbie frantically appealed to her to "do *something*," she had given a garden party and several cocktail parties for Deborah, to which all the eligible young bachelors in nearby Hartford and New Haven had been invited. But nothing had come of all this, and Sybil, feeling she had done all that was possible, had given up trying to make a match for Deborah.

When Abbie opened her campaign, only her disguised anxiety softened the blow of her explosive nerves as she said, "And now she seems determined to *marry* that Mr. Kirby!"

She stopped to see how they were taking the news, and decided that the bombshell had secured the effect she anticipated. Deborah's "thing" with a colored man was now placed on a new, more calamitous plane.

Smith, like the rest of them, was profoundly shocked, even perhaps alarmed by this disclosure, and he asked incredulously, "Marry a colored man?"

Abbie nodded unhappily.

"And what has *she* to say for herself?" asked Emily, truly dumfounded.

"Nothing," said Abbie, in effect pouring kerosene on the fire, "Nothing really."

Emily stared at her, unbelieving, and crushed out the cigarette she was smoking.

Outraged and on edge, Ellery said: "She's quite mad—if you ask me!"

"Miscegenation in the family next," declared Smith, and turning to the ladies, added, "And if you don't happen to know what *that is*, so much the better for you!"

"She doesn't plan to stay in Boston, does she?" asked Kate timidly.

"I expect not," said Abbie.

Thoughtful, Ellery said, "The truth is, Deborah's looking more and more like her grandfather Levi, and she's acting more and more like him every day. Have you noticed, Abbie?"

Abbie had, and her eyes strayed to Levi Comstock's portrait hanging on the wall. She frowned unhappily and made a mental note to have Sarah take it down and remove it from her sight.

"Well, if it's any compensation, I found out a few things about her Mr. Kirby," Ellery said. He paused for effect. "He's a musician, played varsity football at Amherst, age about twenty-six, attractive in an elegant animal sort of way, intelligent, ambitious, and wears his clothes like a gentleman. But there's no getting around it, he's a Negro."

Abbie shuddered and sympathetic waves ruffled the hearts of every Comstock present.

"From all I can learn, he's got no business, no income, and no connections, and his father is an undertaker," Ellery told them unhappily. He had hunted and had discovered every possible detail, in addition to his race, that could be used to damn Jeff Kirby in the eyes of the Comstocks. One piece of gossip he reserved to use later, when Deborah came back.

Their thoughts converging on the man they did not know, but about whose strange influence they had heard, they spent some time going over the particulars of the situation. Aunt Kate was sure he must be something of a black Rasputin whose ghostlike presence was even now haunting the place. They were assembled to make his acquaintance, if only vicariously.

Ellery declared that all this was the result of the way colored people were coddled these days in the name of liberalism—"Simply fashionable nonsense."

Smith passed his hand over his thin, clean-shaven cheeks,

a slight pout gathering on his lips. He finally asked querulously, "Well, what does the girl *really* want?"

Abbie said, "I offered her a year's trip abroad to forget this absurdity, and she unceremoniously rejected it!"

Without looking up, Emily said, "I knew she wouldn't go."

"And she's flatly refused to see a psychiatrist, after all the trouble I went to, to find a man like Seligmann," Ellery said somewhat peevishly. He was convinced she was exhibiting alarming psychoneurotic tendencies; who else but a psychopath, or maybe a nymphomaniac, would think of marrying a Negro!

Gerrit, who had long carried around a grudge against his brother, turned to him. "Ellery!" he said sharply, his voice rising to a tremulous falsetto. He paused for effect, and there was a girlishness in his gestures. "It's a pity," he said, "you don't have more to do with your time. Deborah may be guilty of stupidity, but she's certainly no lunatic!"

Above the drone of talk, they heard footsteps on the polished floor and Ellery turned to see Deborah standing in the doorway.

As Deborah entered the room with the tray, they all swung around to face her. Deborah felt trapped as she faced her aunts and uncles with the unspoken accusation and horror on their faces. Putting down the tray, she hugged her sister, kissed her three aunts, and shook hands one by one with her uncles. Cousin Agatha, her dress rustling noisily, bustled up to her. From the excessive warmth of her cousin's embrace, Deborah knew that her mother had already announced her intention to marry Jeff.

She felt a surge of indignation. Her mother (without consulting her) had not only discussed with them her relationship to Jeff Kirby, but Deborah suspected she had summoned the family to bring pressure on her collectively. Tangled in

[129]

a web of duty, personal animosities, and ties of love and loyalty, she found herself trying to fend off their curiosity. Nor did she mean to try to get out of it by vulgar explanation. A sense of futility stifled her. How could she describe the depths of her feeling, how justify, even explain, Jeff to them?

Breaking the silence, Abbie said defensively, "We were discussing your Mr. Kirby."

"I know," Deborah's voice was curt.

"Why, Deborah, why!" cried Sybil.

"Have you thought of what would happen if you had children?" asked Emily.

"What about it, really, Deborah?" coaxed Gerrit, his manner friendly and encouraging. They all watched her.

"*Frankly*, Uncle Gerrit?"

He nodded.

"Jeff has asked me to marry him," she replied. Her experience with her mother earlier in the evening made her omit any mention of her own love for Jeff for fear someone might jeer at her.

"That's your last word, then?" her mother asked. Her voice lifted pleadingly at the end and drifted off.

Coughing lightly, Ellery prepared himself to deliver the clincher.

"Then I must inform you, young lady, that your Mr. Kirby has a colored friend—a Miss Desvigny, a cabaret dancer."

"Perhaps," Deborah said, fully aware of his insinuation. "He has lots of friends."

The aunts' back stiffened visibly. Deborah had not exactly locked the door against her family's demands and tears, but she easily detected an undertone of bitter hostility.

To his dismay Mr. Channing, who had been watching her carefully during this exchange with her family, saw tears fill her eyes. Childless, he was really very fond of her, almost as if she had been a daughter. He got up from his chair and went over to her. He felt he must protect her. He thought: "Nothing of her father in her face except a slight cleft in her chin—and lucky for her." Aware that his expression was softening as he looked at her, he frowned to preserve the un-emotionalism proper to a lawyer. Then, slipping his hand under her arm, he drew her aside and spoke to her.

"We're all fond of you, but if you'd only—" He was going to say "behave yourself," but he changed it to, "if you'd only think more clearly! You know, my dear, your mother talks of disgrace to the family. That's old-fashioned talk. But the way I see it, you're taking a terrible risk. Marriage is not just a name, marriage is blood, culture, family, race and children, my child."

"And why should mine turn out badly?"

Mr. Channing replied gravely: "Because you're involved in an affair that cannot last forever. What you have now, and what you will have, if you should marry this Kirby fellow, is a back-street arrangement at best. His friends will resent you; your family and friends will disown you. He's un-doubtedly attracted by your color, and you're intrigued by the excitement of revolt in being with a colored man when society says 'No.' All this is incompatible with a healthy mar-riage. I have been married twice, neither marriage was deliriously happy; but we got along and lived together pleasantly. What you're about to do is to jump into a mael-strom—"

"Marriage is always challenging, no matter who it is," she said. "And I'm tired of hearing about maelstroms and in-fernos!"

"I can hear your grandfather's voice," he said softly. And he added, "Jeff Kirby must be a superior young man."

"He is, he is."

Mr. Channing put his hand to his ear.

"What?" he said. "I don't hear anyone too well."

Deborah repeated her praise of Jeff Kirby.

"Ah!" he said.

The color deepened in Deborah's face, and Mr. Channing watched her suspiciously. She became silent. There was something in her silence of obstinacy, and yet he felt he had made no progress in dissuading her from taking a ridiculous course. An odd impersonal jealousy stirred in him. He could not understand this. After all, what he sought was only a prudent solution of her difficulty. There was something that angered, amazed, yet almost amused, him about the way in which she disregarded his and her mother's wishes. It was really as if she were hugging to herself the thought of triumph over them both—and their generation.

He walked away from her sadly, and rapping on the table with his knuckles for silence, began trying to shape in his mind how to bring to a summation the thoughts of everybody toward this dilemma involving Deborah. He took a commanding position, his back to the fireplace. He held himself extremely upright, and his shrewd, steady eyes shone on the Comstocks. With his white hair and white mustache, he had a patriarchal look.

"Love is a curious thing," he began philosophically, "fatal alike to rich and poor, white and black. Now, all this—mixed marriages—is very new (he stifled the word 'modern') to me. Love triumphs over everything, or so the young think! But we must deal with realities, and I do not think young Deborah has."

In his dry, matter-of-fact voice he declared that in his judgment the fact was incontrovertibly established that Deborah's "colored gentleman" was an awkward reality that must be kept secret at all costs. As he looked back at her, an odd feeling crept over him, as though he had come across something strange and foreign. He thought: "Now, what is she thinking about, sitting like that?"

Emily tried to say something nasty in a pleasant way. "And how will dear Deborah like living in Harlem?"

Her incomparable instinct for the wrong approach had not failed her. Everyone flushed.

Deborah suddenly leaped into anger. She replied acidly, "Of course she'll like it; why shouldn't she?"

Emily was properly squelched, and her sly smile faded. Her own marriage, poor thing, had been a dreadful mistake, but having enough good sense and enough feline cunning to scheme, she forced her husband into a compromising position, and she herself went through divorce proceedings without public censure. They had actually been miserable together, emotionally and sexually. They needed to be separated and the court—thank God—was persuaded to perform the operation.

A brooding look had come to Deborah's face after her outburst, and even Mr. Channing became conscious of her withdrawal from them. He nevertheless plunged on and declared that since no one had been able to prevent her from trying to make a sticky mess of her life, it was tacitly understood by everyone that if she married the gentleman in question, she would discreetly keep him as far from her family as possible, and not unduly embarrass her family.

He allowed himself a moment to look around to see how his words had affected his listeners. They were looking at him approvingly. He fixed his glasses firmly on his nose and continued as though he were presenting a court brief.

Further, if anyone inquired about Deborah, or her whereabouts, it was agreed that she was to be reported as being in New York studying. This arrangement, charitably enough, didn't preclude her visits to her mother. As Mr. Channing observed shrewdly, this would be a good thing as people would see her from time to time and not concoct wild stories about her sudden and mysterious disappearance.

"Good sense!" Ellery applauded. "Good advice!"

Tears came to Kate's eyes. She bent and kissed her niece with fervor, and with tremulous little steps left the room, overcome.

Deborah reddened, but said nothing.

Ellery said, "I suppose this is what comes of my introducing her to Knox Gilbert. Play with dogs, and the fleas bite you!"

"If you want to know how *I* feel—I admire her courage," said Gerrit; but no one cared how he felt. He was regarded as only an effeminate watered-down version of a Comstock.

Deborah said, "Thank you, Uncle Gerrit."

"Well, she won't get a cent from me, if she marries *that* man!" was Abbie's final, pathetic gesture of protest. It actually was a form of retaliation, as Deborah had inherited a little money from her father which had been left in trust, with her mother and Mr. Channing as co-executors.

Deborah seemed outwardly indifferent, but inwardly she was dismayed by her mother's devious vengefulness.

The really remarkable thing was that Deborah, twenty-two, with no practical or worldly experience to speak of, in the end overwhelmed Philip Channing, seventy-one, heavy with experience. He was himself upset. He felt beaten, depressed, and very old.

More than anyone else, though, Abbie recognized what damage had been done by her hastily summoned meeting. She had forced her daughter to declare publicly her affection for a Negro; worst of all, she had little hope of shaking her resolution now, and she had visions of Deborah holding firm to her declaration. From childhood on she had sometimes been obstinate as a mule.

Abbie would like to have felt her daughter's head in her

lonely lap at this moment. To receive her confidences and caresses, to plan the trousseau; but under the circumstances that was impossible. Yet the conflict between mother and daughter had its roots not in Deborah's intransigence about a Negro but in a turmoil deep in the complicated personalities of both. Deborah's involvement had merely given it blazing focus. There was another, subtler aspect. Her mother's attitude, indeed the family's, gave Deborah the feeling of being driven from her own kind.

The two women looked at each other steadily now. Both knew that their lives were about to be profoundly affected, and neither chose to halt the headlong drift. But the flinty quality of understanding in the Comstock family had made the relationship between mother and daughter a brittle thing, and before their eyes a deep emotional illusion was suddenly shattered forever. For in Abbie's view, Deborah had embraced the cheap fanaticism of Levi Comstock and in the process had brought shame and crushing humiliation to her family.

–4–

Levi Comstock had been a vivid presence in the room, ghostly but real. Squint-eyed and bespectacled, with the bony cheeks of the ascetic, he, like Deborah, had been only twenty-two when he felt impelled to join the radical wing of the antislavery movement. His hatred of slavery had come swiftly and uncompromisingly after listening to William Lloyd Garrison in a fiery speech at the Park Street Church. The next day he announced his mission to help save the Negro race. He was an internally religious man, a sincere Congregationalist, and because he was also essentially a tortured soul, the freedom of the Negro became his personal crusade. His logic was simple: slavery was wrong; any effort to end it was right.

Beyond agitation, he gave practical action to his philosophy by participation in the Underground Railroad. His house in the South End of Boston was often a haven for runaway slaves. When a Negro escaped the South, Levi opened his door to him, fed and hid him, and then hurried him along under the protection of night. His greatest personal triumph was in convoying twenty-nine slaves to freedom by organizing them into a funeral procession.

However, after years of useful and selfless work, his career was brought to an abrupt end by a galling sense of monstrous guilt: this dedicated man believed that in a crucial moment he had failed the Negro race.

Late one evening in 1860 a Negro, one Derry Harth, turned the key in his employer's butcher shop and started down the street on his way home. A white man, watching from the shadows of a nearby doorway, signaled to three men in a grog shop across the street, and they rushed out and seized the Negro. They carried him bodily to a courthouse, where a marshal standing at the entrance hurriedly motioned them indoors. At nine o'clock the next morning Levi Comstock was walking past the building on his way to his law offices, when he suddenly heard the shrill call of his name. He turned and saw a man he knew beckoning urgently.

"They snatched a Negro!" the man said breathlessly. "The marshal's got him now—"

Levi ran up the steps, pushed into the official's office, and planted himself beside the hapless Negro.

"I'm a lawyer," he announced. "I can help you."

"It's no use," the Negro mumbled dully. "They'll swear I'm a slave and take me back South, and I'll fare worse if I resist."

Levi Comstock noticed the Negro's scarred hands and face, urged him to put up a fight, and assured him that he would never be taken back. The prisoner brightened perceptibly and stoutly declared he was a free man but had been seized as a fugitive slave; that he had been born a slave on the plantation of James Kephart of Fauquier County, Virginia, but that he had bought his freedom. He had come to Boston several years ago, and had since procured employment, married, and had children.

It soon developed that Derry Harth was a victim of an infamous gang of cutthroats, called the Blackbirders, who operated in Boston, New York, and Norfolk and were involved in the criminal business of kidnaping and selling free Negroes. They made nightly forays, seized unsuspecting Negroes, and with the connivance of corrupt officials carried them to ships lying in the harbors and shipped them South. Each one brought them $500. In this case, they had falsely sworn to an affidavit declaring Derry a fugitive slave and themselves slavecatchers who were returning the culprit to his rightful master.

"It's plain this man is held unjustly," Levi Comstock exclaimed.

"It is not for us to determine whether the statute is harsh or not," declared the marshal. "We must bow to the plain letter of the law. He must be surrendered and formally delivered to his master in Fauquier County."

Word about Derry Harth's predicament spread rapidly, and indignation swept across Boston. Even the most temperate people were outraged, and resistance crystalized instantly. By midday sixty-odd abolitionists, led by Levi Comstock, had met in his office to decide on a course. They broke up unable to agree. A few stayed behind and, when Levi insisted, agreed to free the Negro by direct means if necessary. They quickly scheduled a public meeting for Faneuil Hall. That night the hall was packed. Speakers piled taunt upon invective to rouse the crowd. The audience cheered when Levi declared, "I am ready to trample any statute or any man under foot, when there's a possibility of saving even one Negro!"

By prior arrangement he slipped away while the meeting was in progress and took a position near the courthouse jail, where Derry was held a prisoner. There he waited the signal of his co-conspirators. The crowd back in Faneuil Hall, as expected, had been whipped into a fury, and soon Levi heard the rumble of their voices and the heavy thud of their feet as they swept around the corner. When he received a nod from a confederate, Levi pushed his way up front. With the aid of several men he battered down the jailhouse door and dashed in, closely followed by a handful of men. They were beaten back by a dozen special deputies, and before long police reinforcements arrived and started to disperse the crowd.

When the people failed to rally to his support, Levi, in rage and pain, stumbled back down the steps, blood dripping from his blond beard, shouting, "Cowards!"

"When I look upon this unhappy race of blacks," Levi Comstock declared afterward, "I say, 'My curse upon the Constitution of these United States!'"

He stoutly urged his colleagues, who had regathered at Faneuil Hall to lick their wounds, to forcibly rescue the Negro, as their sworn duty before God. They argued the uselessness of such a course.

"If Derry Harth is returned to shackles," Levi declared heatedly, "I, Levi Comstock, could not stand before my Maker and exult in the fact that I am a Christian. Should I make the attempt, the recollection of my failure would blister my lips and cover my cheeks with blushes of shame!"

His friends finally persuaded him to let the law take its course and assured him justice would triumph. He bowed with misgivings. The next morning Levi Comstock, discouraged by the court's refusal to intervene, visited Derry and told him: "There isn't humanity, there isn't Christianity, there isn't justice enough to save you—you must go back." Derry, trying to show as little emotion as possible, was plainly stunned; but he stabbed Levi with these words: "Suh, yo' all done sold me down de river and thrown the noose ovah mah head."

The Negro, trembling in a new suit provided by the slave-catchers, was taken from jail and led through a passage of soldiers with fixed bayonets to the ship that was to carry him back to slavery. As he lumbered by, people shouted at his captors: "Kidnapers!" The authorities, expecting trouble, had already notified merchants to close their shops. Soldiers were ordered to fire if the crowds became too unruly. Houses were draped in mourning, and church bells tolled. From the thousands lining the sidewalks there were groans and hisses as Derry was hurried on board the south-bound vessel.

Levi, standing bareheaded on the steps of the Old State House, his shock of blond hair blazing in the sun, compared the scene to Milton's Hell and wept. But this was not the last he was to hear of Derry Harth. As each new report trickled back, it wrenched his heart and shook his soul. For upon arrival in Fauquier County, Derry was turned over to Norfolk's notorious slavedealer, Robert Lumpkin, who promptly chained the Negro to the floor of his slave pen. The alleged fugitive suddenly became a profitable curiosity, and people paid admission to see: THE NIGGER WHO WANTED TO BE FREE. Old P. T. Barnum, when he heard that the famous fugitive was being exhibited in Norfolk, offered Lumpkin $500 to allow him to repeat his story for five weeks in his New York museum.

Levi groaned. "They want to show Derry like a monkey!"

The Negro was finally put up for sale. Levi, in shame at

his immense failure, raised enough money to redeem him and wrote Lumpkin for his release. He never received a direct reply. But some months later the Boston *Post* carried a notice announcing that Derry Harth, "late of Boston," had died of unknown causes, and that the Church of Jesus Christ in Norfolk had refused to give him a Christian burial, because he had "absconded from the service of his master and refused to return voluntarily, thereby disobeying the laws of God and man."

Levi Comstock was humiliated beyond recovery, and from that day he never left his old frame house; until in 1889, toward the end of his life, aroused by the widespread lynching of Negroes, he emerged and made one wild, desperate foray. He traveled to the South, and by himself stormed Fauquier County jail and tried at gun point to free a Negro he thought might be lynched. He was caught and executed as a criminal.

His last will and testament contained this statement: "I, Levi Comstock, am now quite certain that I failed the race of black men. My guilt will never be purged away, except by my blood, and the blood of my children, and my children's children."

So even today, his hand had reached from the grave to tug at the Comstocks.

–5–

Back in her own room upstairs, Deborah stood at the window. The rain had stopped and she looked up at the moon which had come over the plane trees. Her mother had gone to bed and the house was silent, free of relatives. She thought bitterly of the evening's events.

Now, her eyes wet, she thought of Jeff Kirby. Had she failed him? Should she have been more positive? She threw herself across the bed, muffling her bitter sobs against the pillows, and finally fell asleep.

When she awoke she remembered a dream sequence in which she had seen the swollen face and reddened eyes of an agitated Levi Comstock. He had been weeping, but she could not tell if he wept for himself, for her, or for the unhappy blacks.

IX

Both Deborah and Jeff would always remember this snowy winter evening. Deborah, delayed at her office, was late in keeping an appointment with Jeff. Meantime he, not finding anyone at her house had waited on the steps of the building. The street was deserted and bleak. The snow had stopped but the wind blew bitterly, so he had gone to a cocktail lounge, called Julian's Bar and Grill, on the corner of Deborah's street.

As he pushed open the door, even with the gay clink of glasses and hum of voices, he instinctively felt that the atmosphere was hostile to him. But when the agate-eyed bartender looked over toward him questioningly, he relaxed and ordered a drink. No one apparently had noticed the Negro stranger, at least so he thought, and he felt somewhat secure in his anonymity. But it was inevitable that at least a half dozen men in this neighborhood tavern would recognize him from his several visits there with Deborah or sometimes with Deborah and Tina.

He lit a cigarette, leaned against the bar, and was slowly sipping a highball when he felt someone edge near to him. Then he heard a man speaking softly.

"I think," he said, "you're in the wrong place. You fellers belong uptown in Harlem."

Jeff could not believe the speech was intended for him; he had been preoccupied with watching through the window for Deborah to pass. In any case, at first the idea did not penetrate. When the meaning began to dawn on him, he could not resist looking over his shoulder, slightly at first, to make sure he had heard correctly, and he discovered that a short, stocky white man was talking directly to him.

The face reminded him of a face he had seen in his childhood that he could not drive from his mind, often from his dreams.

Jeff said, "I'm minding my business, what about you minding yours." And he returned to his preoccupation with the window and his highball.

"Well, I'll be damned," the man said, raising his voice. Then he addressed the world at large. "Listen to how this nigger's talking!"

A hush, oppressive and dangerous, blackened the place.

"Why, I'll kill you—you black sonavabitch!" the short man hissed.

"No you won't," shouted a tall, red-necked man as he approached stealthily. "Anyone kills this nigger—it's me!"

By now several men had crowded around Jeff.

"But, I don't understand—"

Two men roughly seized his arms and pinned them to his sides. The stocky man in front moved swiftly, with force, and, with his hammerlike fist, rammed Jeff a blow under the ribs. Jeff winced and strained against the viselike grip of the two men. When Jeff, using his head as a weapon, tried to butt his assailants, they yelled for reinforcements. But the stocky man jammed his forearm under his chin, and with a swift knee action, caught Jeff in the groin. Under their concerted blows he fell to the floor limp.

"That'll take care of him, boys," the bartender said matter-of-factly as he came around from the rear of the bar, reached down, pulled Jeff to his feet, and half dragged him to the front door.

"That'll teach the black bastard to stay 'away from white folks!'"

Just then Deborah turned the corner and heard the commotion inside the tavern, looked in, and gasped when she saw Jeff being pushed through the door, bloody and helpless. Ashen-faced, her voice trembling with anger, she cried, "My God! What have you done to him!"

"Hey, lady, did you bring him here?" the bartender shouted angrily.

"No. But I'll take care of him," she said as Jeff staggered toward her and almost collapsed in her arms.

"Well, he's yours, sister."

"You beasts! How could you!"

Her tone was hard, but it could not conceal the tears in her throat.

The white man was startled. He recovered swiftly enough to shout, "Well, keep the nigger outa here—and you stay out, too! Your kind louse up a decent place!"

He slammed the door viciously.

"Beasts!" she screamed.

In the immense quiet of the deserted street Deborah and Jeff were the only human figures; the people who created violence, and the people who deplored violence, were both out of sight.

Jeff was barely able to walk. He staggered to the support of a lamppost, while she caught her breath and tried, with numbed fingers, to hold him.

Deborah finally half led and half dragged him to her house, helped him to mount the stairs and stumble into her apartment. He was almost a dead weight and it was the longest journey of her life. His clothes were filthy from his rolling on the tavern floor. She undressed him, got him into her bed, and called a nearby doctor.

Waiting for the doctor, she tried to ease his pain with cold towels. All the while she had the strangest feeling of guilt. Sick with shame and rage, tears filled her eyes.

The doctor had come at last. He was white, and was brusque and sarcastic when he spoke to her after she led him into her bedroom, where Jeff was obviously in agony.

"Kicked, was he?"

"I—I think so," she said.

"Barroom brawl?" he asked as he went about his professional ministrations, searching with his hands, pressing, and watching the spastic movements of the knees.

"I—I don't know just what happened—"

"Weren't you with him? He your husband?"

"No—no. I'm—" she stammered and drifted off helplessly, almost on the verge of tears again.

" 'No, no,' what?" he asked irritably. "Either you know or you don't!"

"He's not my husband. We're friends."

"Your boy friend?"

Deborah bristled at what was intended as a nasty insinuation, but said nothing. And a look of astonishment that became contempt spread across the doctor's face.

He walked briskly into the bathroom to wash his hands. Deborah covered Jeff and waited.

"Is he all right, Doctor?" she asked finally.

There was no answer.

Then he came out as briskly as he went in, wiping his hands with an air of distaste.

"Won't be much of a lover for a while now," he said crisply.

He fished a pad out of his pocket and wrote a prescription."

"Sedative," he said as he handed her the slip of paper. "Cold compresses tonight and tomorrow—nothing serious."

Then he crushed his hat on his head.

"Ten dollars, please," he said. Ordinarily he charged five dollars a visit.

Deborah realized he had exacted a tax for Jeff's being a Negro. She was shocked, but paid him without protest.

Tina came in finally and when she saw Jeff's condition and Deborah's disarrayed appearance, she worried about what the landlady would say, but she pitched in energetically and helped her roommate minister to Jeff, and offered to make excuses at the settlement house the next morning as to why Deborah had failed to appear for work.

Jeff woke up, conscious that many things were wrong. His entire body felt as if it had been run over by a truck. He moved his head on the pillow. For a moment he was convinced that his skull had been fractured. Then slowly his wakening mind grasped the fact that he had been in a bad fight and that Deborah had somehow helped him. He got himself up on one elbow as she came to his bedside with a tray of eggs, toast, and milk, and smiling ruefully, he apologized for having inconvenienced Tina and her.

Deborah, herself still in a state of emotional suspension, straightened the bed clothes around Jeff and then sat at the foot and looked at him. His face was unmarked, but his eyes betrayed his feelings eloquently. He was grateful and said so, pathetically. Whenever he talked like that he tore her heart. This was, indeed, the first time in her life someone had ever needed her, needed her desperately. The circumstance had raised her courage and self-esteem. She felt a new sense of responsibility and competence—"Kid, you did your-self proud," was the way Tina phrased it.

"Jeff, I didn't know quite what to do about your people, whether to call them or not. I didn't want to alarm them."

"No harm done," he reassured her. "They're not worried about me. I'm sure they think I'm in my studio working."

That evening she helped Jeff into a taxi and took him back to Harlem. When they reached his house, he let himself in with his own key, and Deborah was about to retrace her steps to the taxi, when his sister, Priscilla, came to the door, followed by her mother. As he predicted, not too much concern was shown by his absence, but Mrs. Kirby was some-what startled to discover that Deborah was a white girl. Mr. Kirby, hearing the commotion in the hallway, came to the door and he too raised his thick eyebrows when he was introduced to Deborah. She declined their invitation to come in, herself unprepared for this meeting with Jeff's family.

—2—

The next evening they were sitting in The Back Door and Deborah said, "I had a feeling your father disapproved of me—"

The jukebox unexpectedly started to clang out the hyster-ical phrasings of "Flamingo" and no one seemingly was bothered enough to stop the machine. Jeff reached into his pocket, and drawing out a monogrammed leather case, a gift from Deborah, offered her a cigarette and took one himself. He struck a match deliberately, leaned across the table and lit hers, then his own. He took a long draw, and exhaled slowly, thoughtfully, as the bell of Bethel A.M.E. Zion Church tolled the hour.

He looked at her fixedly with his frank brown eyes. The

empty glass slipped out of her fingers when Jeff suddenly broke the silence after a long pause.

"Do you believe in God, Deborah?" he asked.

He was the kind of person whose thoughts gave birth more to questions than answers. His inquiry had a curious effect on her.

She said, "Of course. Why?"

"This may sound crazy to you, but my father actually called on God's support to oppose my marriage to you!"

"God's everybody's crutch, Jeff," she said, and thought of the petitions her mother had made to God asking Him to intervene to prevent her marriage to a colored man.

"My father took my hand between his and said, 'Sit down, Jeff, and listen to what I'm telling you. It may be that you won't understand, though it's no fault in a young man to lack understanding, even when he's got an education. Wisdom only comes with age, I suppose. I got nothing against your young lady, Deborah, but, Jeff, Negroes should marry Negroes, and whites marry whites. God planned it that way. Anybody who tampers with His plan is riding for a fall, believe me.' "

She said, "Sounds like my mother talking, Jeff."

"Well, I said to him, 'Dad, white people don't seem to follow the dictates of the Lord, and yet they're happy and prosperous.' " Jeff paused. "Deborah, he was scandalized!"

There was an instant of silence. Jeff looked like a man trying to untangle a puzzle. Then he plunged on, "I said to him, 'I guess it's all in the ability to say as white people do, "Yes, this is the Christian thing to do, but it isn't practical or expedient." ' "

Jeff acknowledged that he might be able to tell his father many things about Shakespeare, describe the influences of Debussy's modern music, and tell him something about the techniques of the theater; but he had to admit there was little he could add to his father's understanding of the Sermon on the Mount. So he had listened carefully when his father said to him, "Son, the white people you're talking about don't go to heaven; they don't go to hell. They go to God's waiting room."

Jeff conceded there was a logic of sorts in what his father had said, but he was unconvinced. Deborah saw he had recognized an ethical dilemma that white men have never resolved, and Jeff was as bewildered as any Negro might be. She herself was unable to offer a logical explanation, so she simply remained silent while Jeff continued to probe his memory and emotions, opening the door slowly on the inner Jeff Kirby.

" 'Look at all the nice girls in your own race,' my father said '—colors from chalk to charcoal! And you pick a *white* girl—why?' "

Jeff sighed unhappily, wearily. The "why" was an albatross around his neck as he splashed about like a mariner lost in a sea of prejudice and ignorance. There was no inventory he could produce that would explain his reasons for choosing to marry a white girl.

Deborah watched him through the thin haze of smoke.

"You know, Jeff, you look like your father, and he might have looked like one of Rouault's kings—human and tragic—if Rouault had painted dark kings."

Jeff smiled.

"Yes, you do look like him, especially in your build and features."

"Not in his thinking, I hope," he said smiling.

"Well, hardly."

"He's a slave to what people think."

"Aren't we all?"

"I suppose so to a certain extent."

"That might be the reason why he's unhappy about us, Jeff."

"It's that—and more."

"What?"

"Well, I suppose Dad feels as though the Lord had let him down, though I think he is as much concerned for me as for himself."

"Perhaps he feels God trampled on him personally."

"He does, Deborah. Anyway, I tried to show him that our plans to marry weren't so horrible a crime, and violated no church law."

"What did he say?"

"'Son, I'll take it the way God sends it!'"

Deborah could tell by Jeff's expression that his father was inconsolable and defeated, especially since his son had shown no sign of remorse. Momentarily she felt triumphant. Yet, like all those who probe themselves, she recognized that Jeff, like herself, often failed to realize that he lived in relation to other people. She could not close her eyes to the fact that their decision might hurt people close to them, and she felt a wave of sympathy for Jeff's parents.

She said at last, "Jeff, your father is a strong man and a good man."

He drew a long, sighing breath. He said finally, "I love the old guy."

For a moment memories swarmed around Jeff. Then he bent close to her. "Deborah, I remember one evening when I was ten, my father said to me, 'Son, I'm going to take you to see the great Kid Flowers, a man who's a credit to his race.'"

"We waved good-by to my mother and set off for the old Madison Square Garden. We took the el downtown, where my father only went about once a year. The streets and faces were strange, ghostly white, and I was afraid. It was dark when we arrived, and as we went into the place there was a loud rumble of voices. The faces of white people seemed funny to me, yet I feared them. And they just stared at us. My father was so calm as we walked into the darkness of the arena, lighted only in the center where the ring stood. I couldn't understand how he could be so calm when the air was crackling with hostility to us. I looked around me in fear. Nothing but white faces peering through the darkness. I could hardly take a breath, because then I would have given cause for anger, and that was dangerous. I thought it meant they would kill us. I remember quite well that's what I thought then. It was terrible.

"Hugging close to my father, I whispered: 'Dad, why do they look at us so?'

"'It's nothing, my boy,' he said, taking my hand.

"'Yes, Dad, it is—they'll kill us!'

"'No, son, you mustn't think that. Not when we know there is a God.'

"I felt lonely. It was so strange that only I was afraid, and he wasn't. What he said didn't help me, not even what he said about God. My heart tightened, as though through the darkness all those ghostly faces would squeeze me to death somehow. Mother was always afraid something was going to happen when Dad took me with him, but nothing did happen, nothing had happened as yet.

"Then, as we sat down near the ringside, the lights went up and we heard a mighty roar behind us! Two men—one white and the other black—climbed through the ropes and into the ring and the roar was for them—at least, for one of them. My father's eyes brightened happily when his boxing idol, Kid Flowers, recognized him and saluted us with his gloved hand. And father pulled me closer to him. The next thing I remember was the gong sounding and the two men were squared away in the middle of the ring—sparring and feinting.

"Suddenly we heard a voice near us. It was terrible and sizzling with hatred. It cried out, 'If McCoy loses, I'll kill me a nigger tonight!'

"And like a great Amen—a rumbling roar of approval rolled across that huge auditorium and lashed back at us. Then, voices pin-pointed from various directions, like sparks whirled out into the night, and the place was suddenly alive with the chant:

'Kill the nigger!

'Kill the nigger!

'Kill the nigger!'

"The man who had first shouted just stared straight ahead, intent upon the bruising and bullying in the ring, his features as though turned to stone. It was horrible. I was beside myself with dread, and I unconsciously jumped to my feet, panting, gazing at this furious vision. My father took my hand firmly in his; and we hurried away—back to Harlem.

"He said; as if talking to no one in particular: 'Strange, very strange people—these white folks.'

"Then, he walked on in silence. I was shaking all over.

"It was for me, Deborah, for my sake my father had taken me to Madison Square Garden. And now I sense what it all meant: he was trying to prepare me for the racial ordeal to come, all that he knew about but wouldn't be able to protect me against; that the ways of white folks, like God Himself, are mysterious, and that's the way life would be for me. It wasn't a logical world, a real world—not the way God had ordered things!"

—3—

It was a bitter cold day in February when Jeff and Deborah decided not to delay any longer. The afternoon

after Lincoln's Birthday they set out to be married. They had
gone to their own doctors for their blood tests. They had
already accumulated a little furniture, had scouted and
found a Sugar Hill apartment in Harlem, and had gathered
some savings before making the plunge. Jeff collected his
sister Priscilla, and her fiancé, Dr. Cass Watkins, and they
started off on their romantic journey blithely enough.

For reasons unknown to everybody in the bridal party,
Jeff chose Newark, New Jersey, as the place they would be
married. But a snotty clerk at the City Hall where they had
procured the license suddenly developed a deaf ear when
they sought his cooperation in finding someone to marry
them. The judge at the courthouse across the street was
much too busy, they were told by the attendant policing the
door. A call at the rectory of a nearby white church brought
the news that that minister was out of town. They hunted
and found in the telephone directory the address of a Negro
clergyman with a reputation for loud and zealous liberalism;
but this poor gentleman, they discovered upon arrival, was
ill and unable to rise from his bed, though Jeff recognized
his healthy features peeking through the curtains as they
walked away from his door.

By now Jeff's patience was becoming somewhat exhausted,
so he hailed the first Negro taxi driver he saw, and dropped
his problem in the hackman's lap. The cabbie, eyeing Deborah carefully, said he knew just the right man, the Reverend
Ignatius Love. (A man who perhaps would split the fee with
him.) And he drove them across the railroad tracks deep
into the colored section of Newark.

They entered a cluttered, unpaved deadend, and halted
before a small dilapidated frame house dirty with the soot
of years. The bosomy woman who opened the door identified herself as the parson's wife, and yawned as she invited
them into a small living room with green wallpaper, a big

pot-bellied stove, and a beaten old harmonium. The minister was not at home, she reported, but promptly sent one of her brood to fetch him at the railroad station nearby where he worked as a porter.

Jeff's fastidious sensibilities seemed ready to give way to the woman's practical solution. And momentarily Deborah had a sinking feeling. Maybe, after all, she had misjudged him completely. Her sense of propriety and feeling for the esthetic were outraged by the place; but when he turned to her with love and happiness so obviously in his face and shrugged a helpless appeal to her for a decision, she felt warmly reassured.

"What can I say, Jeff?" she said in a voice that expressed everything. "Do whatever you think best."

"He's probably one of those jackpot preachers," he replied in an amused aside to her. "But the ceremony will be just as legal as if the pope himself married us."

They both smiled in understanding at the tragicomic elements in the situation; though Priscilla and Dr. Watkins saw no humor.

Nearly an hour passed before the door opened and in walked a spare man of dark complexion, with a little boy who looked like a black leprechaun trailing at his heels and several other older children of varying sizes and shapes. The Reverend Ignatius Love, a freelance functionary of the Pentecostal Pilgrims, had a pontifical face. He gave the impression of being a small man, though he was only slightly under average height. Deborah noticed that his hands were black and small, with pink palms; his body thin and concave about the stomach; his voice soft and high-pitched; his manner apologetic, even perhaps obsequious. When he smiled rather tentatively, she caught a glimpse of small, gleaming white teeth, which somehow gave his face a bewildered, haunted look.

He apparently had left work hurriedly, as he was still wearing the trousers of his redcap's uniform, though he had taken time to change into a long black coat shiny at the elbows. His eyes bulged when he saw the blonde girl with the pale white skin. He saw immediately that this was not an ordinary, workaday ceremony, but fabulous doings with a touch of provocative unreality. He started by examining the license with the air of a man about to do something fraudulent. Perspiration wet his forehead. He gave a nervous cough and licked his lips uneasily. Jeff himself, as he walked into position, tripped over an upturned corner of the ragged rug. Deborah, in spite of the bizarre quality of everything, was in full possession of herself.

The Reverend Love adjusted his spectacles and began to read mournfully from a black book with a purple marker hanging from it; while his wife was at the harmonium playing "The Wedding March" with the beat of a dirge. When the preacher reached the place where the question is asked, "who giveth this woman—?" Deborah was struck by the utter fatuousness of the passage. It put the minister himself in a ridiculous position, forcing him to overlook the fact that the bride's people were eloquently absent—no!—not absent—but probably in the vicinity now, gun in hand, beating the bushes for the runaway couple, and would presently appear to halt the ceremony. He was obligated to put the query, but he was aware that in this case it carried the implication that perhaps *no one* would really wish to undertake this dangerous mission, even the other young man with them, colored though he was. When the minister finally came to the usually-rhetorical, "If any man can show just cause why they may not lawfully be joined—!" his pace accelerated noticeably as though he expected the long arm of the law (or someone) momentarily to reach through the window and yank him off to jail.

[155]

Deborah had given her hand to Jeff and said, "I will." But as she performed the simple act, she was conscious that something deep within her had ripped slightly. She smiled wryly as she thought of her mother—for years she had hoped her daughter's perfectly managed wedding would be the focus of the Boston social season, preceded by months of fussing over clothes, making invitation lists, lovingly if possessively taking innumerable details into her own hands. Deborah, according to custom, had not forgotten to bring along something old, something new, something borrowed, and something blue. But her mother would have found it incredible that even this detail had fallen into place without her supervision. She undoubtedly would have been outraged that her daughter was being led into matrimony in these miserable surroundings, in the presence of only Priscilla and Dr. Watkins and a handful of poverty-stricken Negroes. . . . And Deborah realized abruptly that the ceremony was all over!

Then, because custom decrees that the minister kiss the bride, an awkward moment developed. He politely allowed Priscilla and Dr. Watkins to kiss her first, then, when Deborah tilted her head charmingly, the Reverend Ignatius Love hesitated to perform this venerable rite. In justice to him, it was a thunderous fact to him that the bride was a blonde white girl, even though married to a colored man. The pontifical face of the minister broke out in a new shower of sweat, and Deborah suddenly became vividly aware of his nostrils, which were unusually wide and were now working in and out like bellows. He blinked his eyes unhappily. He hoped no one had noticed his hesitation, people are so quick to attribute such fumblings to alcohol; or, maybe, to a fear of asserting oneself in the presence of white folks. The ceremony had confused his mind. Normally he was a law-abiding, God-fearing man. But the adventure of marrying

Deborah to Jeff had upset him. He had fallen under the spell of Deborah's bluish-gray eyes. And suddenly he felt the contrast between his own shabby spouse and this beautiful white girl. ("Make a man blow his top!") And he was filled with longing, and he hated Deborah for having tantalized him into this unchaste feeling.

He looked coldly at his wife now. Her face was black and plain. Her unshakable composure irritated him. Why was she unable to give herself to love like this white girl? He thought of his first night of marriage as they lay in the small, cluttered room upstairs with the large flowers splashed across the green wallpaper. A little China lamp with a pink shade stood on a table beside the bed, and its light fell on a scene that had haunted him, for ten years! His wife had fallen on her knees and loudly prayed to God to bless the holy bonds of matrimony, and asked forgiveness for the sexual act she was about to perform. How he suffered that night, waiting through an hour-long supplication, trying to appear at ease, and finally striving to hide his embarrassment when she got up, turned out the light, and clumsily climbed into bed—and indignities of indignities, she proved to be no virgin!

He sneaked an envious glance at the bridegroom, who seemed to accept this white girl's attentions with casual naturalness. Jeff's poise upset him, and resentment engulfed him. He felt like a prisoner. Would he ever escape? Was it too late to live like this crazy nigger? But how could he escape? There were still the installments to be paid on the furniture, and six mouths to feed. He looked at his unheated shack, with its dank rat-infested toilet, footworn linoleum in the kitchen, the dirty walls. From the dark, unlit hallway he could smell the old musty odors, and he felt stifled. As he saw it now he was doomed to live in this slum corral: forever nickel-and-dime tips, hand-me-downs, fat meat and greens, and the three gold balls of the pawnshops.

He recoiled from his vision, and tears started to his eyes. . . .

Meanwhile Jeff, sensing some of the reasons for the clergyman's hesitation to kiss the bride, settled the man's dilemma by quickly seizing his hand and pumping it heartily. The Reverend Ignatius Love gave him a relieved and grateful smile, and offered his congratulations. Then, in a gentle reminder to Dr. Watkins of the marriage fee due, he said: "Ten dollars, please. Always a little more expensive in cases like these, you know."

PART TWO

I

"I deal in flesh," Knox Gilbert said to Perky Sparhawk. "And sometimes I get too much of it. Too much white hair, Perky. We ain't gettin' younger."

"Don't worry 'bout the snow on the mountains long as they's fire in the furnace." Perky's moon face stretched to a grin and his gold tooth glimmered.

"Deborah Kirby's a problem."

"How's that goin'?"

"Business is fine as you damn well know from your per cent, Scrooge. Marriage? As full of hurricanes as Florida in a bum year."

Perky shook his head. "Never did cotton to it. Jake," he called to the old bartender, "bring Mistah Gilbert more of the same." And Perky waddled off, leaving Gil tracing the bright checkers of the table cover with his long fingers.

The night crowd was beginning to drift into The Back Door. Gil was hungry. Would he wait for Deborah, who had asked him to meet her here? Yes, he'd wait. He saw apprehensively that the Desvigny woman had come in. The dancer was glittering in a flaring green-and-yellow gown bright with rhinestones and emerald-colored sequins that picked up the green in her eyes and her tawny skin. Deborah wouldn't be pleased. Fortunately Perky's Sherl wasn't here to muddy the pool. Was Jeff coming also? He hoped not. A new combo, Ivory Colum's, one of his own stable, was improvising; sweet and whining. Meanwhile to their sad accompaniment he thought over the events of the last months, months in which Jeff Kirby, now "The Tan Troubador," had filled his coffers with money and his life with complications. As old Jake had once said to him, "Mistah Gilbert, ef yuh run, yuh keeps runnin', suh."

—2—

It wasn't long after the February marriage that the strain between Deborah and Jeff was plain. The Harlem flat was no honeymoon nest. Any conventional marriage would have festered from being too close to the in-laws. This one was overburdened by complicated disapprovals and envies. Deborah was outwardly calm, but Gil sensed that she shrank from the necessity to make friends with numbers of people she would have disliked whatever their color. She had kept up her job at the settlement, although Jeff urged her to give it up. "And we live on what?" she had demanded. To Jeff's assurance that he'd get a part-time job, she smiled caustically.

Gil hadn't waited long before he began insinuating that Jeff was forcing her to make sacrifices unnecessarily. Abbie Comstock had not withdrawn all funds. She was too clever to do that after the inevitable had happened. But if it seemed a pittance to Deborah, who told herself that more than ever she must keep up appearances, her own money wasn't enough. She wanted clothes. She must have them. The apartment must be beautiful. She knew that she needed a setting: the right curtains, soft gold wall-to-wall carpeting, good pictures, bookshelves. Most irritating of all was housekeeping. She couldn't cook well enough to enjoy it. She despised cleaning. Helpers proved unhappy and intractable. She was ashamed that she might be getting like her mother, but there was no question that girls recruited from the neighborhood resented her.

To Gil's delight, after six months or so, she had pushed Jeff toward allowing the manager to carry out his plans and launch him on the troubador route. This was sweetened by Birnbaum's consenting to do Jeff's songs at a Town Hall concert and a promise of future performances. No eating money there. But the money from the rise of Jeff as a popular star eased some of Deborah's concern, although not Jeff's. He had little time to compose. He had to be away from New York. Meanwhile Gil became closer to Deborah. So far, Jeff did not seem jealous but tense and occasionally off beat. He was drinking, not wildly but steadily. That they were still violent after over a year in their sex absorption with one another was clear, but there was more abandon than content. Deborah spent much time at The Back Door. Rumors skipped around the entertainment world. "Yes, suh, cain't hide nuthin' in Harlem," Perky said. "Even walls got ears. People just hears things."

—3—

Deborah arrived alone about two-thirty. As always her entrance created a stir. She wore black, a black-and-gold scarf over her hair, a black velvet cloak blowing open as the spring breeze from the door followed her. Her knitted sweater was tight, so was the trim skirt. Her pearls were new and larger, several strands of them. Perky brought her immediately to Gil's table. Floyd, the waiter, soberer than usual, supplied the drinks.

"Jeff not here?" She seemed surprised.

She threw off scarf and cloak.

"New talent?" she asked Gil.

He nodded. Ivory Colum, tall, powerful, looked up from the piano, smiled and waved. He was bigger than Jeff, a shade darker; otherwise the two men were alike except that in Jeff one quickly recognized sensitivity, in Ivory brutality was near the surface. Colum smiled.

Deborah inclined her head.

"Introduce me?"

"Later. Jeff doesn't like him."

She laughed. "I might."

"Not for you, dear. You're a one-man woman. Or if not, remember me."

"Why not just say, 'you damn well better.' "

"Edgy tonight, huh?"

Deborah didn't reply but sat with her eyes down, fiddling with her cigarette. Glancing up, she saw Jeff come in. He stood looking things over. His dark eyes seemed preoccupied. He gestured toward them, then saw Zabee at the bar and went over, sat down beside her, ordered drinks. Jake served them. Perky, standing at the end of the bar, frowned. Jeff leaned toward Zabee. Their heads were close. His scarlet jacket and black slacks contrasted boldly with her costume.

Deborah reached for Gil's hand. She gripped it, he thought to keep from shaking.

"Introduce me to that piano player now!"

"No. Be nice. Don't play your bitch bit."

"I'll go over there. It's the tramp not the bitch in me!"

He knew she'd go. He sighed. Ivory was looking up again now. He trailed off a quick crescendo. Gil motioned him over. The big man pushed through to them.

"Ivory, you haven't met Mrs. Kirby."

The huge man dwarfed Gil. He reached a hand—not slim

like Jeff's but gnarled—took Deborah's, and raised it to his lips.

"No—and she's lovelier than I'd heard."

"I could get mischief outa this," he thought. "And would I like it for sure."

They formed a tableau, everyone watching. Jeff turned and swung across toward them. Gil got up awkwardly, his short legs uncertain. Zabee stood with her back to the bar now, her arms stretched along it, her smile slight but not gentle.

"Well, well, my dear." His voice was gruff.

"Evenin', Jeff." Ivory stepped back.

"Play us a tune, boy." Jeff's voice dismissed him. Ivory went back to the piano.

Jeff muttered as he sat down, "Just the kind of guy who'd pick up a phallic symbol as a stage moniker—and a lousy pun at that!"

"Drinks, Floyd! Everybody same!"

There was no relaxation as they sat, Deborah between Jeff and Gil. As the combo begun to play, Jeff, startled, seemed about to jump to his feet, then sat again.

"Nervy sonofabitch, he's playing my song!"

Deborah reached for his hand. He pulled it away. She found herself remembering the night at Town Hall when she had first heard it. It had been exciting, then; it was exciting now, but bitter, painful, and ominous.

—4—

That blustery February evening, almost wedding anniversary time for the Kirbys, had not kept the crowd away from Town Hall. Birnbaum's orchestra had grown in popularity. His interest in the modern contrasted with his love of the classical. Bach and Mozart shared programing with

Roger Sessions, Bartók, Hindemith, Howard Hansen. To-
night the first half of the concert was excerpts from opera:
Bellini, Donizetti, Verdi; the last half German lieder, with
Jeff's two songs as the final numbers.

Their seats were in a mezzanine box. They had invited
Priscilla, her doctor fiancé, Tina Viviera, and, of course, the
ubiquitous Gil. Deborah and Jeff arrived early and first, Jeff
correct in black tie, Deborah in a low-cut evening dress,
straight lines, jade-green. They had bickered over the high
jade choker and the heavy earrings. "Shouldn't cover too
much of that skin, my alabaster doll," he had said, and then
threatened to order a scarlet dinner jacket. "Down, boy, let
your music blast for you!" Deborah had replied.

In the box next to them were Tom Tobin and his family
and friends. Tom's daughter Dolly-May was to be the soloist
of the evening. Dolly-May's career had been not unlike
Jeff's in some ways. However, Tom, not disapproving like
Jeff's father, had energetically furthered his daughter's
operatic ambitions and pinched pennies to keep her out of
night clubs where she could have shone.

Harlem was proud of Dolly-May, and so was midtown
New York, where Tom was the beloved keeper of the door
at one of the oldest private clubs. Deborah had once been
invited to an afternoon of music at the club (Segovia shoot-
ing sparks toward heaven from his guitar), and she had
watched Tom greet everyone with precisely the correct
serene or sunny countenance for each. Now she noticed
around her and in the orchestra seats below distinguished
members of the club who had come to applaud Dolly-May
as one of their own.

Why had the girl chosen so lighthearted a name as Dolly-
May? This baffled Deborah until she learned that along with
scrupulous honesty as an artist she had insisted on her own
name. Dolly-May Tobin it was. So it would remain.

From singing in a church choir on Lenox Avenue, Dolly-May had graduated to the chorus of the Metropolitan Opera House. Her industry and talent impressed all who heard her. A fine teacher reached a knowing hand, and scholarships, special concerts, and Birnbaum's interest followed. One day the Golden Curtain would shine behind her as she took her place with Marian Anderson. "All God's Chillun," Deborah whispered to herself as Tom Tobin leaned across to greet them and wish them well.

"Proud night!" he said. "Mighty proud!"

Their guests had all arrived, Gil with a low, "Lordy, you've outdone yourself tonight, gorgeous!"

The music moved over and around Deborah, who was conscious of Birnbaum's clean control, of Dolly-May's voice, which could be bell-like at one moment, or again dark, or almost belted out with hammer force. The first half closed with Desdemona's "Ave Maria." The bravos and applause brought up the lights.

Attention engulfed the Tobins at the intermission. Deborah performed mechanically, aroused to quickly stanched fury when she saw Zabee threading down from the seats back of them, "Dressed in the undressed, as usual," she thought as she met insinuation with hauteur. "I know what she is," Deborah told herself. "Jeff loves to compare everyone and everything to his pet paintings. His precious Zabee is a desiccated Gauguin."

The lieder, for the most part by Brahms, were lovely. They calmed and uplifted Deborah. She was ready for Jeff's songs, and if she had resented not having been allowed to hear them before, their strength and beauty were full recompense and far beyond her hopes.

As she listened, her pride was in Jeff, but her enveloping ego told her that this was her own too. Hadn't she suggested it? Here was the perfection of the syncope. There was Basin

Street here, and the deeper, warmer, alive echos of Charleston and rhythm that she could not recognize, rests and breaks that were shrill and nerve-tormenting, hints of mammy songs. There seemed to be no striving to make it concert. It was Jeff, she recognized, not Bix Biederbeck or Ellington. She held herself taut as the brasses engulfed the hall, she was lifted by the glorious voice used as a trumpet, and she wept at the simplicity and tenderness of the low sobbing.

The pieces, she realized, were short oratorios rather than songs. The first, Jeff had titled, "He Is My Gracious Friend."

Around Henry Vaughan's mystical poem Jeff had woven his own awe at things eternal. This was the wondering and questioning Jeff, retreating from that God of Vengeance his Baptist forebears had revered. The Christ child became the black baby in its black mother's arms. Here too was the Black Virgin, high on her rocky hill, or the Gullah mother and child in the swamp. This was reverence laced with irony, sweetness sharpened by the almost but never quite bitter. This piece ended with the exact quote from Vaughan:

> *My soul, there is a country*
> *Far beyond the stars*
> *Where stands a winged sentry*
> *All skillful in the wars;*
> *There, above noise and danger,*
> *Sweet Peace sits crowned with smiles,*
> *And One born in a manger*
> *Commands the beauteous files.*
> *He is my gracious Friend . . ."*

During the applause she reached for Jeff's hand and pressed it. His eyes seemed to her gentle and brooding in the dark. She had never seen them quite like this.

He had called the second piece "Leda." Where the first had been for the most part quiet, this was impassioned, often strident. The dominant was sex, twisted, complicated, accented by harsh trumpets, tortured oboes, drums underlying the voice, now guttural, now almost miming the climax of fornication. Yet there was love, too, in this passion. The black swan and the white, the awful presence of Zeus. As the music ripped her apart, she found herself in that well-recognized state between agony and ecstasy. At the close she heard the words: "I cannot reach you, Leda, I cannot touch you, Leda, are you my spouse, are you my demon, are you my child? Do not destroy me, Leda."

She thought she had fainted. But no. Cheers, to which Jeff had responded, raising her beside him. They had called him to the stage where he and Dolly-May and Birnbaum were overwhelmed. There was a party afterward in the green room. Champagne, more cheers, shouts, speeches. She had hated it all; it was taking him away from her. Later, he had torn her clothes from her, flung her on the soft gold rug of the huge living room, and their love-making was the fiercest they had ever known. Yet in the midst of it she found herself thinking, "I am losing you, but I'll fight! You'll be what I make you. You are not my child, you are *mine!*"

–5–

The combo had finished, packed up, and left, Zabee along with them. At the end of Jeff's songs those left in The Back Door had applauded; but not the trio sitting nearby chain-smoking and drinking.

The quiet among them was brooding and Gil felt it might sputter and flame into a scene at any moment.

Deborah glanced at her wrist watch, nervously.

It was now four-thirty in the morning. Perky's curfew had

tolled. The night had closed in. The brightness and glitter gone, Perky's place had become dark and barnlike. The noise and bustle and music had evaporated.

Gil had the feeling that he was in some strange foreign land as he caught the voices of the retreating customers talking their unintelligible jargon. "See you at two chimes!" "Take it easy, Greasy!" "Plant you now, dig you later."

Now the three of them, each raging with inner conflicts, sat in the spill of the work lamp, in a sea of up-ended chairs piled on tables, as the stench of stale cigarette smoke enveloped them.

"Like a big-three conference at the top of a rat hole." Jeff's voice was still angry.

But Deborah quickly turned the cold, chiseled exterior to sparkling animation, the blue-gray eyes shone, and every now and then she laughed heartily as Gil and she tossed nebulous quips.

Jeff still brooded silently. Perky joined them at the table, followed by Floyd, who with his unfailing instincts had brought a round of drinks for smoothing action.

Perky squinted at Deborah to pierce the shadows made by the dim work light.

"What have you done to yourself?" he asked.

"Nothing, really—only a new hair-do."

"No wonder I didn't recognize you."

"That's a man for you, Gil," she said. "And he swore to be my friend for life."

"I never forgets."

"Do you believe him, Gil?"

Gil nodded assent.

"You've always been kind," Deborah was obviously sincere. "And I still think of you as practically my only friend in Harlem, Perky."

"Married over a year now, eh?"

"Practically newlyweds," Gil said.

"Yes, exactly thirteen months now." Deborah's eyes sparkled.

"And you've already got him seeing where his bread is buttered."

"I don't like it," Jeff said. "It's already interfering with my work at Juilliard; I don't like shoveling ashes for beauty. And how!"

Deborah's eyes hardened. "Jeff, sometimes you're simply impossible."

Gil said, "Jeff, I think you're a lucky fellow. Not every man has a woman in his corner."

Someone broke into the conversation to congratulate Jeff on one of the recent rave reviews of his night club act, but cut his speech short when he looked at Deborah.

Jeff floundered through a polite thank you.

"And who would that be?" Deborah asked, manifestly irritated by the interruption.

"Just a fellow I know."

He was plainly annoyed by the query and added, "You could at least treat my friends civilly, Deborah."

"I'm not a madam, darling. Why don't you ask your Zabee Desvigny to be civil to your friends. She has the talent."

"I will."

"Listen, kids," Perky said as he sliced through the red middle of a filet he was having for breakfast. "This is the kind of thing old married folks on television do. You're both sweet kids. Now, forget that stuff!"

Perky was attempting to play Pilate.

"I must leave," Deborah announced unexpectedly.

"Not feeling ill?" Perky's tone was anxious.

She shook her head.

"Maybe it's too hot and smoky?"

Deborah was silent while she methodically entered lip-
stick, powder, and cigarettes in her pocketbook.

"What's the matter, then?"

"Oh," she said wearily, "I just think I should go."

Jeff said, "Maybe a nightcap will help."

"You've had enough already."

"That's the sort of stuff makes a man blow his top," Perky
spoke under his breath, but his tone was fierce.

Jeff blushed crimson under his brown skin, looked at his
watch, and started to get up. "Okay, let's go!"

"You may stay and finish."

"As you choose."

Her icy voice alarmed Gil. He felt Jeff was provoking her
unnecessarily. He had often been conscious of the way Negro
men in The Back Door treated white women; men commanded and women obeyed. As most white men would have,
he resented the equation. As Jeff asserted this over-drama-
tized masculinity, Gil felt it might foreshadow something
violent and dangerous.

Deborah still did not move.

Gil said, "Maybe we all ought to be going—it's getting
pretty late anyway."

"Now what?" Jeff asked when he noticed her petulant
stubbornness. "Well, if you'd rather not talk about it—"

"Well," she said finally, "if you insist. I think you were
childishly ridiculous tonight."

"And why, please?"

"That little interlude at the bar."

"Frankly, I don't follow you."

"Logic is an important attribute of the human being," she
said. "But you can certainly be obtuse when you choose.
Need I say more?"

"Sure, speak your mind, because I still don't get this. Don't
mind Gil and Perky, they're practically in the family now."

"All right. The reason that you're silly is that I was looking at you and Zabee Desvigny."

Jeff said nothing.

"Why did you keep talking to her when she was so obviously trying to embarrass me?"

"That's a crazy idea." His voice became heated. "She's an old friend—we grew up together, as you very well know."

"So?"

"And anyway, she was giving me a few pointers. Surely you can't object to that!"

She seemed to stiffen inside. "You think it's all crazy imagination."

"Very crazy."

"Then, have it your way. I'm leaving!"

Jeff excused himself and stalked toward the men's washroom, with Perky's voice trailing after him: "Watch them beer crates near the door, Cuz." And in a side-mouth comment to Gil, "Whipping's too good for her!"

Deborah retouched her face in a compact mirror, seeming unruffled now.

"Well," Gil said, rising along with her. "You're not really going?"

"Yes, I think I must."

"Jeff will be back in a moment."

"I must go now."

Her voice was emphatic and unhappy.

Jeff was so long returning that Gil said, "Wait! I'll see you to a taxi."

"No need. There's always a taxi out front, but thank you."

Gil hesitated, then quite unable to follow the subtleties in the relation between Jeff and Deborah, he picked up a lace-trimmed handkerchief she had forgotten and went after her to return it. He called out to her, caught up to her, and handed her the lacy trifle.

"Thanks a lot," she said. "You're a very nice person, Gil. And thanks for everything."

Gil bowed in mock courtly fashion and said, his voice jocular, "I hope you'll have need of my service again, madam. Call on me, any time."

Suddenly she clung dizzily to the door. Her pocketbook dropped to the floor.

As he hurried to hold her up, he felt a wisp of her hair against his cheek. Her body was alive, luxurious, and an erotic impulse stirred in him.

"I'm quite all right now," she said after she had caught her breath.

Her skin was ashen but her eyes hinted her gratitude before she stepped into the night.

Perky eyed Gil steadily as he walked back to the table.

"That girl's got guts, Perky," he said.

"You mean gall—but, what a piece of woman!"

—6—

As Gil was starting to leave a half hour or so later, the telephone next to the bar rang.

Jake, who was removing his white jacket, wearily reached for the instrument. "It's for you, Mistah Sparhawk."

"I wonder who in hell—"

Frowning, Perky picked up the dangling receiver. His eyes popped. It was Deborah herself.

"Come on!" he yelled, and bolted through the door hatless, with Gil close at his heels, onto a gray, eerily deserted Lenox Avenue. "He's killing her!"

"Whose killing who?" Gil shouted as they tumbled into a taxi parked before the door.

Perky said matter-of-factly, "Well, the white bitch asked for it."

[174]

The cabbie wouldn't drive fast enough down Lenox Avenue, west across 125th Street and down Morningside Avenue, even with Perky barking top-sergeant directions. Finally it entered triangular Rochambeau Square at the southernmost tip of Harlem, a fragmentary neighborhood, predominantly white. The area, under the gothic shadows of the Cathedral of St. John The Divine, had an air of decaying grandeur. The taxi pulled up alongside the bronze weather-beaten statue of the Revolutionary War general astride a horse which stood at the triangle's point, directly opposite the awning-shaded doorway of the building where Jeff and Deborah lived.

Perky and Gil raced through the sumptuous old lobby and, discovering no elevator service in operation, dashed up the winding carpet-covered stairs.

Perky knocked at the door. Silence within.

Gil said, "Maybe they're both dead in there?"

Perky turned the knob. The door opened and they went in.

The room beyond the foyer was a shambles: chairs overturned, draperies askew, clothes lying disordered and tangled in corners where they had been flung.

There was every sign that two people had met and battled. But there were no bodies lying lifeless on the floor, no trails of blood.

Perky touched Gil's arm and pointed to the bedroom. They peered in and distinguished at last the shape of a human form—no, two human bodies so closely intertwined they seemed one.

They had battled, blended, and subsided.

Deborah and her husband were fast asleep in each other's arms.

Perky and Gil stepped back out of the room and closed the door.

II

Why Jeff's father had asked Gil to visit his house was not clear to the agent. Perhaps he felt that as a white man Gil was removed from the pettiness and squabbling of Harlem and could be sympathetic, but probably it was an accident of mood coupled with the fact that as his son's business agent Gil had a certain status in the old man's eyes, though he was by no means sold that being a crooner was a worthwhile substitute for his own aspirations for Jeff, aspirations which had been shattered by the unfortunate marriage. Even now, with Jeff married nearly two years, it was clear that he hadn't become reconciled to the fact.

There was no reason at all for this calamity to have befallen him, he honestly felt. After all—

He was a deacon in the church.

He was a Republican and an Elk.

He lived by proprieties and conventions.

He was a successful undertaker, whose letterheads described him as an "underground specialist."

And Mr. Jefferson Kirby, Sr., was listed in *Who's Who in Colored America*.

These distinctions may seem trivial and inconsequential,

but to Mr. Kirby they were profound social realities. Not only did they give him a feeling of superiority over other Negroes, but it made him feel superior to poor white people as well. The truth is, he reacted to the same illusions that feed the vanity of white men.

In a community where the local newspapers in those days, dubbed anyone a "sportsman" who earned five thousand dollars yearly, Mr. Kirby was a millionaire. Actually, he wasn't even well-to-do. But in spite of the Depression he made a moderately comfortable living, which enabled him to buy his own home and put his children through school decently. Until today, whenever Gil saw him they exchanged the superficial remarks of two people who don't know each other very well, and he would mostly talk about his children, telling Gil that Priscilla was doing well at Hunter; she had pulled down two A's this term. Then his eyes would cloud. "That boy of mine made a mistake not coming into the business." He would think this over for a moment and then confirm it with: "Yes, he's made a big mistake all right."

Asked to describe Mr. Kirby, people probably would have said he was a "typical businessman." He had all the conservatism inherent in his class, and struggled hard to realize the values that gave status within his group. He was so much like his counterparts beyond Harlem that he appeared almost a caricature of the type. He regarded the kind of work a man did as the only index to his character. If his wife, Narcissa, failed to have dinner ready on schedule, he grumbled good-naturedly about the lot of the tired businessman. He spent his evenings attending meetings or serving on committees, or when the weather permitted, doing little chores about the house, which he owned with only a first mortgage. His conversation, outside of his undertaking business, dealt with local affairs and frequently those of the church. His views on public questions were considered entirely orthodox, and his

[177]

membership in the Bethel A.M.E. Zion Church was of a piece with his general solidity. He played whist at the Elks Club, was popular, and though boisterous, he paid for the drinks with good grace when he lost, and gloated humanly when he won.

Mr. Kirby moved smoothly and complacently within his own segregated orbit. The fact is, he was not known to have been out of Harlem more than six times in fifteen years. And then he had gone downtown only briefly to replenish his wardrobe. In all probability he would never have seen the city beyond Harlem if some twenty years ago Rogers Peet, a clothier in the Fifth Avenue shopping area, hadn't enterprisingly attempted to capture the Negro trade by employing a Negro salesman, a Mr. Fred P. Hayes. This gentleman wrote a number of letters on the firm's nicely engraved stationery to prominent colored people, soliciting business, but not without carefully observing that "Rogers Peet is the first and only prominent house that has employed a colored salesman." Mr. Kirby naturally was one of those to receive this flattering correspondence, and he declared it a "race duty" to patronize such an establishment, and in the years that followed he had made a half dozen pilgrimages to this temple of racial enlightenment.

–2–

The day Mr. Kirby felt impelled to talk at some length with Gil, he had invited the agent to dinner at his home, where Jeff would join them. It was suggested that Gil pick up Mr. Kirby at the undertaking establishment so that he could show Gil the way to the house.

Gil found Mr. Kirby seated in the late sun in front of his cheerful-looking establishment, a sturdily-built structure facing Lenox Avenue at 130th Street, about a stone's throw from The Back Door. The Kirby edifice was a streamlined mortician's palace, as modern as jive talk, and had by several years anticipated in design the bizarre Angelus in Los Angeles. A broad driveway curved up to the canopied double-door entrance at which a uniformed doorman stood. The uniquely constructed building, resembling a squat cathedral, was surfaced with Indiana limestone and glazed brick, and was surrounded by landscaped grounds with hedges. Before this imposing building a big sign was erected on stilts and bore the legend: JEFFERSON FUNERAL SYSTEM, and below neon letters spelled out the slogan, "We Satisfy the Dead, So We Satisfy the Living."

Mr. Kirby greeted Gil's arrival with a dry cough. He was a very dark man. The late afternoon sunlight seemed to bounce off his shiny bald crown. Perspiration trickled along the corners of his nostrils from which hair grew. His eyebrows were bushes of hair, and a certain weary patience played about the eyes. He was an imposing man, even though below his ribs a heavy paunch swelled. Mr. Kirby was now sixty-one, big, booming and blustery. He had worked with his bare hands in pulling himself up by the bootstraps. He had trudged into Harlem in 1916 penniless, but cautiously clutching round-trip tickets back South in one hand and his son in the other. Narcissa trailed her husband with Priscilla in her arms. He was buoyed up only by a burning ambition to win security for himself and his family, and was not dismayed that his meager schooling limited his aspirations. "A Kirby knows without having learned," he always said. He had been working as a dining-car waiter for the Pennsylvania Railroad, when an old crony, Rice Williams, persuaded him to quit his job and become his partner in a funeral parlor. Mr. Kirby, he said afterwards, wore a tuxedo with the impeccable air of a polished gentleman, and thus would give "tone" to the undertaking business.

Impatiently ambitious, Mr. Kirby lost little time reorganizing the business when Williams died. He quickly took advantage of the fact that Negroes were beset with fears they might die without receiving a decent funeral, and also were unable to buy insurance from reputable white companies. He started his own burial society to which people paid small premiums for burial insurance; and he started a funeral company to which the policyholder's insurance was paid at death to provide funeral services. The twin operations he called the Jefferson Funeral System. He insured people merely on their "looks." That is, no medical examination was required. And he asked no searching questions about the cause of death even when violent, for he was well aware of the hazardous nature of life in the streets of Harlem. His risks were few, because delinquent policies had no cash surrender value, and he knew the bulk of his policyholders intimately as friends, neighbors, and fellow lodge members.

"This is quite a setup," Gil said, surveying the building which represented rags-to-riches success.

"Even a blind pig gets an acorn now and then," Mr. Kirby said modestly. "But sometimes I think my people don't appreciate what I'm doing for the race, or the sacrifices I've made to build up this business."

Mr. Kirby had convinced himself that he was performing a racially patriotic service that contributed to the happiness and well-being of Harlem.

"Trifling Negroes think ownership of a business is all home cooking," he said ruefully. "Why, I was nearly wiped out once—and all because I tried to do something for my people."

He described this as a case of misplaced confidence. When the Afro-American Bank & Trust Company, a brand-new banking outfit owned and operated by Negroes, opened lavish offices in Harlem, it had necessarily to compete with established white institutions. The Negro directors of this company promptly made a distinct racial appeal for depositors. Mr. Kirby was one of the first to respond. He deposited about five thousand dollars, but within a very short time the bank collapsed, and he was caught without a cent of cash. He was unable to meet his payroll. His back was clearly against the wall—a situation, according to him, that required "pushing a camel through a needle's eye." With the consent of Narcissa, he quickly raised a mortgage on his own home, and before long he was out of the tall grass. "Today I'm sitting pretty," he admitted. The experience, however, had in no way dampened his enthusiasm for the success possible for Negroes in business, even though he hadn't noticed they had arrived belatedly on the scene of capitalistic plunder.

"Because of all my speech-making, Mr. Gilbert," he said, apologetically, "you've only seen the outside. I know Mrs. Kirby is expecting you for dinner, and I suppose you want to see Jeff, too, but I think you'll have time to see the place —come, let's go inside."

The interior was furnished in somber good taste, but even with bowls of roses there was the usual clinical odor. The lobby had dark oak paneling, red spongy carpeting, and red leather chairs and divans. Under a portrait of the founder sat a mortuary hostess giving softly modulated information to some potential customers. Indirect lighting reflected a pervasive amber glow. Two side corridors led to sumptuous "slumber" rooms, where the wakes were held. Big pickled-oak doors opened into a low-ceilinged chapel, which had an air of discreet nonpartisanship, and could easily seat about a hundred people in an atmosphere of serene fluorescent lush. There also was an amiable staff, composed of a cosmetician, two embalmers, a chaplain, and a few clerks and chauffeurs, who ritualized this business into an assembly-line efficiency, and somehow managed to dispel the crepe-hanging gloom so characteristic of most such places.

Gil was impressed and said so, though he found it difficult to imagine Jeff happy in this unctuous setting.

Mr. Kirby seemed scarcely to hear his compliments. He was peering at the place with the gimletlike air of concentration that one employs when viewing things through opaque windows. "I'd miss this place if I had to leave it," he said as they slowly descended the steps of his establishment and headed in the direction of his home. He usually walked home evenings, picked up his copy of the *Sun* at the corner newsstand, and confidently saluted his friends and neighbors he met along the way. This evening he seemed to be avoiding them—at least, he was preoccupied and perhaps hadn't noticed them.

Something in Mr. Kirby's voice had startled Gil, so he quickly asked, "You're thinking of leaving?"

"I might—and soon."

There was no reason whatsoever to associate Mr. Kirby with scandal. So the thought of his pulling up stakes seemed ridiculous to Gil, even flighty. Gil was speechless. It might be, as some people claimed, Negroes have no roots. In that case, he couldn't figure what kept them in places like Harlem, unless it was just plain inertia. Sometimes the young people moved away because of new opportunities abroad, but for a man of Mr. Kirby's age, connections, and stability to pick up and move seemed utterly fantastic.

"Kids are grown now," he said, like a man completing an inventory. "Jeff's on his own and has no mind for business. And Priscilla will be marrying soon. Think maybe Mrs. Kirby and I will go back South—to a nice, quiet farm."

"You're joking, Mr. Kirby," Gil protested, growing more and more puzzled.

"I don't fit in anymore, Mr. Gilbert," he said bitterly. "Ever since Jeff married that girl."

—3—

The first hint of a changed attitude toward Mr. Kirby had come at the annual elections of the Elks, when he had lost the Exalted Rulership, which he had held for a number of years. The community's reaction to Jeff's marriage had been slow, taking several months to gather momentum. When the whole scandalous mess was dragged into the open, people's first reactions were mixed. The men felt it an act of stupidity, since a colored man didn't have to marry every white girl with whom he had slept; and many of these, nudging each other, recalled nostalgically their youthful philanderings with "pink meat." Those unlucky fellows who had never enjoyed the delights of "gray frails" declared loudly that only bums, hustlers, pimps and racehorse touts associated with white women—not well-brought-up lads like Jeff. "If whites could see some of our beautiful Negro girls," they said, "they would understand why we are perfectly happy to forget about white women." And they told the old, old story of the monkey who lost his head over a piece of tail.

These were purely masculine views.

Before a local columnist first printed the story, the women already had heard that Jeff was having "a thing" with a white girl, and they had dismissed the gossip as the monkeyshines young men get into while sowing their wild oats. But when he married the girl, they were faced by a concrete fact. The women were shocked and unanimously denounced the relationship, though the young girls were romantically excited, if a bit startled. Their mothers strongly resented Deborah's intrusion—after all, they had daughters to marry off, and by taking unto himself a white girl, Jeff had narrowed the field of eligible young men. They were convinced, without ever having seen her, that Deborah was nothing more than cheap, poor white trash: "Who else would marry a Negro?" they asked, not expecting any answer. The mulatto women, often enjoying a position in Harlem far beyond their actual personal worth, were especially incensed and declared both Jeff and Deborah were without race pride.

"How do you account for all the uproar?" Gil asked after Mr. Kirby outlined the situation.

"Mr. Gilbert," he said gravely, "Negroes, I am sorry to say, all have a cruel streak in them. They have known so much of hard times that maybe this is natural."

Everyone's misgivings about Mr. Kirby himself sprang entirely from the conviction that he must be a rather unsound man; obviously, a man who can't manage his family affairs, can't manage other people's affairs. Those in the church had said more than once that "old Kirby" was extremely able about handling money, as he undoubtedly was, but they now became obsessed with the idea that as church treasurer, if he continued to have charge of the funds, he might squander them on "some wild scheme." Mr. Kirby's removal seriously hurt his pride, especially when the local newspapers handled the story as though he had been discovered to have been a criminal.

Mr. Kirby's friends and neighbors had not really reacted to his difficulties with outright hostility, though beyond his hearing there was mean-spirited gibing. Actually, they liked him as much as ever, but they regarded him simply as incapable and unpredictable now. His companions of the past felt uneasy in his presence. And his business suffered; this was an especially hard blow to him. There is no denying that the ferocity of gossip, dredged up out of the gutter and dumped into the local newspapers, was enough to topple the stoutest soul. So it was natural that he would have betrayed

[184]

considerable irritation during his spell of notoriety. He told everyone, "What's done, is done!" and met the onslaught stoically. He stood staunchly by his son and refused to admit publicly that Jeff had made a grave mistake—or that he had betrayed his race, as so many people charged.

—4—

By now Mr. Kirby and Gil had turned the corner of 138th Street at Lenox Avenue. Suddenly they heard the howls of a child seated in a wooden box on the sidewalk. The older man looked down at the squalling infant and patted its head thoughtfully. He perhaps reflected upon his own hard lot along the way. "The Jones' kid," he said, as he pushed aside the miserable clutter around the child's makeshift crib. He cooed to the baby to hush its cries. It was abundantly evident he loved children and was stirred by the poverty in this tableau.

Gil suspected he would send the mother a check the very next morning.

"No, Mr. Gilbert, I don't fit in anymore," he said sadly, as Gil fell into step alongside him. "They won't accept me anymore."

"You shouldn't feel that way," Gil said. "Things will blow over eventually."

"Maybe. But people don't trust radicals—and that's a damned radical thing Jeff's done. Why, he could have run for Congress one day. Now—?"

The thought made him miserable.

Gil said, "Of course they don't like radicals, but Jeff's going to be a big man—and you and everybody will be proud."

He wasn't convinced.

"There's nothing shameful in what he's done," Gil added, hoping to reassure him.

"Of course there isn't." His voice was sharp. "But nobody believes that. It's taken me nearly twenty years to make a place for myself, and one thing like this wipes it out in a minute."

To Mr. Kirby, establishing a business had meant more than economic salvation; it was his way to escape the white man's dining room, and indeed become an important person in the community. And he had been in the vanguard of his race's economic and social progress, and had constituted a leavening influence in Harlem, until his descent in public esteem.

"They even think I'm a Communist!" he added bitterly.

Gil couldn't help smiling. Mr. Kirby wasn't even a noisy Roosevelt-hater, though he thought the President was throwing the country back into bankruptcy. But, for all that, he would not think of discontinuing his insurance business, which covered all contingencies in this world if not the next.

"You think it's funny," he said. "You'll find out that a government can't run forever giving people handouts—destroys initiative. And all this worry over foreigners. Take these America Firsters. Seem to have the right idea."

"Do you really think so?" Gil said, sparring.

"Not only that, but the government is pampering the people. Look at the way labor is getting out of hand these days. Why, I myself have worked for five dollars a week and thought I was well paid."

Mr. Kirby probably had the gravediggers in mind. They were at the moment on strike, though he didn't mention this fact.

The conversation had taken on an oblique quality. So, as they approached Mr. Kirby's house, Gil thought it appropriate to mention that the son of Eustace L. Bradhurst, a rather well-known realtor, was married to a white girl, and old Bradhurst was apparently prospering. This suggested that it was possible for him to live in Harlem and enjoy the respect of his neighbors.

"Bradhurst is different," he replied. "He's always been peculiar, they expected it of him. I don't mean that I don't like him, because I do frequently talk with him at the Association of Trade & Commerce, but he's so crazy in his views that nobody pays any attention to what he and his family say or do—s'help me, he even joined a *white* church, Dr. Fosdick's, I believe! And he belongs to all these anti-Nazi fronts. Jeff favors them too."

Gil almost laughed to himself. "But there's nothing *peculiar* about you, Mr. Kirby," he protested.

"Of course not. And I'm no Communist either. But they don't know what to expect from me now. Besides, think how Jeff and Priscilla will feel if their father has no responsible position in the community." His voice had a stricken note and he paused thoughtfully. "I've worked hard to become a respected citizen. Time was when everyone used to be glad to get Kirby's opinion. They used to say, 'Old Kirby knows his onions.' Now I'm supposed to be a lost ball in high weeds."

—5—

The prim, tree-dotted street where the Kirby's lived was one of the better-kept areas of Harlem and had the air of cherished solidity. The home was a modern, three-story dwelling, one in a group designed by Stanford White, situated on 139th Street. Mr. Kirby had bought his when white people, fearing the encroachment of Negroes, had fled in panic as from a black tidal wave and had unloaded their property at prices far below their actual assessed values. The shade-freckled houses, uniform in architecture, contained fourteen rooms, two baths, French doors, and hardwood floors, and were sold for as low as six thousand dollars apiece. The area afterward became the most fashionable in the city for colored people, and a stronghold of Negro society.

This evening Mr. Kirby entered his house, workingman fashion, by the rear entrance with Gil trailing at his heels. Odors of greens and ham cooking assailed them as he opened the door. Narcissa at the stove gave a half turn, a half smile, a half kiss that flew in the general direction of her husband's bent-down face. She was a comely buxom woman in her late fifties, neatly spic-and-span in appearance, the belle of the ball in her day, when the social élite gathered at the New Star Casino and danced the fox trot. Up to now, knowing exactly where she stood with her man and her children, she had been a happy woman; but lately clouds had come on her otherwise serene horizon.

"Oh, Mr. Gilbert," she said with sincere warmth, as she made a full turn and spied Gil. "Please, please do come in. The place is a mess, but Mr. Kirby will show you the way to the living room."

Piano chords and a voice he recognized drifted into the kitchen. Mr. Kirby cocked an ear. "That's Jeff," he said to no one in particular. Gil followed him into the living room through French doors that separated it from the dining room with its Adams Cameo set. A winding stairway in the foyer, opening into the living room, led to the room upstairs. The place was attractively if conventionally furnished. There was orderliness and here and there a hint of luxury. The living room was painted a buff color and contained overstuffed chairs and a divan, delicate bric-a-brac, a deep-pile rug, a Hepplewhite occasional chair, and bowls of synthetic flowers. The floors were parquet, and on the walls hung a picture of a meadow at dawn and, of course, there was the

GOD BLESS OUR HOME. At an upright piano flush against the wall sat Jeff, wearing slacks and a bright sports shirt.

"Hiya, Gil!" he shouted between chords. "Did the old man sell you any insurance today?—maybe a nice plot in Greenhaven?"

Mr. Kirby's eyes were a mixture of love and mild annoyance. "Mr. Gilbert is a fine young man," he said, and added in gentle reproof, "And he's got a good head for business." Then, with his spectacles and newspaper, he sat down in a big armchair near the wide bay windows and stretched his legs out full length on the silk-fringed hassock. He wheezed and groaned with obvious pleasure as he settled himself into the downy comfort. A green lamp caught a glimpse of his profile, as he prepared like one who reserved judgment to concentrate on his son's improvisations.

"Jeff," he called suddenly, pitching his voice above the music. "Prissy. Has she come home yet? Who's going to help your mother in the kitchen? . . . Where's Priscilla?"

The questions came in a staccato jet.

"I'm coming, Dad," a voice called musically from the floor above.

His daughter swept down the stairs breathlessly, and bounced into the room with a delighted smile at the sight of three males. Not too subtly her eyes conveyed the idea that this was as things should be. Lovely was the word for Priscilla. No wonder, Gil thought, Jeff guards her so jealously that he scares the men away.

"Hi, Gil—Jeff!" she greeted them warmly, tossing her head with the air of a girl who is confident about her good looks.

Then, kittenlike, she sat on the arm of her father's chair, and embraced him as he grunted with pleasure. The sight was a pleasing one and did them both proud.

"Someone call me?" she asked in playful innocence.

"Why aren't you helping your mother instead of fussing

[189]

with yourself. She's breaking her back in the kitchen," Mr. Kirby declared. "Now, you run in there and give her a hand."

Priscilla at nineteen was fragile, a beauty, a peach-brown doll's face amazingly smooth, but pouting now with mock discontent. She had been washing her hair, drying, combing, and redoing it in this style and that for the past hour, and now it lay in a lustrous black aureole around her head. Snatched from an incomplete toilet, she half expected her brother to defend her against her father's mild rebuke. She went over to Jeff, sat on the edge of the bench beside him at the piano, planted a resounding kiss on his cheek, and smiled. He chucked her under the chin affectionately and turned to his father. "Aw, Dad, give her a break—Prissy's got a date tonight!"

"With that Watkins fellow, I suppose," Mr. Kirby said with the weary air of one tired of the man who came to dinner.

"And what's wrong with Cass? He's the smartest interne at Harlem Hospital and he's going to be a good doctor, too," Priscilla said, beginning to bristle.

"He's all right, I guess—but he's got no background. Who's his people? Has he even got any?"

Priscilla turned defiant. "Just as good as ours!"

"What the heck does that matter anyway, as long as he's a first-rate guy and will do right by Prissy," Jeff said, annoyed because this subject had been kicked around endlessly.

When Mr. Kirby tallied his daughter's assets, which he had built up carefully, he was convinced that the upstart Dr. Cass Watkins was unworthy of his daughter's hand in matrimony, especially since his prospects as a physician in Harlem were none too bright. Priscilla was beyond the reach of the cruder aspects of racial prejudice, because she lived and played almost exclusively within her own community. She had made her debut into society, and a stunning one it was, too, thereby observing the social amenities. She attended a top-rank college, belonged to a Greek-letter Negro sorority, and was popular with her set. Her clothes bore the labels of fashionable Fifth Avenue shops, and she wore them with considerable style and verve. And, above all, she was a *Kirby*. Priscilla had the routine assets of any girl of her sort, but in Mr. Kirby's eyes she was a priceless gem, attainable only at considerable cost.

"First thing you know," Mr. Kirby said, turning squarely at Jeff, "she'll be doing one of your tricks—walking off and getting herself married to a nobody without her family's consent!"

Jeff ignored the thrust at Deborah and himself, but he made a spirited defense of Priscilla's right to choose her own boy friends, even the man she would eventually marry. He always defended her. And his loyalty and affection was reciprocated in equal measure by his sister. She had defended his right to marry the girl he loved, even to her stunned parents.

"After all, Dad," Jeff said, "according to you *yourself*, we've got some no 'count characters in our own family!"

The sardonic reference to his forebears fell on Mr. Kirby's ears like a thunderclap. "Let your mother and me decide what's good for your sister," he shouted, then suddenly clamped down his voice as if he caught the neighbors listening. "I want no more of this wrangling, do you hear—Jeff, Priscilla?" And by way of changing the unpleasant subject, he repeated his order that his daughter go to the kitchen and help her mother.

She left obediently.

"Play something, Jeff," Gil said in an effort to relieve the tensions.

"Sure. Dad, anything you want to hear specially?"

"Anything that'll drown out this arguing."

His son whirled slowly on the bench; but before he could strike a chord, Narcissa, who had had things well in hand back in the kitchen, called her family and Gil to the dining room table.

Dinner at the Kirby's was a one-dish affair. Barely had Mr. Kirby finished the grace when Narcissa began heaping the first plate with collard greens, boiled potatoes, slices of ham, and a big spoonful of piccalilli for relish. And Priscilla filled the glasses with buttermilk. In his home Mr. Kirby was always served first; even now with a guest at the table Narcissa followed this ritual and gave her husband precedence.

"Never keep a man waiting for his food," she said, passing him a laden plate. He waited until everyone was served, and fell to his food zestfully.

"Do you know, Mr. Gilbert," he said between forkfuls, "there's still nobody that can turn out a meal like Mrs. Kirby."

Jeff chimed in with, "You can say that again, Dad."

Narcissa smiled shyly, deprecatingly, her eyes lowering to the handsome silver service before her.

"How's Deborah, Jeff?" Priscilla suddenly interpolated.

"Fine as wine—went to Boston to see her folks. She'll be back tonight."

Deborah, as always, struck a dissonant chord in the harmony of this household. Not that there was anything explosive about Mr. and Mrs. Kirby's reactions now—rather it was the tired patience that is characteristic of people who have suffered much. Deborah had become one more cross to bear—one more imposition by the white folks, and like wars and depressions had to be borne philosophically.

"Jeff and Deborah are going to have cute kids—and no kinky hair either," Priscilla said, laughing impishly. The idea intrigued her. "And I'll baby-sit."

Gil suddenly thought of the possibility: a white girl with

a black baby! The image of Deborah nursing a Negro child was nightmarish.

Mr. Kirby interrupted the vision with, "She'll never have a Negro child."

"How can you say that, Dad?" Jeff said, astonished.

Priscilla sounded a jocular note: "She looks like the twin-type to me!"

Mr. Kirby shook his head unhappily. "The more I look at that boy, the more I feel he's the spit image of his grandfather."

"Grandpa was a radical, Gil," Priscilla confided, proudly.

"A damned fool, if you ask me," Mr. Kirby countered.

He had struck a pose of superiority, but underneath Mr. Kirby was upset. He was embarrassed by any mention of his father, not only because he had been a slave, but because he was a loud-mouthed radical who, as a man, had been a failure. Mr. Kirby said finally, "And like him—you've tried to bring unhappiness to your mother and me."

"No such thing," Priscilla said stoutly. "Jeff's the nicest brother a girl ever had, and I know he never meant to hurt you both."

"Never mind, Prissy," Jeff said, toying with his food.

Mr. Kirby shrugged wearily, unhappily.

Narcissa opened her mouth to say something, but her throat became choked and no words came. She merely sat helplessly and remained silent, and picked aimlessly at the greens on her plate. She knew well that Grandpa Ditcher was an inflammatory subject and the cause of endless quarrels between her husband and her children. And she dared say little, for fear of throwing kindling on the blaze, because her own highly respectable parents had objected to her marrying a son of Ditcher Kirby. But she was apparently unaware that in reality this bickering between her husband and son was a defense by each of his own meaning of life.

Gil was startled by the vehemence, however.

The coffee was served in silence. And they returned to the living room for innocuous conversation.

The Kirby bell rang. It was now about eight-thirty; the young Dr. Cass Watkins had arrived.

Mr. Kirby took his cue, said good night to everyone and went upstairs to bed.

A curious hush had come over the house now.

Priscilla and Dr. Watkins made the most of the poor privacy the living room afforded. In the kitchen Narcissa was doing the final fiddling before herself going upstairs for the evening. When Jeff and Gil ambled in, the maker of this home gazed up at her son with a matter-of-fact affection.

"Dad's not really mad with you, Jeff. He really loves you and Priscilla both. But he is so terribly disappointed—that it makes him angry!" She patted him affectionately. "Sit down. You, too, Mr. Gilbert, and have a piece of cake and a glass of milk before you both go."

"Okay, Ma."

Jeff sat at the kitchen table and watched his mother set out the bottle of milk and cake. Her hair had become disarranged during the evening, and her light brown skin, ordinarily clear, now was muddy under the shaded electric light. Her neglected hands were tired, and the red nail polish had begun to peel. Gil was surprised that the Kirbys didn't have a servant. Mr. Kirby was a kind man, and manifestly considerate of his wife, but it apparently had never occurred to him to employ someone to help her with the household work; and possibly the idea had never come into her head either. This seemed characteristic of most Negro households.

"You must be tired, Ma."

"No," she said cheerfully. "I was tired sometime back, but not now, son."

Narcissa cut the cake, poured the milk into two tall glasses, and sat down opposite them. Her forearms, still plump and shapely, lay on the white porcelain table; her eyes, brown as the cake she had baked, were fixed on her son as he drank the milk.

"Gil, I used to really eat this by the ton," he said. He turned to his mother for confirmation. "Didn't I, Ma?"

"Mr. Gilbert, I remember everything about my boy. The bicycle he always kept in the backyard, the dogs he would never let sleep outdoors, the piano lessons after school, the football in winter and the camping in summer, and that time he wrote a composition for his high school orchestra. I remember every bit of it, son—including the girls you were wild about, not to mention the ones that were wild about you. That Zabee Desvigny was an awfully nice girl!"

Narcissa paused in her nostalgic recital.

There's something I've wanted to ask you, Jeff, ever since you told us you were married—"

"Ma!" Jeff interrupted, indicating Gil's presence.

"I hope you don't mind, Mr. Gilbert," she apologized. "But I see so little of him these days, what with his tours and everything—but, after all, this isn't a secret to you!"

Narcissa turned to Jeff. "Tell me, son—tell me the truth. What made you go against the wishes of your father and me —we only had your good at heart?"

Jeff pondered the answer he should give his mother. His feet scraped uneasily under the table. He fumbled in his mind a moment. Dare he reveal the hard truth that his love for her, great as it was, could not be compared with the feeling that had drawn him, and now bound him, to Deborah? How could he tell her that the depth and power of his love for his wife was such that it filled and dominated him, that it was different than any love a son could possibly feel for a mother?

He spoke as honestly as he could to the tired woman opposite him. "Ma, I know you always wanted me to marry Zabee, but I married Deborah because I loved her. It's as simple as that."

The worn corners of Narcissa Kirby's mouth trembled. "That's what I hoped you'd say, Jeff. And now you're happy, I hope."

"Of course, Ma."

He was as grave as a judge who had handed down a death sentence to an innocent person. Gil sensed that Jeff felt his answer had somehow left his mother still puzzled. He started to say something, when he looked at the kitchen clock.

"Nine! And I promised Deborah I'd meet her."

"Oh, my," Narcissa said, "you mustn't ever keep a woman waiting, son."

"Let's shove off," Gil said quickly.

Gil could still see Mrs. Kirby's eyes, as they walked swiftly across Seventh Avenue. They told the poignant story of a mother's soaring hopes for her son—and they had been dashed. For, not alone had he married a white woman, but, as his father observed contemptuously, he was "only squawking for a living."

The light summer rains began falling as they came within sight of Perky's neon sign. An indescribable joy suddenly seized Jeff, and he said to Gil, "What did you think of what Priscilla said?"

"About a child?"

"Yes. About Deborah having a child."

"I don't know, Jeff."

III

Knox Gilbert had fled to The Back Door in the late afternoon of a sultry June day. He was concerned about the state of the world. He didn't much care about the world except as the rushing events in Europe got in his way and the reactions of his friends and clients endangered their careers and his own peace. Universal peace was only a pleasant umbrella where his own concerns could bud and blossom. He resented the rattling of sabers when they crashed on the borders of his personal life. He resented his friends' involvement in these alien concerns. As if their own complicated lives weren't strained enough without their confusing them with the distant marchings of Stalin, Hitler and Mussolini. Mr. and Mrs. Roosevelt were bad enough on the home front.

He found Jake (but no Floyd) poking around in the back, sat in a small pool of light at a table, and sat looking at a drink. His major problem was still Jeff Kirby and, of course, Deborah. The fact that Jeff was also now his number one source of income, while pleasant, was increasingly perilous.

Gil remembered when he had been bickering with Perky over the contract agreement for Jeff and how they were to launch him.

"Well," Perky had said, "At least we can ship him along T.O.B.A. which routes colored shows through the South. He'll make it there."

"Why not Broadway?" Gil had said, the big stakes always top of the mind. "If I can build him into an attraction, he'll make the grade with whites, and we always can squeeze bigger prices from the colored houses."

Gil felt he had long ago learned the secret of selling to Negroes.

Perky had pursed his thick lips. "Not *black* enough," he had pronounced soberly.

"Meaning what?"

"His skin ain't the right shade. Now, colored chicks really go for his type of cool brown. But white—"

"Oh, I've—"

Perky had interrupted, "Excuse you me, but I never saw a white man who didn't like his colored folks black and hot, specially when he's paying good money at the box office."

There was something in what he said, and Gil had admitted the combination was an asset in the variety theater.

"But even so," Gil had said, "he's a cinch to make good on Broadway. He's got the personality of a Paul Robeson and the polish of a Roland Hayes. With these he can't miss."

He hadn't missed. The "Tan Troubador" was now thoroughly launched. Gil had borrowed the term from Perky's rich lexicon. And, with Deborah's help, they had pushed him. It took only a few months under Gil's management to transform Jeff into a busy, tireless performer.

Being Jeff, he liked the swift motion and was quickly fascinated by the comings and goings. While he pretended not to care, the attention also pleased him, and particularly Deborah's delight in it. Gil didn't explain to them some of the angles involved in the sudden interest the New York press had shown in Jeff. That, for example, Miltie Shoop, in repayment for choice morsels Gil had slipped him now and again about Sherl, had written a rave notice about the unknown Jeff—simply a case of washing each other's hand.

It was after this Gil had told Perky, "He'll make money like a slot machine."

—2—

Gil remembered, too, Jeff's return from one of the early out-of-town trips—to Baltimore. Gil had decided not to meet Jeff at the airport but at The Back Door. Deborah was in Boston visiting her family; otherwise they both would probably have met Jeff.

"Hiya," Jeff said, as he came in and joined Gil in the murky quiet. It was his stock greeting but delivered with little of his usual bounce. He wore a tweed suit, his "working clothes" as he called them. He often wore tweeds these days to effect a kind of conventional belonging when he had to rub elbows with white people.

He had just completed a two-week engagement at the venerable Booth Theatre in Baltimore, a landmark along Pennsylvania Avenue.

This Baltimore stint had been something of a triumph, and pointed to smooth sailing from there on out.

He was the first Negro to appear at the Booth Theatre, and Gil felt proud of himself (and Jeff) for having turned this difficult trick. The theater's manager, Morrie Kaplan, had signed a contract for his appearance under subtle duress. He had had misgivings about booking a Negro; and, instead, had sought the established Sherri Shannon, who by now was a big moneymaker. Himself Jewish, he was afraid the innovation might provoke a racial incident, and bring down on his head the wrath of a city hostile to both Negroes and Jews.

But Gil had insisted that he take Jeff or else no Shannon,

knowing that Morrie was also under pressure from liberal groups to alter his racial policy. Morrie was partly mollified, and his fears temporarily allayed, when the newspaper columnists, who had caught wind of the negotiations, vigorously applauded the manager's courage in advance notices. Kaplan quickly came to terms when Gil agreed to shave Jeff's fee and the next week bring in Shannon on a percentage basis so that he could recoup any losses he might incur in presenting a Negro attraction.

Gil was capable of some sharp trading; what agent isn't? But this backstage business, involving several weeks' haggling, would have made Jeff flush with anger had he known, perhaps caused him to refuse to perform; so Gil was careful not to mention any of the details to him. He had him billed simply as the "Tan Troubador"—discreetly omitting to mention in the publicity releases and newspaper interviews that he was married to a white girl. For impact on his audiences Jeff depended not so much on his feeling for the voice as an instrument as on his charm, and so Gil was elated when one reviewer dubbed him the "Sepia Russ Columbo," and a photograph caption in a lady columnist's report tagged him "Tall, Tan and Terrific."

As things developed, the package deal proved to be a double triumph: when Gil ran down to Baltimore to check the box office receipts, he discovered to his delight that Jeff's appearance was a sensational success, and, Morrie, who overnight had become a local hero, was prepared to offer him a return engagement.

Yet Gil realized, then, that Jeff seemed unhappy in his work—at least, he was bothered in his mind. And this naturally disturbed Gil. With his natural talents as a performer, he was moving along smooth pavement. He, apparently, was indifferent to this fact. Equally talented colored people in Harlem obscurity were crying for the opportunities he already enjoyed and the many that lay ahead. The irony of the situation made Gil think of one of Perky's homely sayings: "Dog that got bone, ain't got no teeth; and dog that got teeth, ain't got no bone."

—3—

And now in the late afternoon, Jeff and Gil were in Perky's, feeling the grayness of the day. Jeff was irritable and restless. Jake, absorbed in his own thoughts, was peeling an apple with a long knife, his elbows propped on the bar. And when they ordered martinis, he merely glanced up, his eyes filled with unwearying patience, and like a high priest before his temple altar proceeded to observe the ritual for thirsty pilgrims. He lumbered to their table with the drinks, grumbling all the while because Floyd was absent without leave and he had to do the table-waiting chores.

Then Jeff suddenly got up, and leaving his drink untouched, walked to the piano nearby, sat down, and for an hour or so he improvised. He just sat there and played. He never moved, and he never said a word. What he was trying to say through his music was not easy for Gil to know—he just played. There was imagery in his phrasings, each one broad and fanciful, sweeping along in a rush of purple wash. His dissonant harmonies had a quality of their own—remote, otherworldly, Debussyian perhaps, always saying something on the verge of words. He was inspired, almost in a trance. And then, as suddenly as he had sat at the piano, he got up and came back to the table.

Gil had caught a glimpse, too, of his depths as a person. He felt a sneaking guilt.

"How'd you like Baltimore?" he said, hoping to change Jeff's mood.

Jeff smiled across the table. "Do you know Countee Cullen, Gil?"

"Cullen?" Gil said, wondering what earthly connection this person had with Baltimore. "The poet?" he asked, vaguely remembering a scrap of doggerel that had come his way from somewhere.

"Yes."

"Nope. I know very little poetry—most poetry never touches me, except to make me restless and nervous."

"Then, try this one for size."

"Okay, shoot."

" 'Once riding in old Baltimore,' " Jeff quoted, " 'heart-filled, head-filled with glee, I saw a Baltimorean keep looking straight at me. Now, I was eight and very small, and he was no whit bigger; but he poked out his tongue and called me nigger.' "

"That's pretty sour stuff, Jeff," Gil said, disappointed that he hadn't exulted about the trip.

"Listen," he interrupted, and quoted the final stanza. " 'I saw the whole of Baltimore, from May to December; of all the things that happened there, that's all that I remember.' "

His smile made Gil uncomfortable. "That's all that I re-member—about Baltimore," he said, repeating his Cullen.

"Come, come, now," Gil protested, slightly annoyed. "Things weren't that bad!"

"Maybe not."

"Well?"

"The joker, Gil—there's always a joker in the deal."

"How do you mean?"

"I mean—even the good things come to us in a sort of backhanded way." He smiled wryly to himself.

His meaning escaped Gil.

"When I was in college, Gil, I took a course in Bible—I don't know why, especially; maybe, because I could skip a class or two during the football training season. I found the stuff awfully dull. But when I received a big round D at the

end of the semester, I was disappointed, because I felt I had
studied enough to have gotten at least a passing mark. I
made no fuss about it, but the dean called me into his office
and said he was quite surprised that I had done so poorly,
and quizzed me about the prof's attitude. I told him that
maybe I hadn't studied enough, but the dean was sure I was
trying to cover up for the prof. Anyway, he raised my grade
to a C—but not before he had offered the opinion that everybody knows Negroes are deeply religious, and, if they didn't
know anything else, Negroes did know the Bible!"

Gil could think of nothing to say.

"Oh, well," Jeff said, "I don't want to lie down in green
pastures along with Marc Connelly, but I have no desire to
wear an eternal sword and buckler."

–4–

Jeff relaxed now, and pushed his hand into his pocket and
brought out a small, blue-suede-covered box. "For you, Gil,"
he said, handing the box over with boyish enthusiasm. Gil
opened it. In it were a pair of beautifully handwrought
silver cuff links that looked like replicas of a Florentine me-
dallion. "Ought to go nicely with your noisy shirts," he said,
laughing.

Gil laughed, too. "Where in the world did you find these?"

"Between shows—did a bit of browsing—and just happened upon them and thought of you."

Gil was touched, and thanked him.

"Baltimore wasn't so bad—after all, eh?" Jeff said, smiling
broadly, as if to say he had tossed off his unpleasant memories. "Now, let me show you something, Gil—something
really exciting!" He reached under the table for a package
he had brought in, untied the strings, carefully unwrapped
the brown paper, and, from a big bundle of tissue paper

gingerly drew forth an ebony statue of a man. He held it between his thumb and forefinger admiringly, and then stood it up on the table. It was about a foot high, and two fingers in width. "I've christened him Sultan," he said happily.

Gil examined the handsome, odd-shaped figure. It was a dramatic piece of primitive art, feelingly executed. It represented a Negroid type, barefoot and wearing a straight, ankle-length gown, with long arms in wrist-length sleeves, and on its head perched a tall, square turban. It was shiny black, elongated and round, firmly erect, and chisled with a purity of line that would delight Picasso. No other detail decorated this inspired conception of the human form. Its stylized proportions were seemingly calculated to heighten its erect length, and thus the piece had the starkly brilliant beauty of a steeple.

"It's a magnificent thing," Gil said after a pause.

"It's Deborah's present," he said simply, and he tightly clasped the delicately sculptured figure with long fingers, almost lovingly, possessively—and smiled thoughtfully. "When I first saw him, I thought of her right away—just felt he belonged to her—and so I tried to buy him for her."

Gil wondered whether this was one more example of Jeff's uncanny intuition. For the manner in which he had acquired Sultan was characteristic of Jeff; characteristic, too, of his subtlety of feeling for Deborah and, indeed, human relations generally.

Jeff's spectacular success at the Booth Theatre had made Negroes in Baltimore very proud of him, and this fact brought him a dinner invitation from a very old widow, whose husband had been a missionary in the bush of Nigeria. Jeff had wanted to refuse the invitation but felt he couldn't because the distinguished man had done much to advance the cause of his race. When Jeff arrived at her home, his eyes immediately lighted on the ebony figure, one of several the old lady's husband had collected as examples of the African's capacity for creating art. He promptly offered to buy it. The woman was reluctant to sell. So he used all his charm on her, sending her flowers and tickets to the theater. She was enchanted with him, and when he told her finally he wanted it as a gift for his wife, the old widow relented and gave the piece to him.

"Think Deborah will like Sultan, Gil?"

"Jeff, I'm sure Sultan will make a big hit with her—and she'll appreciate the feeling that goes along with him."

Jeff said, as if talking to himself, "I suppose this is the reason I'm a crooner: to earn enough money to do things like this—bring beauty into Deborah's life."

–5–

Jeff had weathered that critical period, when a singer discovers that either he must rise to the challenge of his work or lie down and accept mediocrity. He had reorganized his life on a basis of rigid economy, and with the cooperation of Deborah had ruthlessly lopped off activities that invaded his work schedule, including his studies of piano and composition at Juilliard. He refused all social invitations, smiled less often, lost some of his boyish charm, and often had to apply a brake to an occasional display of peevishness. He only allowed himself the indulgence of one or two leisured drinks a week, a big sporting event once in a while, and from time to time a piano concert.

The practical necessities of the new career were dangerous to the tension of the marriage. Yet Knox Gilbert felt that he must disregard them. He felt compelled to insist that Jeff travel without Deborah—any other course, he felt, would have been disastrous, not to mention the money invested that would have gone down the drain if his marriage to a white girl became public knowledge—at least known beyond Harlem. Besides, her presence on tours would have been very inconvenient, to say the least. Such commonplace doings as procuring hotel reservations and being served food in restaurants were for them nearly impossible. Few places would accept a mixed couple as guests; Jeff himself had had to stay at the homes of colored friends and eat in nearby hash houses, because the hotels and restaurants operated by whites didn't admit Negroes. Jeff himself was too fastidiously racial to accept the hospitality of the ramshackle places that announced in neon-loud signs, "Colored Accommodated." And even these would be squeamish about renting a room or serving a meal to Jeff and a white wife, perhaps in fear of police retaliation. Even in New York one evening the three of them happened into a dining room where the waitress pointed to Jeff and said, "That colored man will have to eat in the kitchen."

Jeff had seen the practicality of Gil's insistence that he travel alone as a way of avoiding unpleasant incidents and nasty publicity, and he had acquiesced, however reluctantly. But he was constantly bothered by a guilty conscience, and was frequently tempted to fling the fact of his unorthodox marriage into the faces of everyone. So whenever he played a theater anywhere near New York, Gil insisted that Deborah make a one-day trip to see him perform, and thus placate him somewhat.

Gil usually accompanied her. And elaborate precautions were always observed. When they arrived at a theater, especially one outside New York, they allowed the managers, newspaper people, stagehands, and musicians to assume that Deborah was Gil's companion. She and Jeff were of course careful not to make any show of affection or familiarity that might give away the masquerade. If they had to eat, they sent out for sandwiches or ate in Jeff's dressing room. They always had to be alert under these circumstances to a sudden opening of a door or even a peeping Tom.

The duplicity upset them both, because they were fundamentally honest people, and it was undoubtedly the gnawing frustration of this complicated arrangement that was the reason behind Deborah's unexpected flare of anger the afternoon they went to the Bijou Theatre in Wilmington, Delaware. Deborah and Gil had arrived by train too late to go backstage and see Jeff before the show started. So they went directly to seats in the audience. Before the curtain went up an announcement was made from the stage that Jeff was ill and would not sing this afternoon's performance. Actually, as they afterward learned, Jeff had developed laryngitis.

A man sitting next to them suddenly threw his hands in the air and cried out, "That nigger's drunk again!"

Deborah was startled, and shocked, too, by the man's ugly vehemence. "I cannot permit you to talk like that," she said angrily.

Her voice was flat and harsh, and she was trembling. Her even, pale skin grew red in splotches. Suddenly all attention was centered directly upon her. But before she could say another word, the astonished man was out of his seat, and like a bat out of hell, left and never came back.

What incensed her particularly were the words "nigger" and "again." She had said to Gil, "You see, Jeff's not a 'nigger' and he's been drunk only once since I've known him —and that was the night you offered him the contract."

Her protective attitude startled Gil. He had never thought her capable of so tender a feeling for Jeff as a man. Maybe it was not Jeff at all; perhaps she was unconsciously defending her marriage to a Negro. While she recognized the handicaps involved in his being a Negro, she always tried to protect him from any harsh manifestations. But it was a dangerous point of view, because it was the sympathy one extends to a cripple. He was, in a sense, her baby, because she was seemingly unaware that Jeff already had lived his life as a colored man and had sufficient strength of character, or perhaps resilience, to meet the exigencies of that fact. Her overprotective attitude was clearly destructive of his manliness. It was one of the evidences of the numerous imperfections developing in the whole relationship.

They were, perhaps, too much alike, both with inherited radicalism, warring with inherited conservatism. Levi Comstock and Ditcher Kirby, both of their father's compromisers, the Christ and the Anti-Christ.

—6—

Deborah gave Jeff a merciless account of the episode in the theater, relating chapter and verse. Gil was surprised by this twist in her character. Jeff would once have blazed with anger; now he could let the barb bounce off harmlessly. Gil noticed the difference in his attitude and said something to Deborah about a thick skin being one of the prerequisites for success. She nodded assent.

"I suppose, you think I'm an idiot," she said afterward, embarrassed.

"No, Deborah," Gil said, trying to comfort her, "I think you're quite a remarkable person."

"I don't know why I allow characters like that to upset me."

"Characters like that—I can take or leave."

"Silly of me."

"Not at all. Things like that can't be helped."

"You're always so gentle with me, Gil," she said, recovering her poise.

Gil was incensed by the thought that if she weren't mar-

ried to a Negro, she wouldn't have to suffer so many indignities, and for the moment he was annoyed with her for her
having married one. He said, "I guess being Jeff's wife is no
bed of roses."

"Please, Gil! Don't pity me—there are many, many com-
pensations."

"Meaning what, precisely?"

She bristled, her chin lifting slightly. And her voice became cold. "I'm speaking from a woman's viewpoint. You
see, I love my husband."

Gil was startled into silence.

"You're inclined to be morbid, aren't you, Gil?" Deborah
said thoughtfully. "In the way you look at things generally?"

"No one ever said *that* to me before!"

"I think you are—just a little, anyway."

"If I am—maybe, it's because I'm alone a good deal."

"Well, maybe not so morbid, but I should say at bottom
you're very emotional!"

Gil was aware that he was often dangerously near wanting
Deborah for himself. Yet, how deeply, and to what purpose?
What did he want to prove? He took a good look at her. He
felt himself wanting to say, "Deborah, you're not constructed
to marry a Negro and live happily ever after."

Jeff had urged them not to catch his last show; otherwise
they might not get back to town until late. So Deborah and
Gil left Wilmington by train about eight P.M. and arrived at
Pennsylvania Station in New York before midnight.

Her catnap aboard the streamliner had refreshed her.

"At the risk of compromising you, Deborah," Gil said with
a grin as they headed for the taxi-stand, "can I take you to a
quiet place I know and give you a drink? It's not so late, and
I'm sure you need one before going to bed. This has been a
harrowing day for you, I know."

"I'd love to, Gil."

They got a cab.

The streets were gravy-thick with the smell of the river.

The taxi carried them crosstown to East Fifty-third Street and dropped them off in front of the Cafe Delacroix—a small, sub-basement dining room fitted with a dozen or so tables and a walnut buffet. Reproductions by French cubists lined the walls. It was a French restaurant operated by an Italian. They were obsequiously conducted to a corner by a French-man. He arched his brows, smiled incessantly, as they read the wine list. They were the only guests in the place. It was a dowdy establishment, though the wines were good, the food delicious, and the prices modest.

Deborah, who saw the inside of such downtown places less frequently nowadays, surveyed the cafe with undisguised pleasure, and sighed the sigh of a felon who had escaped prison.

They ordered drinks, and the waiter presently returned with them.

Deborah tasted hers, and half talking to herself, said, "I guess we always expect the other fellow to be clairvoyant—and it isn't quite fair."

"How's that again?"

"Gil, this morning before we left for Wilmington I re-ceived a letter from a woman friend of mine that upset me—and I don't know why it should have, especially. Maybe it's the reason I've been in such a foul mood all day."

"Bad news?"

"No. Simply that the wife of an old boy friend . . . had a baby. He wired my friend in Chicago, who is also a very dear friend of his, announcing the birth, and she wrote to me thinking I'd like to know. Somehow the news affected me quite badly for a while today."

"Really?"

"And a *son*, too," she said, adding ruefully, "Other people have babies—Deborah has Jeff."

"No reason why you can't have one, too."

"I don't know, Gil—"

"Jeff's anxious," he said quickly. "Nothing would please him more."

She flushed. "I know. He said something only a few days ago about, now that he's making some money, we ought to start thinking about a family. But, Gil, I just hate bringing a child into a world that offers it nothing but unhappiness—and pain."

Unlikely, Gil figured. But this was important to her, so he nodded. "Why not? Others do it."

"Colored children have a frightful time of it. Why, just the other day a colored mother was telling me that the white youngsters won't play with her boy in kindergarten. The poor thing doesn't understand why, and he's too young for her to explain."

"Deborah, that's like saying only white people should have kids! You don't mean that, do you?"

"I know I don't sound logical, but that's not quite what I mean."

She was hedging, Gil thought. So he pushed her, "Well?"

"Maybe it's crazy, Gil, but I don't see why—if I have a child—why it should be called a *Negro*—and treated like one!"

"I admit it doesn't make sense; yet not to have a child—why, that's carrying a protective attitude to absurd lengths."

"Gil, you've only a nodding acquaintance with the Negro's problem. You don't have to live with it twenty-four hours a day. I didn't either, once. But now I'm learning the hard way—and it's often pretty ghastly."

"Negroes survive," Gil said.

"Perhaps. But if I were a Negro, I would live in constant

fury, and probably would beat myself to death against the bars they meet everywhere."

"As far as I can see, they get to live with it—and Jeff's a prime example."

"I doubt it, Gil. I'll give you an example. One afternoon Jeff and I went to the zoo in Central Park. We were standing in front of a cage watching the antics of the monkeys and feeding them peanuts, when a little white boy came up and excitedly shouted, 'Oh, Mama, look at the niggers!' Now, this remark was meant innocently enough, I guess, but, Gil, I was mortified for Jeff as well as myself. I'm sure he turned crimson inside. No, you don't get used to that sort of thing happening to you daily—I know *I* don't!"

"That's pretty awful, I must say," Gil said.

"Well, that's what throws me. I'd go stark, raving mad if a child of mine had to undergo that sort of thing in and out of season—especially, when there's nothing *I* personally can do to protect the little thing against such cruelties!"

"I see what you mean," Gil said and wondered what psychic injury is done to such a child.

"You know, of course," she said, "that the child of a marriage between a Negro and a white or red, yellow, or even a brown person—no matter how little its appearance resembles that of a Negro—is considered *Negro!*"

Gil nodded, but he wondered whether if at the root of her objections to having a Negro child was her own latent, undefined, perhaps unconscious fear of racial extinction. For, after all, in one way or another, we all seek immortality through our children.

"Why—" Deborah added almost fiercely, "why, it's enough to make the angels neurotic!"

"What does Jeff, say?"

"Naturally, he wants kids; but, frankly, Gil, I simply can't bring myself to tell him even what I've told you."

"Why, not?"

"It simply might crush him—and his ego, too."

"Of course," Gil answered, though he thought the idea of crushing Jeff's ego was so much rubbish.

Deborah stared at the room, empty of all but the Frenchman and two or three pairs of people who had wandered in as they talked. The place, however, was full of piped-in music, in a light opera mood.

—7—

A couple of weeks later Gil wandered into The Back Door in the early morning hours. He told himself it was to check up on Ivory's combo, but when he saw Zabee sitting at a table surrounded by a group of eager young people, he admitted to himself that he had hoped she would be there. Both Jeff and Deborah were out of town and he might therefor have an opportunity to talk with Zabee alone.

He sat at a table by himself, ordered a drink, acknowledged Ivory's wave, bowed to Zabee and tried to watch her without seeming to stare. The long blue-black hair was set as usual in a neat bun at the back of her neck. But what he always noticed first were the emerald-green eyes. She reminded him more than ever of the statue of Nefertiti. She might be unpredictable, but there seemed nothing formidable about her, he thought. One felt she had a deep potential that reached longingly for an emotional equal, that essentially she was merely a passionate woman, unashamedly so, whose exotic beauty stirred erotic images in men.

After a half hour or so, her companions left, and she sat alone sipping her drink, a book nestled next to her ashtray. Gil glanced at its colorful, stylized jacket, and verified the title: It was *Lady Chatterley's Lover*.

"Exploratory?" Gil asked across the tables, smiling.

[213]

The question seemed to startle her.

"I wondered," Gil said, "why you were reading this particular book, and in my curiosity started talking out loud."

She smiled, too. "Perhaps," she said.

"I'm all ears, then. May I join you?"

She offered him a seat beside her. She slowly moved her glass like a pawn across the red-checkered tablecloth, then sipped the last of the amber drink.

Finally she said, "You're making quite a boy out of Jeff."

Gil wasn't quite sure what she meant, but he said, "Yeah, he's getting to be a big man in this town. Did you see what Milton Shoop said in his column?"

"Yes, I saw the write-up, but I wonder whether it's the sort of big man Jeff wants to be!"

She seemed to wince slightly and slowly undid the catch of her jacket. She was wearing a suit of dark green velvet with a sheer white blouse, and a startling bracelet of Afro-Cuban design with red and green stones mounted on a broad brass band. It was an attractive outfit that left enough of her arms and chest bare to reveal the smooth skin.

Gil asked her if she cared for another drink.

She nodded. "Beer and ginger ale, and lots of ice."

"Beer and ginger ale, mixed?"

"I know it sounds outlandish, but it's a delicious drink I picked up in the tropics."

Gil caught Floyd's eye. As the waiter approached, he glanced appreciatively at Zabee's voluptuous figure and grinned at Gil understandingly, as though they were fellow conspirators in a planned seduction. When he returned with the order, she supervised the mixing of the half-and-half combination. Gil picked up her check and his, signed his name, and handed Floyd a third big tip—knowing it was too much—knowing that he was crudely buying good will. The extravagance would pay off ultimately, he rationalized, but he was annoyed with himself, and annoyed with Negroes, too, for the subtle pressure he was feeling more and more as the days went by.

"Gil," said Zabee, "I came as near praying you'd talk to me tonight as I get to prayer. When you asked about the book—I liked to fainted with gratitude."

"No such thing," Gil said. "I already felt I knew you well."

"Never mind the chivalry—I'm still happy you spoke."

"Why? Lonesome?"

An expression came into her eyes that was part exploring and part caution. "Isn't everyone?"

"Yes, I suppose so. And like all bachelors—I'm always a little lonely."

Zabee laughed flirtatiously. "You, lonely! Not with your dark good looks."

He laughed too.

She thought awhile. "You meet a lot of women."

"I meet a few."

"Interesting ones, I mean."

"But few like you."

"Do you mean that? Or are you trying to be sensational?"

"Both."

"Seriously, Gil, I really—"

"Need money?" Gil interrupted. "Do you want to borrow a little something?" Then he wondered if he ought to lend any more money. The poverty in Harlem was grimmer than he had imagined, and these people would be hard pressed to return a loan.

She smiled ruefully. "Money, I could use—especially nowadays, when the kids can't pay tuition at the school. No, that wasn't why I wanted you to speak." She fumbled a moment. "Oh, heck," she said finally. "What I want to say can be put in one word. And yet—well, I've got to talk with someone. And you're elected."

"Okay, shoot."

For a full minute she sat there saying nothing. Then she pushed back a wayward wisp of her black hair and looked at Gil squarely—with an expression in her eyes that he remembered a long time afterward. "I'm in love. And the man's married—actually jilted me for a white girl." She turned away after that and looked toward the doorway unhappily.

"Jeff?" Gil asked, but without really entertaining any other possibility.

There was a silence as Gil underwent the experience that goes with sudden realizations. He thought of several responses and picked one carefully. He said, "Jeff's a nice guy, and as far as I can see he's devoted to Deborah."

"I know," she said, unconvinced.

"Love isn't always logical."

"Sex isn't either!"

"Sounds like a problem in semantics."

"But she doesn't understand him, really," she insisted, ignoring Gil's stress on the meanings of words.

She was talking absolute nonsense, Gil thought. If she possessed even a little insight into that pair, she might be a happier girl. And he also thought that any attempt to supply the insight would only tighten the hold of her small, personal problem.

He said, "Oh, I don't know. Perhaps, she understands him better than we think."

She said, "When he married her, I wanted to die. Gil, believe me, she's bad, very bad for him—and by that I don't mean she's not a nice girl personally!"

"You'll get over this. Maybe, not tonight—or tomorrow—but you'll laugh at yourself someday, and even might be sorry you ever told me this story."

"I doubt it. I don't love easy."

She blushed a lovely peach tinge. Gil believed her.

[216]

Then, as if talking to herself, she said, "I never wanted
Jeff for myself, but for himself. What attracted me to him
wasn't sex alone, or even love alone, for that matter. It's simply something about him that suits—the way he moves, the
way he talks, even the mean little expression he has when
he thinks. We like the same foods, drinks, joints, and people—maybe, it's simply that we belong to the same tribe. . . .
Do I bore you?"

"Not at all."

The expression on her face when she talked about Jeff was
revealing, to Gil, of many good qualities—of loyalty, tenderness. Suddenly, Gil understood Jeff's warmly flattering remarks about her, and his lingering attachment to her, mani-
fested in postcards he never failed to send her while on tour.
She was good for a man's ego. What she felt was not bold;
it was not arch; it was not mercenary; and it was not selfish;
it was simply a distillation of her own responses, like the
neatly curved shape of her eyebrows or the impeccable bun
on the back of her neck—no more and no less than that, and
revealed as naturally.

Unexpectedly Gil felt a deep longing for her—to possess
this girl himself.

Zabee caught him musing, and, he suspected, divined his
thoughts. She blushed a little, looked at her glass, and then
raised her eyes—but whether anxiously or in a repetition of
the look, Gil could not tell. She knew enough not to surrender her person instantly.

Gil thought that presently he ought to halt this confession.
It was awkward. He wondered vaguely whether she was not
straining her tenuous connection with him.

And then, as the music quickened, Zabee plunged on rapidly. "And if she understood him and they had a good marriage—at least for his sake I *would* forget. But it's wrong

—all wrong!" Then, after a moment of silence, she added fiercely, "After all, Gil, she's *white*, and he's a *Negro!*"

Her meanings were pregnantly clear to him, and he was surprised more by her racially inspired vehemence, and amused, too, by the ludicrous position of this girl, who, to all appearances was a white person, stoutly arguing for a loyalty to black folk. Gil might have laughed if the posture she had assumed was not without poignant irony, and she innocent of the grim joke implicit in her words. But he said only, "If Jeff's marriage is a failure, he's never given me any hint."

"Perhaps not, but I can read it in his face." She smiled to herself in tender remembrance of an incident. She said finally, "He used to be so gay, so alive, ambitious. Now he's got a hang-dog look. I can't bear it!"

Gil thought: The link between masochism and sex may be composed wholly of frustration.

He said, "You might be reading something into the situation that doesn't exist, Zabee."

"No. I don't think I am—call it a woman's intuition if you choose. Gil, I believe Jeff's too loyal, too stubborn to admit he's made a ghastly mistake."

"Well, as a friend—if you feel so strongly about it—why don't you talk it over with him? I'm sure he has confidence in your opinions."

Zabee shrugged. "No use. He's got the idea that he's engaged in some sort of holy mission—a personal crusade to prove that a marriage between a Negro and a white person can work. That he, and we, and people like us, can make a go of such a relationship if we only try."

"That's an awfully odd reason for a marriage."

"That's Jeff. When it rains, he says, 'it's Nature's weeping.'"

"Deborah's bright," Gil said, "as well as attractive. Maybe they'll work out their problems." He wondered if his words sounded as false to her as they did to him.

She nodded. "The girl does have a sense of drama. Maybe this will save the situation."

"And Jeff's a poet at heart."

"Not a poet. A patriot. When everything is tumbling on top of him, he's still waving the flag." Then she added softly, "Maybe, the poor guy is just plain stuck."

"And what about Deborah?"

Her green eyes were bitter.

Gil took a long breath. "Zabee, if you don't mind my saying so—the trouble with you colored people is that you carry your feelings too close to the skin. No toughness. No facing the facts. When problems develop, everyone seems to fall apart at the seams."

Her eyebrows arched slightly, and she looked at Gil steadily, silently. He saw his kernels of wisdom fall on barren soil, and by way of changing the subject, he asked if she cared to dance. He stood and held out his arms in a gesture of invitation. "Do you mind?"

Zabee wouldn't look at him then. She reached for her glass and drank deeply—stood—and in tempo glided gracefully into his arms.

Her body was unexpectedly responsive. He could feel her thighs warm, clinging. She was, as several dance critics had already testified, very good. Gil said, "I'm not too good at this sort of thing. I'd starve if people paid me for tripping the light fantastic."

She just smiled, looking at nothing for a long time, and finally looking up—softly—into his eyes. He could smell her perfume now—or at least became aware of its pervading presence. It was Chantilly, a subtly provocative fragrance. A dark feeling stirred in him. He held her a little closer.

After a while she said, "I think I'd better sit down."

They went to the table, and she declined another drink. He noticed her face was damp, a darker color now than peach; perspiration formed tiny beads on the upper part of her lips. She was panting—slightly—and trying to disguise it; but he could hear the rhythm of her breathing and see the dilation of her nostrils.

"That music does things to me," she said quietly.

"Women respond to men," Gil said.

"It's no good, Gil."

"But it could be, Zabee."

She spoke petulantly. "No, Gil If it's wrong for Joff, it's wrong for me, too."

Gil wondered if she thought that since he'd seen her sensual impulses were not confined to one person, he'd written her off as a slut. Suddenly fragments of the evening's conversation formed a design, a meaning. He had learned a curious fact about this creature: She considered love, or sexual attraction between a white person and a Negro so overwhelming that no amount of will power could resist it. If a man and woman found themselves behind closed doors, nothing could prevent their embrace; chaste inclinations, marriage vows, and even racial taboos were of no avail. But in the end such scalding embraces were disastrous, lingering agony and thus created their own disasters.

Gil took a good look at her, and mentally looked back at her disciplined education as an anthropologist. He laughed to himself. Hers was not the logical reasoning of a scientist; not the proverbial wisdom of an old woman, nor the gossip of a busybody; it was simply an ancient sigh of her people echoed as fact, and dealt with pitilessly and without moral judgment; and there was neither blame nor anger in her ambiguous smile now.

—8—

Until now they had paid very little attention to the surroundings in Perky's. But noisily now, two konk-headed tap

dancers, Bob Nots and Two Chops, took the floor and were
going through their noisy, vigorous paces with much grunt-
ing and grimacing to extract a handful of applause. Finally a
loud sustained chord by Ivory's combo drew attention to the
concluding stunt of their act: while the drum rolled, one
fellow gripped between his teeth a table with a chair piled
on top, and danced. Gil had often seen them before. He had
made money on them, because there was a class of people
who enjoyed Negroes in such darky roles. But Gil always
felt their broadly Negroid antics more embarrassing than
amusing.

"Pretty awful, don't you think?" he said, clapping perfunc-
torily.

"Not too good."

"I booked them downtown once—and they're not only
lousy performers, they're ignorant, unreliable fellows."

"Maybe they wouldn't be hoofers at all if they had the
chance to be, say, engineers. Who can tell?"

"They're naturally unreliable!"

"Gil," she said deliberately, "I like you—like you very
much—but I'm afraid you're headed for trouble."

"Why?" he asked, startled, and thought, "There's that
Negro sensitivity again."

"Because—well, simply because you don't understand us.
Nor does Deborah, if I may drag her in by the heels."

"What us?"

"I mean—Negroes."

"I'm no missionary, if that's what you mean. But you'd be
surprised at all the heckling I take on Broadway because I
represent Jeff, a Negro, and many other Negroes. That
should prove something about my attitude toward your people! They even call my office Uncle Tom's Cabin."

"I wonder . . . After all, Gil, one's motives are not always
apparent, even to the person himself."

"Okay, okay," Gil protested. But he was annoyed at her sensitivity, and wondered irritably what she was trying to prove.

"Take him," Zabee nodded to a sallow-skinned white man listlessly trailing a mop after him. "He's what I mean."

Pop Tubs acted as a porter and sometimes as bus boy. He was dirty and often smelled of stale whiskey. He was often spat upon and the object of cruel ridicule. Perky had told Gil his story, how he had once had money, fallen in love with a spectacular Negro entertainer years before, set her up in a luxurious apartment, then squandered everything he had on her, and when she deserted him and had milked him dry, took to dope and drink and had become one of Perky's pensioners.

Gil was unable to see this as symbol or parallel. Did she mean that Knox Gilbert was in danger of ending up like this crazy old man? This was nonsense! Women were his tonic, black or white. He could and would keep after Zabee. He'd find a way to bring her around, perhaps even cause her to ease up on Jeff and Deborah. He'd make them all need him. They all needed him right now, in case they didn't know it.

He frowned as he looked at Zabee.

"You think I could be like that?" he said.

"Why not?" she said.

"Why, you—"

"Say it," she said, " 'you yaller bitch!' "

"No!"

She let her smile grow warmer.

"You're really all right, Gil. But I have to show you the way I feel. I think this mixing things up is bad medicine—bad for you, bad for me, and especially bad for Jeff. Deborah can probably take care of herself. In a way, I hope so. I wish her no harm But I'd certainly like my man back and I don't make any promises not to try."

She got up. Gil started to rise.

"No, Gil," she said. "I'm going home—and by myself."

He saw her to the door, then went to the bar and ordered another drink.

"Trouble ahead," he thought to himself, wishing Perky were there to gossip. "And, Knox Gilbert, you'd best have a care. You're already in it up to your ever-loving neck."

IV

The warm, shining, mid-June day had blessed her party, Deborah thought as she stood looking out from the apartment through the leafy park and up toward St. John the Divine. Ever since the Town Hall concert she had planned to give this party for Dolly-May Tobin, but the apartment must be ready, it must be truly impressive; now it was! Yes, it was; her apartment, Jeff's too, of course, but essentially hers, her created setting for a spectacular couple. Today it would blossom as her salon.

She looked around, walked around, feeling the softness of the golden wall-to-wall carpeting under her gold slippers, touching an object now and then, savoring the sweep and color of the huge oblong room. One of New York's most successful Negro lawyers had once lived here and he had made one spacious apartment out of two. She let down the venetian blinds so that sunlight lit sparingly their ocher-tinted walls and ceiling. There were broad windows all along one end of the living room. The heavy curtains, emerald green, were caught by gold loops, and the valence at the top was gold. At the other end of the room were bookshelves, ceiling to floor. Deborah had chosen their content patiently, as much to exhibit a startling patchwork of bindings as to announce their owners' somewhat esoteric literary taste.

The furniture, of varying periods, was pulled together in effect by upholstery in golds and greens. Although she had had to raid many antique shops, the result was what Deborah had wished—primitive, almost barbaric, but never old-fashioned. Chairs, love seats, several divans, and ottomans were arranged to form islands of comfort for groups of people. For today, the small sand-colored rolling piano had been moved in from Jeff's music room. It stood over against the bookshelves.

Deborah faced the south wall now, as those who entered the apartment from the lobby did. She knew how beautiful it was, and she had been told often enough, not only by the flatterers but by the sincere. Even Uncle Ellery had approved with, "Magnificent! It's early Comstock come late, and at its perverse best!" Her relations with her family were now practically nonexistent except for Uncle Ellery who kept in touch.

She had been able to be lavish in spending when money sharply ceased to be their problem. Jeff's tours now vied with royalties from recordings of his songs. The latest of these, "Return Ride," for which he had also written the lyrics, was currently at the top of the hits. She had remembered how proud he had been when they were able to buy the paintings she was facing now: the delicate Picasso nude; the early Marin, a purple-green shadowy and poetic landscape; the Degas. How angry she had been when he insisted that one of her own paintings hang on the same wall, a bold still life of scarlet and yellow fruit. But the whole room was drawn into focus by the fireplace, the mantel, and the portrait above it.

The fireplace, now logged and ready, pine-cone sprinkled. The marble around it was good, and happily pink and rosy-veined. The mantle above Deborah had kept clear except for the erect ebony of Sultan (Jeff's gift from Baltimore) at one end, and a brass Maltese cross at the other. The portrait above the mantel commanded the room. Deborah looked at it now as the blazing substitution and yet reincarnation of Levi Comstock. Here was Jeff: as bullfighter, as toreador, as ruler of this domain.

Jeff had not wanted the portrait, but it had been Tonio Diaz who had suggested it. He was their friend. He was hard up. This was the way he saw Jeff: the tamer, the champion of causes, the dark figure arrayed in rainbow colors. Together, Deborah and Tonio had persuaded him. So now, lit by an overhead glow, the dark eyes and brooding triumph of the toreador looked down, and for a moment Deborah trembled as she remembered Levi Comstock's dying statement: "My guilt will never be purged away, except by my blood, and the blood of my children, and my children's children."

–2–

This was morbid. She must get hold of herself. Here she was, about to be hostess at the most distinguished affair ever given in Harlem, more distinguished even than James Weldon Johnson's literary evenings had been. Music and poetry, twin themes of this triumphant June afternoon, to blot out the ominous shadows of world affairs—an oasis of harmony and understanding, no matter how close to the figure of General Rochambeau in the square outside.

When she and Jeff had talked over the party, he had been immediately enthusiastic. He had wanted, however, to invite old friends: Perky, Sherri, some of his other cronies at The Back Door, even Zabee. He thought his father and mother should be asked, but with Gil's aid Deborah had persuaded him that this was wrong for what she was attempting to do, that she was indeed furthering the serious side of his career. He had been somewhat mollified when she invited Cartwright. Cartwright was his favorite teacher at Juilliard; Deborah liked him, although she was fearful of his attempts to secure a large scholarship grant for Jeff. She came more and more to resent anything that took him from his life as The Tan Troubador. She even resented his going with the USO to camps to entertain the draftees. Gil, however, had explained that Jeff's outstanding popularity with the troops was giving him new fans and obviously increasing the sale of his records.

So the guest list had been kept to the noted and, where publicity demanded, sprinkled with the notorious. The noted would have been climaxed by Mrs. Roosevelt, who would have accepted if her schedule had allowed. Deborah was satisfied, but she was nervous. She looked over the rest of the apartment. In the dining room where a bar had been set up, she poured herself a generous drink of bourbon. She knew she shouldn't drink today. Certainly not too much. When Priscilla had been there earlier, helping, Deborah had been snappish with her. Remarks about how much lovelier the apartment would be when there was a child to grace it had made her face flush and her hands tremble. Priscilla would be back soon now, with a friend who had offered to help with the drinks. Deborah must be pleasant to them. She must be pleasant to everyone. There would be gossip, there would be envious remarks. She must ignore them. Nothing must spoil this afternoon, least of all herself. She freshened her drink, carried it with her to the bedroom, sat down at her dressing table and faced the mirror.

The slightly dawn lines of her face did not worry her, nor the shadows under the eyes. She knew they emphasized her pale beauty. She smoothed her hair, sipped her drink. She

had chosen a low-cut dress, emerald-green bodice, soft flow-
ing white skirt, gold and emerald necklace, the gold shoes.

She finished the bourbon. Would the people she wanted
really come? How silly of me, she thought. Already many
flowers had arrived from well-wishers, and only a few tele-
grams of last-minute regrets. She decided on long earrings,
again emerald and gold. As she was putting them on, the
doorbell rang. Guests? Surely not this early.

It was Floyd from The Back Door, almost sober. He carried two huge trays covered by napkins.

"Perky say they fo' yuh success fo' party, Miss Deborah."

He brought them in and when she found they were dozens
and dozens of canapés, of all sizes and colors, she had Floyd
bring them to the bar, found him a tip, and watched him
shamble off.

This was kind of Perky, she knew, but there was reproof
in it also, she felt. She knew that many people at The Back
Door thought she had grown withdrawn and snobbish, even
questioned whether or not she really meant her friendliness
toward Negroes. She saw that her scheme of things for the
afternoon was already being twisted.

When Priscilla and her friend came back, they found
Deborah pouring herself another drink.

"Pretty early?" Priscilla asked.

Deborah's voice was cold. "I'm quite all right, Priscilla."

—3—

"Came early to help our Madame Récamier," Tina Viviera
greeted Deborah. Cass Watkins, laden with buckets of ice,
was right behind her, followed by a bartender and his wife,
hired for the occasion.

"Why don't you two help Priscilla get coffee and tea

started?" Deborah said, then exclaimed, "Here are the Tobins!" She rushed to greet Dolly-May and her father.

With them was Mrs. Kean, Dolly-May's singing teacher
and coach. "I want to congratulate you, Mrs. Kirby, on your
husband's beautiful 'Return Ride.' No wonder it's so popular. Will he sing it for us today?"

"If you ask him, perhaps. Believe it or not, he can be
bashful. I'm troubled that he's late. I can't imagine . . ."

Deborah led the Tobins and Mrs. Kean to a divan and
chairs, where Tom watched over his daughter adoringly.

"You look prime lovely," he said to Dolly-May as he eyed
her oyster-white gown, her scarlet toque. "You'll sing lovely,
too."

Gil arrived now, blustering along with Miltie Shoop, who
ushered in a tall blonde girl in a dress too flamingo for a June
day. They plunged directly toward Dolly-May. Gil kissed
her hand. "I never forget"—he paused—"a figure!"

"Or a business opportunity." Miltie giggled. "He's got you
in his talons."

"Some other time." Dolly-May was gentle but definite.

Deborah had joined them. She was drinking another bourbon now. Abruptly aware that things were out of hand here,
she was too confused to cope.

"Well, Deborah, my beauty," Miltie said as he bowed
before her. "I almost dragged Garbo along, but I figured two
white flames in the same digs would spontaneously combust.
Instead"—he presented the blonde—"I've got Mollie in tow.
She's my gal Friday, Sat'day an' Sunday. Special for Sunday.
She's hot stuff all right. Her longest suit is red underwear, ha!
ha! I hire her to keep me out of trouble. Trouble is, it's what
she gets in. Even in zero weather she spots a frying pan to
jump into."

Guests were arriving fast now, happy with the June sunlight and pre-party drinks: Owen Dodson, the poet and

dramatist whose all-Negro production of *Hamlet* had been applauded at Howard University; Langston Hughes, the more strenuous poet, voice loud, mellow and rumbling; Walter Winchell, his staccato periods bashing the unbashable Miltie Shoop; Carl Trent, a young novelist protegé of Perky's.

Knox Gilbert crossed the room to Deborah. She had never looked more beautiful, but he knew that, unlike her at moments of crisis, she had been drinking.

"Where's your boy friend?" he asked.

Her blue-gray eyes sparkled with anger. She turned away without speaking and went to the Johnsons.

Gil reflected: "Parties, they can be many things. This one could make or shatter Deborah. The party circuit can be a damnable short-circuit. In this town, parties are used for status, for seduction, for nothing. But Deborah is one of those people who uses a party like a spiked cudgel."

Gil turned. Jeff had arrived with his friend Cartwright from Juilliard, and Carl Van Vechten, eternally the cherubic high priest of Harlem. Jeff was smiling, correct in white, one of his Brooks Brothers moods. He was immediately surrounded, but he went to Deborah.

"Sorry," he said. "I've just been leisuring around." And Gil saw that she was weeping as Jeff held her lightly for a moment.

—4—

Cavaletta, a client of Gil's, had fluttered in with a couple of sinuous boy friends. They immediately began twittering and drinking. Cavaletta looked like a flower maiden from *Parsifal*, from the buxom era. Gil wanted her to demonstrate vocal ability immediately, but Jeff quelled him.

Now people were crowding in and nobody leaving. Leonard Lyons was darting among the groups like a dedicated garter snake. Irita Van Doren graciously smiled on all with exactly the appropriate words in her husky-sweet voice. After her came Arlene Campbell, the poet and essayist, almost Indian-like with her straight black hair and bronze skin. There was the usual number of Negro fanciers and exploiters. There was the ex-Baptist shouter who had become a Roman Catholic, taken to confession, and wore the ashes of his repentance with no humility whatsoever. Birnbaum had arrived, John C. Wilson, Richard Watts, Marc Connolly.

The crowd was dividing in islands and patterns. It was so far a successful party. The drinks were appreciated. Some of the women huddled together ominously, while others merely cuddled.

Karl Trent, always belligerent, had cornered Gil. "Understand you're buffing around Harlem these times," he said. "Remember what Perky always says: 'Play with dogs and the fleas bite you.'"

Gil flushed but restrained himself. "Why don't you stick to grinding out your novels?"

"Why don't you leave Jeff alone to write his music, 'stead of balancing his balls like a trained Sealyham? Hear you're even getting him a Hollywood contract."

"So what?"

"He's too old. I always say Hollywood's a berg for baby faces with nonagenarian hearts. They calls it cloud-cuckoo land. I calls it cloud-cuckold land." Nodding in Deborah's direction, Karl added, "Say, she seems to be the only one's not cottoning to her own shindig."

Gil left him, and with Cavaletta in hand, now insisted that Cavaletta be allowed to sing. A space was cleared around the piano over against the bookcases. One of the sinuous young men accompanied her. She sang coyly, some tinkling modern ballads.

"She dishes up *à la* D'Oyly Carte." Trent grunted.

[231]

Perfunctory applause and an encore. For the most part now, the tempo of the room was rollicking and high-pitched.

In front of the bar, Arno Stamm and Todd Park were violent and loud in political argument. It was well known that Arno used his voice for moderation in all things, while Todd lifted his for action, most of it leftist.

"Give it to him, Arno. That a boy!" Miltie Shoop shouldered his way in. "Trotskyite—mosquito bite—that red rash is all the same, scratch it and it's communism!"

Others joined. There was almost a free-for-all until Jeff and Gil genially elbowed them around.

On the opposite side of the room a quieter group had formed around Arlene Campbell, who was talking to them in her soft, almost singing, voice.

Perhaps more than any other woman in the Negro literary world, Arlene had won the respect of critics for her writing, which was at the same time both intellectually sharp and yet warmed by a special warmth. Of late it had taken on a mystical quality, and she had attracted followers who revered her. If she had not firmly discouraged them, in these chaotic times, she would have found herself priestess of a cult. She had heard Todd Park's angry voice.

"They think he's a kind of saint." She smiled. "He's not wicked enough to be a saint. These are cruel habitations in which we live.

"I often comfort myself by reading the Seventy-fourth Psalm, then turning back to the Twenty-third. 'They have set fire upon thy holy places, and have defiled the dwelling place of thy Name, even unto the ground. . . . O God, how long shall the adversary do this dishonor? . . . Why pluckest thou not thy right hand out of thy bosom to consume the enemy? . . . Arise, O God, maintain thine own cause, remember how the foolish man blasphemeth thee daily.'"

Her voice was low and vibrating with sternness. "Yes, our God of vengeance has vanished, but remember, we are his children, and he shall be merciful, even as he punishes our enemies. 'Surely thy loving kindness and mercy shall follow me all the days of my life, and I will dwell in the house of the Lord for ever.'"

She stopped. They were quiet as the party noises swelled and whirled around them. . . .

–5–

"Make your bed hard," Karl Trent was saying. "You don't never get anywhere huggin' a soft mattress." The group around Trent and Todd Park was arguing vehemently. Pieces of dialogue leaped out and plagued Deborah as she stood attempting to be calm, as she smiled an yessed Birnbaum's discussion with Cartwright of the development of classic jazz.

"Negroes have memories like mules," she heard. "They never forget, especially when the whites are involved."

She wondered if they were talking about her. But then the exchanges heightened. Arno Stamm had joined them.

"When you want to act it up, pick a town what's got a de luxe jail."

Angry voices muddled. Then Trent's topped the others: "It takes a real gentleman not to spill eggs on his vest."

Stamm answered him. "Take care you don't mess 'em all over your face."

Deborah wanted to join them, perhaps to calm them, but she knew she didn't have the strength. She felt weak. She felt nauseated. She saw that John Campbell had moved in on them. The voices rose and fell. She could not follow them. Then she heard John's voice. "Remember our old friend, the unsuccessful Democratic candidate for President, John W.

Davis," he was saying. "Lots of folks didn't think he fought for us, but he did. Remember he said, 'The great trouble with the truth is that it travels more slowly than the lie.' There's a lot o' lies travelin' around this here room."

Deborah felt comforted.

–6–

Birnbaum escorted Dolly-May toward the piano. She sang "The Willow Song," to bravos and demands for one of Jeff's songs. She sang the "Leda." Everyone had crowded in. They wanted more. Dolly-May quieted them.

"Let's have Mr. Jeff Kirby now," she said. "Let's have 'Return Ride.'"

Jeff went to the piano, whirled it around, and sat to play his own accompaniment.

Deborah stood close to the fireplace. Someone had poured her another bourbon. Gil was at her elbow.

"Isn't he wonderful?" Gil said.

Deborah didn't answer. The whole room seemed abruptly to be falling on top of her. She wanted to shriek out, "Don't sing that song. I can't bear it again. I can't bear any of this." Jeff caught her eyes as he sang. He was singing the sentimental ballad to her. It had been written to her. As she stood there, she was aware of what it had meant to them in worldly terms. It was money as well as dreams. Was there a cynical look in Jeff's dark eyes as he sang? Was he asking her, "What does this mean to you that means so much to me?"

> *"I want to ride back,*
> *Back to the past,*
> *Along the old track*
> *To when I first loved you.*
> *I want to love you again like that,*

I want to hold you again like that;
Feel the hot summer and the winter weather,
Dream the old bright and boundless dreams together.
I want to ride back to the past.

"But there's no return ride to the past;
There's only today and tomorrow,
Our joy and our hope and our sorrow.
Let me hold you, then, quiet like this,
Summer loving and long winter kiss.
Hold it closely, the first and the last,
Keep it tenderly, now, hold it fast;
Ride ahead! There's no ride to the past!"

There were shouts, bravos, a confusion of emotions. People had begun to leave. Jeff was surrounded. Deborah tried to make her way to him. She was stopped by congratulations and chit-chat. She felt hemmed in, frustrated. Priscilla was at her side.

"How proud, how proud you must be," Priscilla said.

—7—

The alcohol, the heat, the noise—Deborah was faint and angry. She paled and half fell onto a chair. Priscilla's arms were around here.

"Deborah, dear, you *must* be careful. I think—I really do think!"

"She thinks I'm pregnant," Deborah found herself saying to herself. "My God, she thinks I am." And then aloud, at first quiet, then louder until it became a scream, "I'm not. I'm not. Leave me alone. Get out. Get out, all of you, get out."

Jeff was beside her quickly, and Gil.

"Get them all out of here," Jeff said to Gil. He picked up

[235]

Deborah, whose fists were beating at him, and carried her to
their bedroom.

Deborah was still in Jeff's arms. As he bent to put her on
the bed, she wrenched herself away from him, her face con-
torted, her whole body trembling. Jeff tried to put his arms
around her, but she beat at him, her hands pounding his
chest, slapping his face.

"Get me a *white* doctor," she cried. "I want a *white* doctor.
No nigger doctor's going to put his hands on me. Nor Cass
Watkins, either. Get me a white doctor, get me a white doctor quick. I tell you, I'm sick and tired of niggers. Get me a
white doctor!"

V

"When are the dog days?" Gil asked Zabee. "Anyhow this late August weather has been feverish this year."

The air conditioning of The Back Door was a benison. Gil and Zabee had come in shortly after midnight. Jeff had been in Boston for some undefined reason and had asked Gil to meet him. The deep voice on the telephone sounded strained and urgent. Zabee had not wanted to come along, but Gil insisted.

Things had been going from bad to really bad ever since the party in June. Deborah and Jeff had been quarreling in front of their friends and drinking immoderately. Gil had found Deborah unresponsive to his own approaches, detached as she had never been before. Gil had never known just what had happened at the end of the party. Priscilla had made guarded remarks. Cass Watkins had insinuated. Had Deborah been pregnant? A miscarriage, or even an abortion?

The reporters and columnists were discreet and flattering in references to Mrs. Kirby's "brilliant salon." Meanwhile, Jeff's career had not suffered too much. His popularity continued. His recordings topped the lists. Gil had heard that

Dave, the painter friend from the old days, and Fess, the high school teacher, were frequently seen with Deborah and Jeff. They seldom came to The Back Door; in fact Gil had not met Deborah here for weeks.

It was Saturday night, and most of New York would be found in the mountains or on the beaches. Perky's place was nearly empty. A couple sat down near the bar; a group of young Negroes were discussing Trotsky's recent assassination, one of them violently proclaiming it had been suicide. A substitute was working for Jake and Floyd. A curly-headed boy pianist drummed languidly on the keys.

Perky had been chatting at the bar as Gil and Zabee absorbed several long cool ones. Now the little man, looking more like a penguin than ever, joined the agent.

"How's you all, Zabee?" Perky flashed the gold tooth.

Gil frowned. "Okay, as you see her."

Perky sat down. "Our other miscegenation not doin' so good. I was sure glad when that Ivory Colum lit out for Miami. How's he doin'?"

"Big time in the clubs. Knows his stuff and makes me a pile of the long green."

"He and Jeff mixed it up proper one mornin' here. I always call a cock a cock, and that sure was a cock fight."

"Are they sore here in Harlem at Jeff?" Gil asked.

"Not sore. He's one of their own. Jest sad. But Deborah? It's jest that some white folks don't never know how to treat coloreds. They have a plain feelin' of guilt about us, and some of 'em gives us money and some of 'em takes out their feelin's in gushin' around."

"I know what you mean. I'm not so sure of my own emotions sometimes."

Perky reached out and touched his arm, showing a quiet emotion rare for him. "You okay, son. You takes us as you finds us. But if the white folks looks for noble savages, they's

[238]

likely get bit by cannibals. *They* find us as they takes us."

A scantily clad pair of girls had come in. Perky went to greet them. He sent Gil and Zabee another drink.

Gil fell to brooding over his own state of mind. It was time he and Zabee broke up. He had been right about her, and she right about him: it wasn't working. There were times when the agent felt like escaping entirely. Yet where? What was his absorption in the Negro race? He was, speaking brutally, exploiting them, but he had felt that his love for them was justification. Yet the marriage of Deborah and Jeff had cut deep like some major surgery, probing for the cancerous reality deep within; he felt caught, suspended. "It's like being in a recovery room," he said to himself. "Hell and heaven were there. You want to come back. You don't want to come back." Where did he want to go, where and when? He smiled across at Zabee.

"Five bright pennies for your thoughts," she said.

Jeff came at last and obviously upset. Dave, who was with him, went to the bar. Jeff came to their table. He looked trim enough. He was wearing an off-white suit, a scarlet ascot instead of a tie.

His usually clear brown skin was clouded by a muddy tinge. Gil hardly needed to look twice to know this spelled trouble.

"And where's Deborah?" Gil asked, suspecting a negative report.

Jeff looked offhandedly at Zabee, and said finally, "Hiya, Zabee."

She nodded, as a look of anxiety spread across her face.

"Where's Deborah?" Gil repeated.

"Deborah's gone," he said, quietly.

"Deborah's gone?" Zabee echoed, then added, "where?"

Jeff groaned and sat down. "I don't know."

And as Perky passed, Jeff ordered a double shot of whiskey. He was genuinely hurt—not his pride alone. And Gil sensed that Jeff disciplined a raging anger with much difficulty.

"That's tough," Gil said lamely.

Jeff glared at Gil for a moment. "I hunted up some old friends of hers," he said, in a voice less pained than his facial expression, "'and they weren't too helpful—neither was her family. I've just come from them. Anyway, a friend of mine is doing all he can to help me—he works for one of those detective agencies. Told him to meet me here if he hears anything important."

"Anything I can do, Jeff?"

He shook his head. "No, Gil, I think not—but thanks a lot."

"She'll turn up soon."

"Maybe," he said unhappily. "But it isn't much fun hunting a white girl in all New York—like coals in Newcastle."

"Why not quit, then?"

"You're kidding, Gil!"

"If all she did was walk out," Zabee agreed, "that's the only thing to do. Sit tight. Have some fun. If she hears you're knocking your brains out to find her, she'll enjoy things that much more."

Jeff turned to her. "You've got Deborah wrong."

"I'm a woman—I should know."

Gil asked, "But what happened, Jeff?"

They wondered how Jeff would frame the story. Gil knew the reason was pretty lurid—at least he suspected as much.

"Argument. And over nothing, too!" His eyes moved reproachfully toward Gil, as if he could read his mind, then back confidingly to Zabee. She had been listening, nodding with understanding, frowning with sympathy, and keeping her red lips parted the whole time. "We had a little scrap. So while I was downtown, she packs and leaves. That was— last night!"

[240]

"What exactly did you fight about?" Zabee asked.

Jeff's expression became vague. "Never mind. It wasn't anything important."

"Are you sure?"

He gave both of them a defiant stare. "Sure I'm sure!"

There was an instant of silence.

And suddenly a short, bespectacled white man with a non-committal face poked his head through the door and surveyed the place with banjo eyes. He said nothing, but Jeff got up and they met at the bar. When Jeff returned, he sat down heavily.

"Well?" Zabee and Gil said in unison, looking at him expectantly.

"She's in Miami."

"Florida?" Zabee asked, incredulously.

"Yeah," Jeff said miserably. "That was the fellow at the agency. Says they traced her to the Everglades Hotel."

"Then," Zabee said, "I'm right. Now forget this crazy hunt. And entertain yourself. Let us do the coming back— since she did the running away."

"Zabee, I wonder—"

"I'm a woman, Jeff. Take my word."

He was obviously perplexed, frustrated. "And how," he asked scornfully, "do I get into my act of being the gay blade?"

"Do the joints—you and I," Zabee said. "It will take your mind off this mess."

"You and I?" Jeff took his first careful look at her since his arrival. He undoubtedly was pleased with what he saw. His wounded feelings needed to be assuaged. But he wasn't quite persuaded, perhaps out of loyalty to Deborah.

"I'd like it," Zabee said. "For a lot of reasons—even if you're a solid blockhead sometimes."

Jeff smiled wanly. "What if Deborah finds out—you know how she feels about you."

"Then, Jeff," Zabee said, "if she wants to raise a rumpus or—quit—nothing would have helped anyhow."

Gil could see him fumbling in his mind with that one. He wanted Deborah, obviously. He was determined to get her back. But she had stalled any logical, even emotional action on his part. Deborah, with almost feline cruelty, had chosen a place where Jeff could not follow her, where, for that matter, no Negro would have the temerity to follow her. She knew, too, this would be a stab in his most vulnerable spot— his helplessness as a Negro. If he were a white man and felt determined or romantic enough, he always could catch a plane, walk right into the hotel in Miami, argue his case, and seal the reconciliation by going to bed with her there and then; or, if he chose, drag her back by the lengths of her hair. But, again, logic didn't apply to this couple, for as a Negro searching for a white woman in Florida, even for a legal wife he had married with the church's blessing, Jeff would be clapped into jail immediately—and, at the very least, treated like a person who had lost his sanity.

Zabee, apparently, had read Gil's mind. "I marvel at Deborah's gift for cultured brutality," Zabee said fiercely under her breath to Gil.

Gil nodded.

Jeff's unspoken dilemma was not without poignancy. Gil could have wept for him. He watched them both.

Zabee was trying to sustain his interest and dispel his near despair. "What about it, Jeff?" she was saying.

Then, not by anything overt, but by some vague, racial nuance, they subtly pushed Gil beyond their emotional selves, as palpably as if a curtain had been drawn. Gil found himself as he often was compelled to feel in Harlem—a total stranger. Zabee had forgotten him now, and he realized that the interest she had shown in him before was motivated not by himself, or any possible charm of his, but by her wish to escape, or for anodyne, or for revenge, perhaps. Such liking as Zabee felt for Gil was merely a consequence of his connection with Jeff. She would have confided in Gil even if she had disliked him.

A curious fact bore down upon him, though he wasn't quite aware of its implications then.

Two beautiful women—Deborah and Zabee—had certainly invited his romantic attentions; but neither one just for himself. Jeff was plainly the pivot in the actions of both. He wondered if he was plagued by an inverted form of chivalry which caused him to feel obliged to respond to every feminine beckon. Suddenly he felt a surge of jealousy. If he had squared the feeling with himself then, he would have had to admit it was racially inspired; for the thought of the fact that every insinuation of his society, yea, every proclamation, had declared the superiority of white men to black, and yet it was of little comfort to him now. Even unreal, fantastic. The perversity of woman's emotions had flung the lie into his face.

And it was a sobering thought.

"Okay, Zabee," Jeff said. "I do need a lift."

"Well, as a start, how about a bite to eat at my place," she said, and as an afterthought, added, "And how about you, Gil?"

He politely declined—and in doing so had a powerful feeling of complicity.

—2—

The Back Door was quiet, as Gil sat there watching them walk arm in arm into the darkness, Jeff waving to Dave as he left.

Gil suddenly felt a great loss. He joined Perky and Dave at the bar.

"So that's that!" Gil said.

He put his arm around one of the girls there, but she shrugged away, smiling.

"So?" Perky said.

"So Dave and I are going out and raise a storm."

They waved to a taxi. It was Sherri Shannon's address Gil gave as they rolled off into the humid night.

PART
THREE

I

In June of 1948 The Back Door had changed little since before the war. It was perhaps brighter. The mural was as horrendous as ever. Perky had ordered new upholstery for the lounges, an even more outrageous scarlet and yellow, and the table covers were fresh in their red-and-white checks.

During the war the military had made the basement club its private possession, the MP's and the Shore Patrol stifling an occasional memorable riot; but there had been no killings, and knife engagements had been minor. Perky's place had fulfilled its patriotic duty noisily but nobly.

"Me, I feels my job is here," Perky would say as Floyd left for the merchant marine and others of the boys around the club volunteered or were drafted. "The rejects wasn't so bad, and I had me a coupla good combos and some boys and gals could belt out a song. The customers didn't do so poorly at entertainin' theyselves. But now it's back to the old days, and I wants it to seem jes like the old days."

It was, indeed, like the old days. Now, in the early after-lull before the cocktail hour, with a light rain falling outside, only a few couples were left over from the afternoon gathering. Floyd, looking not much more venerable, was cleaning up in back, Perky and Knox Gilbert were sitting over drinks, waiting as they had so many times for Jeff Kirby to join them.

"Good to be liftin' with you again," Perky said. "Burn Europe up an' down, did you?"

"Not so hot as all that for me, but Zabee's pulling in the mob in Paris. She's a kind of poor man's Josephine Baker."

"Miss her?"

"Huh?"

"Women, women! I heard you'd took her over there."

The two men grinned at each other; Gil's long nose and sharp features made one think of a hybrid collie; Perky's whole countenance was like a bulldog attempting a smile.

"She'll stay till she gets tired of them or they get tired of her. It's good to have a jealous woman off my neck," Gil said.

"When she comes back?"

"I'm soft. I'll open the door again, I suppose."

"You've had worse. Take me."

"Yeah, take you, you damned old whoremaster! How's Sherl?"

"More like she's a wife ever' day, fussin' an' fumin' an' fussin'. Aint been able to get at my 'electric trains."

"Never knew you had any. Secret vice?"

"Jes one of 'em. Can you imagine, her old ma's gittin' married again. You lucky when you ain't had no more to do with that one. I told her I'd make her ma a good weddin'. That didn' suit her. An' she's always complainin' about the icebox. What's an icebox to me? Maybe an apple?"

"Why don't you send her packing?"

"You know why. I wishes I didn't have a flowerpot to my name. Then mebbe she'd git out herself."

"What you need is to get allergic to sex."

"Me an' sex sure ain't got no allergy. Jes gotta make up my mind; I got Sherl an' she's sure got me."

"Jeff's got a surprise for you."

"I hears there's a dame."

"Don't let Jeff hear you call her a dame!"

"Well, there's nothin' like, as the song goes. What's with 'er? She some hifalutin'?"

"Wait and see for yourself. Fess is coming in here before long."

"Good. I hear he's been seein' a lot of Jeff. Good thing, too. Fess is a right 'un, 'spite all his teacher's learnin'. Jeff suttinly needed a friend. He went kinda loco awhile before he cleared out for Chi."

"Dave's gone off to New Mexico to paint."

"Yes, I hears. Why you not wantin' to talk about Deborah? Holdin' out on me, Gil?"

"How much do you know?"

"Jes heard she died, some accident; ain't heard no more, 'cept gossip. Say, Gil, you think they's gossip in heaven? Must be if they's women in heaven. Poor old Deborah. She was headin' for it. Busy, al'ays busy. But ain't nobody too busy to die."

"I'll tell you all I know."

"Hi, Floyd, fill 'em up. Make it strong—an' speedy."

—2—

"Most of what I heard was from Uncle Ellery, some secondhand through one of Ivory Colum's men," Gil said. His hand shook as he lifted his fresh drink.

"After she lit out for Miami and got herself settled in a Miami hotel, Deborah got more desperate and lonely. As usual, she made an impression. Stray wolves from four seas tried to make time with her. She got more and more remote, turned in on herself, lambasted the old society fishwives who insisted she play bridge with them."

"Weren't they busy with rumors about her?"

"Yeah, but she didn't care. Maybe she *was* a Negro's wife; but she'd left him, and in a strange way her status was rebuilding. She could reassert herself as Deborah Kirby of the Boston Comstocks. She could have, but she didn't.

"Instead, her rebellion reasserted itself. She took to spending her time in those fish-and-crab places outside Miami, picking up waifs and strays who were fascinated by her cold beauty and flattered her."

Perky broke in. "What about Ivory Colum?"

"I'm coming to that. He and his combo had been playing around in various Miami hot spots for some time.

"She still had a yen for him. And she'd go and listen to him. But there couldn't have been a worse place in the world for her. She couldn't even speak to him. Things were so bad in Miami then for Negroes that the two of them couldn't even go out of town without being scooped up, and all Deborah could do was to pass him a note now and then, and maybe sneak a smile.

"Meanwhile, you remember, Jeff was trying to get in touch with her, and she was all churned up. It was a wonder that something wild didn't happen then and there. But all of a sudden, late that autumn Ivory and his combo got a chance to go to Cuba. He got a message to Deborah saying she should follow him. So she did. And there never was a crazier mixed-up place for those crazy mixed-up people.

"Most of what I heard about this was from her Uncle Ellery. They got wind of what was going on, and the Comstock clan sent good old Uncle Ellery down to Havana to see what he could do. He couldn't do a goddamn thing. Deborah took him into her swing. He found himself whirled into a round of Cuban madness and sound. He tried to make sense with Deborah, he even tried talking to Ivory, but got nowhere.

"They were overwhelmed by the heat and color and multi-racial strains of Cuba. Ivory and his combo were performing in an Afro-Cuban club, where they vied for plaudits with a native combo and those folk singers, mariaches or whatever they call them, guitar and voices. If you'd ever hear them sing "Cielito Lindo," you'd pass out. It's hot, yes, it's wild and sad too. Ellery told me Deborah said it reminded her of Perky's. Finally Ellery left. There wasn't anything more he could do."

"What did Deborah's ma think of all this?"

"She was the cold old bitch as always. Even at the end she just seemed to think it had been coming to Deborah. Puritan inevitability. All that. I don't like those goddamn Comstocks."

"White shouldn't mix it with blacks nohow. If one's out to kill the lion, one despises the flea."

"What does that mean?"

"Figger it out fer yerself."

"Well, it seems Ivory had got himself a speedboat, one of those high-powered numbers, and he and Deborah used to go tootin' around in it. One night they'd been hitting it up hot and heavy, and early in the morning one of Ivory's friends saw them roaring off into the dawn toward Florida. Maybe they figured they were going there, maybe not. Anyhow, that was it, that was finish. They were never heard of again, and no boat bottom's up, either."

"She'd have cottoned to that. She'd have liked that, don't you think?"

"I guess maybe. Maybe you're right. I'll never know anybody like her again. I'll never be the same as before I knew her. It's not the same world, Perky, it's just not the same."

"Have another, Gil. We can drink to her, can't we?"

II

The two men sat brooding over their drinks. It was hard to meet the actuality of Deborah's death and the mental changes it meant for them. For Perky, largely in his concern for Jeff. But for Gil, the loss of a symbol, the woman he had tricked himself into believing he had loved. Now he would revert again to what he thought of as the search for beauty. Actually it was a Woolworth tiara that would bedeck his queen; it was prettiness, not beauty, he craved; nor was his passion for true flesh, but the fleshly. This was his business as well as his life. He was unreal rather than phony, a man without focus.

Fess arrived now, his short powerful body shouldering among the tables toward them. As usual, he was dressed casually in sports clothes, a bright blue windbreaker, trousers to match, tennis shoes. It was his effort never to appear the conventional schoolteacher; his straight hair was crew-cut above his smooth tan face, his intense black eyes snapped, his voice was deep and just a shade gruff as he greeted Gil and Perky, requested a Scotch from Floyd, and sat down. Jake was at the bar now, and waved to him.

They were holding special summer classes at the high

school, and Fess had come from teaching one of them. His reputation as a teacher was high after he gave up writing his book and settled down. He had persuasiveness and understanding, warmth but not possessiveness, toward his students, among them several girls who tried to pierce his objectivity. But this he was adept at preventing, the confirmed anchorite, escaping entanglements as he had escaped marriage. Fess liked music and art, but he also liked science-fiction, baseball, and the latest variety of Campbell soup. He had countless friends, among whom only Jeff and Dave were close.

The Back Door was slowly filling with the afternoon crowd. As the three friends sat waiting for Jeff, they were recalling those bad weeks after Deborah had left for Miami. They stirred one another's memories and a sorry picture emerged.

"He was a mess," Fess said, "striking out every time he came to bat." Gil and Perky nodded their heads.

"He was always free-flying," Gil said, "but then he was flying too free and in danger any minute of hitting a charged wire." Jeff had spent hours drinking in The Back Door, indulging his melancholy. He shone with a sort of perverse luster. As always, he attracted stray women, and he spent time and money on them, playing games as an excuse for not living. He would go on long rambles, hanging out in the hot spots, telling himself he was picking up new rhythms. He told people he was composing, but there were no results.

All his friends failed to pull him out of it. Fess tried to get him to the stadium for baseball games, and would make excuses to sit around with him in the taverns. Gil couldn't persuade him to fill engagements except for an occasional stint for the USO. Finances were bad. Perky even refused to take his percentage for a time. Jeff avoided his family. When he went on rare occasions to the Tobins', he seemed

vague and distracted. It was finally Birnbaum and Cartwright who rescued him. Cartwright managed a scholarship
in Chicago, and Birnbaum persuaded Jeff he must get back
to his composing. Overnight the purposelessness was re-
placed by energy. With Dolly-May's help, the apartment was
closed, the furnishings put in storage. Jeff said he would
never live there again, and the Tobins took steps to rerent it.
There was a farewell night at The Back Door, and early in
October Jeff was on his way to Chicago and study in composition at Northwestern University.

–2–

In Chicago Jeff became quickly absorbed by his new life.
His old work disciplines reasserted themselves and were
strengthened. Fess made several trips to visit him. Gil went
out to look over some talent at the Grand Terrace. They
brought back happy reports to the New York friends.

At Northwestern Jeff was involved at once, liking both his
teachers and the atmosphere. His room in Evanston was
functional, in fact his whole new life bordered on the mo-
nastic. He was truly too busy for women, although occasionally he went out with one of the coeds. Trips into
Chicago were to visit the art galleries or to spend a half-hour
at one of the Rush Street spots or at The Golden Lily or The
Cabin Inn or to listen to Sammy Stewart playing at The
Sunset.

Not long after he started his work in composition, he had
an idea for a ballet. Some years before, he had happened on
a quotation, a sermon-chant by a Negro preacher. It was
about the alabaster halls of heaven, the angels and the
sounding of Gabriel's trumpet. It reminded him of *Green
Pastures,* and as acknowledgment of his debt he decided to
call it *White Pastures.* Around this chant he wove a mixture

of saraband and bacchanal, his old echoes of Debussy and folk song. He wrote with speed and fire, calling on his friend Tonio Diaz to design the sets and costumes, trying out parts of the score as he progressed with the student orchestra at Northwestern. In the midst of this activity he heard of Deborah's death. It must have affected him deeply, but it did not slow his activity or shadow his mien. It was not long after that that his isolation was challenged by another woman, and the scars slowly faded.

There had still been time for a USO show now and then. It was Fess who told of a big benefit at the Sherman House in late November. It was that night Jeff met again a high school teacher, Grace Caldwell. Their previous encounters had been casual, but it was after the Sherman House benefit that awareness and delight began.

Someone once said of Chicago: "Ring a bell on the Lake Front and the whole city comes running!" So it seemed that night at the Sherman House. The talent and the townsfolk were abundant. Cocktail parties, small dinners, large dinners, had been given earlier. Here now were debutantes from Lake Forest, dowagers from the Lake Shore Drive gold coast, suburbia and Bohemia in the best dress and undress. The literary world was there to prove the Windy City the true hub of fine letters: Harry Hansen, tall and sardonic; Fanny Butcher, petite and furbelowed; Fred Babcock looking solidly Chicago-*Tribunish*, although he did sport a red vest; Marion Strobel of *Poetry* magazine, destroying reputation with verve; and Mrs. William Vaughan Moody, always the gracious patroness of the arts and good causes.

The great ballroom was smothered under flags and other red, white, and blue paraphernalia: bunting on the platform, festoons, streamers from the chandeliers, white pigeons— probably called doves as lone symbols of peace here—in beribboned cages hung from the light brackets on the walls.

Murmurous, as if participating in a rite, the audience became tensely engaged in this tribal tribute to the patriotic. They sensed that they were on the eve of war, and many of them were impatient for it in spite of the warnings of Colonel McCormick's "greatest newspaper in the world" and his rabid isolationist followers. This varied crowd was involved in the warlike, but held in slow motion by the pause before battle.

The Chicago Symphony Orchestra swept into action, a robust tenor, unquavering, led off in the "Star Spangled Banner." A red-white-and-blue-sheathed soprano sang "This Can't be Love," soft at first, then belted out a chorus, while Richard Rodgers himself, rubicund and perspiring, conducted. From the Great Lakes Training Station a smart Navy band played military marches climaxed by "Stars and Stripes Forever." Carl Sandburg, the benevolent gray lock shielding the blazing dark eyes, strummed his guitar and chanted a Chicago poem. Boy scouts and girl scouts, having escaped their dens, scrubbed bright, sang piercingly a medley of World War I tunes: "My Buddy," "Over There,". . . Jeff, in his Tan Troubador role, scarlet jacket, loose white shirt, sang sentimental ballads, then gave the audience a serious moment with the Vaughan, "He Is My Gracious Friend," and to clamoring demand, "Return Ride"—an ovation! Then followed tap dancers, a juggler, magicians producing flags from outer space. Everything but elephants, seals, and trained fleas. Finale: "The Battle Hymn of the Republic" as balloons and confetti drifted like snow from the ceiling. Cheers. An exploding and jubilant fiesta.

As Jeff rushed down from the platform and made his way toward Fess, he saw Grace Caldwell sitting with a group of teachers. She was striking with her brunette hair, her deep olive skin, her veiled dark eyes. He introduced her to Fess, and met her friends. For a while they stood buffeted by the crowd, then Jeff winked at Fess, whispered to Grace, and folded her in her wrap. Together they went out into the sharp November night.

Jeff and Grace Caldwell were quiet in the cab as they left the excitement and clutter of the Sherman House. They got out at a place near Thirty-first and Cottage. It was a modest club, only half full. A lone pianist was playing and singing softly. The walls were hung with paintings by the Chicago Negro group. Before they sat down Grace led Jeff over to look at them; their bizarre colors triumphed over the gentle candlelight.

"Most of them by my pals," Jeff said. "Like them?"

"Well . . . I suppose I don't really care for modern paintings; often I find the colors stimulating. Perhaps they make me feel inferior because I don't understand them."

"You must just let yourself rip, enjoy them. Same with music."

"I like *your* music, all I have heard. I'm eager to hear more."

"That you'll do."

They sat and ordered drinks. Jeff was pleased by her obviously honest reactions. Later he told Fess that her interest in art and music seemed always to be fresh and entirely free of affectation, that to have liked something because it was the thing to do would never even have occurred to her. He recalled Deborah's poses with sadness.

This was one of those magic times when two people discover one another, sympathies are warm, and facts and ideas are traded.

"You've been through a great deal," she said. "Please don't think I'm patronizing if I say that you've weathered it remarkably well, Jeff."

He smiled, took her hand, and pressed it for a moment.

Because she knew many of his friends and because Jeff's

life was much discussed, Grace knew much more of him than he of her, and Jeff listened intently as she told him of her background.

She had been born in Charleston, South Carolina, where her father was a successful doctor, her uncle a loved and respected lawyer. They were conservative and comfortably well-to-do.

"They've always left me free to do pretty much as I please, and to think freely, also."

"You're lucky."

"Yes, I am. I thought of it the other day when I picked up an Everyman edition of *The Confessions of St. Augustine*."

"Your kind of reading?" he interrupted her. "You scare me."

"Just by chance. You should read it if you haven't."

He shook his head.

"He was the same kind of saint you are."

"Me, a saint?" He whistled.

"You'd be surprised to find what a saint you are. At least, I think so."

"That's good?"

"Yes. Anyhow, St. Augustine wrote, and I blessed my family as I read it: 'No doubts, then, that a free curiosity has more force in our learning these things, than a frightful enforcement.' "

"I wish my folks were like that, particularly Dad. I sure haven't given him an easy time, but it's been difficult."

She nodded. "I've heard so."

"We try to get one another, but sometimes he seems to me to stand for everything I hate. He's the perfect bourgeois. You could plant him spang in the middle of a Kathleen Norris novel. He has those damn labels for everyone—Commies, Jews, Roosevelt lovers, nosy liberals. Yet, in spite of it, I think you'd like him. You'd like my sister, Priscilla, her beau who's a doctor and sounds like your dad. You'd like my mother a lot, and she'd like you."

"You love your father, don't you?"

"Yes, and I admit I wish he could cotton to me more. I never honestly wanted to bug him. Somehow I just had to."

"I understand better than you might think because I've had it, and even worse, in my own family. Why, some of my light-skinned cousins want things that don't matter so strongly that I'm ashamed to say they've even passed for white.

"It often embarrasses me," she said. "In places, like tonight for instance, when I know people take me for Spanish or Creole, I go out of my way to make certain that they know I'm a Negro.

"It's ironical that it's only at such charity affairs that we can really mix. And I know it's better here in Chicago than some other places."

"Not much." His eyes were grim as he said it.

"Why, even at school," she went on, "the white children go across to the candy store each recess and they *will* bring those licorice 'nigger babies' back and show them jokingly to the colored children. I try to persuade them to get licorice sticks instead, to explain why it's bad manners. They can't or won't understand. I suppose it's a small thing. Perhaps I have a chip on my shoulder. Perhaps I shouldn't take it so seriously."

"It does matter," Jeff said. "It is serious. The children are the most of all, serious. You should care. I'm glad you do. We have to care very much. At all times."

—3—

They sat in silence for a while, then Jeff asked, "You like teaching?"

"Very much," she said.

[259]

"And you like children? Sometimes I think teachers can't see children for pedagogy. I feel like telling 'em, 'watch out, sister, your pedagogy's showing!'"

"It's true, unfortunately." Grace shook her head impatiently. "With all their training schools, with all their knowledge of modern psychology, many teachers, supervisors and principals, too, don't apply it."

"Some children are blooming innocents," Jeff laughed. "I was. You wouldn't imagine that sin had to be explained to me. I caught up later, all right.

"But I remember one episode all too well. It taught me a couple of things, one of them that my dad would put out for me in a big way.

"I read early, but I never could figure. Two times two might be five or even six to me. We had a jam-full classroom and so we doubled up and sat two by two on those bench seats. There was a pretty little white girl sat next to me. We were having some kind of numbers test. The kid saw I was having trouble so she showed me her paper. I copied it, thinking she was being mighty kind. She was. The teacher saw and pounced on me. 'You dirty little cheat,' she said and dragged me up in front of the class. I struggled and hit at her and she grabbed my hand and gave me a good whacking with a ruler. 'I'm giving you a note to take to your father,' she said. 'He's to bring you to see the principal before ever you can come back to *this class.*'

"I ran home bawling. My old man was raging. He knew I hadn't cheated. I didn't savvy what cheating was.

"The next day he gave that principal a lecture on innocence and experience. Maybe he was a bit pompous, but I was certainly proud of him. They put me in another class."

"No trauma?"

"Not much, I guess, only I got wiser and maybe trickier,

and it did make me close to Pop. I felt he was always there to battle for me."

"What happened to the little white girl?"

"They clean forgot her in the mess. Maybe they didn't see she was showing me the paper, because I wasn't peeking, I was just looking."

It seemed as though they could go on talking forever, but the place was thinning out. Jeff looked at his watch. It was after two.

"Time to go," he said. "One of those little devils will take a peek at *your* eyes and ask, 'Teacher, who was you out with last night?'"

"This has been good. And I'm glad you like children." Jeff helped Grace into the cab. It was quite a ride to her south side apartment. He put his arm around her and she leaned against him. They did not talk. Jeff was thinking of the many stormy cab rides with Deborah, of the passion, the distress; and the joy, too, he remembered.

For a moment, as he watched the shimmying of the neon lights outside the cab window, he wanted to draw Grace to him fiercely, to find the answer to his loneliness in her lips, but he held himself in check. This girl wouldn't accept an affair.

He kissed her lightly on the cheek as they said good night. Certainly they would see each other soon again.

—4—

On the long ride to Evanston, Jeff found himself ill at ease and uncertain. Would he ever be ready for marriage again? He had been rigorously telling himself that his work was now all that mattered. He was almost for the first time at peace with sex. He mustn't chitter it all up again. There was a war in the making. He had wanted to go into the Army even now, but his draft board had persuaded him that it was more important to keep on with his USO program.

It was almost dawn when he climbed the stairs and he had an early class. He must finish the ballet before too long.

Fess was awake, reading.

"That was sure extra innings," he said. "What's the score?"

"She's a fine woman." Jeff began throwing off his clothes.

"Yeah," Fess said as he turned out the bed lamp. "I bet she hits a grand slammer every time."

"You and your baseball!"

"You and your women."

Jeff's determination sent him quickly to sleep, but it was of Grace and their children that he dreamed.

The news of the bombing of Pearl Harbor hit Jeff when he was rehearsing the orchestra for the ballet. He dismissed the students but they hung around, listening to the radio and chattering. Jeff felt cold, isolated, and lonely among them. He knew that his sister Priscilla and Grace Caldwell were together at Grace's apartment. Priscilla had come to Chicago to see Cass Watkins who was training for the Army Medical Corps in a nearby camp. She and Grace had quickly become genuine friends.

"I must enlist right away. Can't put it off any longer now," Jeff said as he found the girls beside the radio. "Just shows what a heel I am, the first thing I thought of was there probably won't be any ballet now. Hot patriot I am."

"This'll be over quickly," Priscilla said. "We'll put them in their place. You'll see."

"I don't know. I'm frightened." Jeff's face was grim.

"It's frightful, but I presume we can all help by keeping calm and carrying on as usual. Your enlisting now, you'll see, won't make any more sense than it did a week ago."

Meanwhile, the bulletin kept on and the horror was

plainer. Grace found herself quoting *Antigone:* "Many are the frightful things, but nothing is more frightful than man."

They sat up far into the night, listening and scarcely believing what they heard.

The months that followed were tense ones. Jeff was restless. It was difficult to persuade him to go on with his plans, but the ballet was to be another big USO benefit at Orchestra Hall. Tonio Diaz was making the sets now, Colin Streit, Jeff's teacher at Northwestern, would conduct. The dancers were all Negro, recruited from churches throughout the Chicago area.

Both Grace and Jeff spent every minute they could working for the USO—she at the canteens, Jeff at the Army camps. This helped to quiet Jeff's conscience, but he felt separated from his friends who were on active duty, he was journeyfervent, he wanted to be on his way. He thought perhaps it was the idea of Grace that was holding him back, and he resented this and at times, resented her, but he let himself be captured by events.

–5–

At The Back Door Fess and Gil were drinking through the afternoon and waiting for Jeff.

"Those were rough innings in Chicago," Fess said. "Holding Jeff on base wasn't so easy. There were times when I thought he might just light out; but Cartwright managed to make him see how many people's futures were tied up with the ballet, and the duty he owed to them."

"It was quite a show," Gil said. "Wish you could have been there, Perky. Practically everyone else was. The Kirbys, the Tobins, Dolly-May's teacher, Mrs. Keane, Birnbaum, and Grace Caldwell's father and her uncle came up from Charleston. It was a great evening and a great party afterward. You read the critics. Jeff's reputation as a serious musician was secure."

"He was getting purty interested in that Grace, wasn't he?" Perky asked.

"Yes," Fess said. "In a way and in a way not. He wrote her a song you must have heard round about that time. Ballad-type, he called it 'One Quiet Night.'

> 'One quiet night
> I found quiet,
> Quiet in you, around you—
> One quiet night.'

And more of the same. Yes, sentimental for Jeff, but pretty good stuff, too.

"Trouble was, as I figured, she made him feel guilty. Still blaming himself for Deborah. Feeling he didn't deserve hap-piness, and the war pressing on him. Anyhow, the ballet cleared the bases, all right, all right! From the minute they played the 'Star Spangled Banner' and the curtain came up."

—6—

No overture precedes the ballet, *The White Pastures*. The curtain reveals a motionless stage, and there is no sound; the lighting so strong and clear that the white and gold expanse is almost blinding. At the back and high up is a suggestion of the pearly gates, and below a huge alabaster throne; at center stage is a massive white marble table. Abruptly, in a rushing of music and motion, the picture seems to explode. There are myriads of white and gold figures of countless sizes and shapes, some stately and dancing on the ground, others flying through the air and on and off the stage as though in endless streams. At one moment the whole stage is fluid with them, the next they are forming geometric patterns, and scarlet lights make them blaze with fire, circles within triangles, octagons in thin circles; a surging apocryphal rhythm. The music is plaintive, then pounding with primitive jazz. In black and scarlet, his satanic majesty appears; flying, leaping, pursuing.

There is another moment of quiet and silence. Then the tremendous peal of bells and of organ music as the tall majestic figure of a Negro preacher, robed in white with silver-gray hair, appears behind the marble table. The stage is now crowded with figures, but they are motionless. Then, as the preacher speaks, his voice trumpet-loud over woodwinds of sound, a gigantic figure that is Gabriel appears.

On that great judgment day I can see Gabriel—I can see him now—on that great judgment day! One foot he plant in the bottomless pit of hell—wid dat other foot he reach up and touch the pearly gates. I can see him now, as he reach over behind the throne—I can see him now as he rest his hand on the white marble table and reach over behind the white alabaster throne. I can see him now as he reach over behind the white alabaster throne and pull out the golden trumpet—the golden trumpet with pearl keys. I can see him now as he pull the golden trumpet from out behind the white alabaster throne—he put it to his lips—the golden trumpet, he put it to his lips—Good God Almighty —hear him blow—*Ta ta ti ta ta!*

As the preacher finishes, Gabriel blows, and then lines of angels appear with trumpets. They cross and recross the stage, their trumpeting takes on jazz rhythms, punctuated and dominated by Gabriel's trumpet, the stage is crowded with motionless figures, some in the air, some on the ground, the figure of the preacher seems to take on the majesty of the Lord, Satan grovels at his feet, and as the curtain falls, we know it is the Day of Judgment.

—7—

Jeff had triumphed. As a benefit, the ballet had been highly profitable. All of smart literary and social Chicago was there. A number of out-of-town critics had come. His students and friends had arranged a party afterward, and the enthusiasm for designer, conductor, and composer was spontaneous, even overwhelming. But for Jeff, the greatest triumph was his father's capitulation. To those who knew them, it was poignant to see the two together. Mr. Kirby put his arm around his son.

"Looks as though you were right. Why, I can see that was a good show. I enjoyed it. An old man can admit he was wrong, can't he? I'm mighty proud of this son of mine."

It was obvious, too, that Mr. Kirby liked Grace and her family. He made a point of inviting them to Priscilla's wedding. Cass Watkins was to get leave soon, and go to New York to be married. The Caldwells liked the Kirbys, including Jeff.

Priscilla had asked Grace to be her maid of honor. They drew aside at the party.

"Everybody's like a big happy family," Priscilla said. "I'm so glad for you and Jeff and especially, too, for Mother. Look at Dad and Jeff. It couldn't be better. You and I can be amused if some of it's for the wrong reasons. Of course Dad's impressed by what he'd call the solidity of it all. I heard him say, 'Those Caldwells are my kind of folks. Good solid citizens and no nonsense.'"

"It doesn't matter," Grace said. "They're happy."

"Now, let's hope you'll be happy. I suppose Jeff will go into the Army, but I have a feeling, and my feelings are apt to be pretty accurate where Jeff is concerned. I have a feeling that it won't be too long before he'll be coming home, and that Grace Caldwell will be a big part of home."

She put her arm around Grace, who flushed, and they went back to join the others who were by now riotously toasting Jeff and singing. "For he's a jolly good fellow."

III

"It didn't take him long, did it?" Fess said, still reminiscing with Gil and Perky at The Back Door. "Once the ballet was over he seized that little white pearl, as they say in Brooklyn, and off to the wars he ran with it."

" 'Zactly what did they do with him? It never was so plain to me," Perky said.

"They made him a tech sergeant," Gil said, "assigned him to Special Services, and sent him all over hell and gone to entertain the troops."

"Jes what he's doin' before. Army's screwy." Perky shrugged.

"Well," Gil explained, "Jeff felt better about it, particularly being in uniform. Made it official like."

"What did the new gal do?" Perky said.

Gil smiled. "Went on with her teaching and her canteen work. And wrote letters to Jeff, I fancy."

"And Jeff got back to home base now and then," Fess said. "At the start he was mostly around the U.S.A. Came back to do a big war bond rally in Chicago and was on here one day for Priscilla's wedding. Didn't you see him, Perky?"

"Naw. He dropped in, but I was off gallivantin' round somewheres. Left me a *billy do*."

[268]

"From what we heard, he was taking Grace Caldwell more and more seriously," Fess said. "He even wrote her another ballad, a mighty soft one. The chorus went:

'At War's End
You will be waiting,
Waiting for me.
There I shall find you,
Watching and waiting,
Waiting and loving,
Loving me, waiting,
At War's End.'

"People liked it, though it never caught on quite like 'Return Ride.' Grace proved how human she really was once when she admitted to me that she was jealous of that song.

"The time came when they were sending Jeff overseas, to North Africa, to Hawaii, to Alaska and Iceland, to England and, later, to Italy, France and Germany."

Fess found himself remembering the story Bones Cobb had told him about Jeff in Algiers.

Bones was a combo player, one of Gil's boys. He'd been with an antiaircraft battalion outside Algiers after the North African landing. He met Jeff and heard him sing and play. It was a whale of a night.

—2—

After the American landings, the city of Algiers gradually revived. The shop windows were no longer empty, but strange wares were displayed in them, as though attics had been rummaged through to seek marketable objects. Motion picture theaters were opened, and one or two variety shows. There were the off-limits cabarets near the Casbah, like the

Lizard, with its native dancers. The cafés put on a good show, but there was practically no food in them. One sat under the striped awnings and drank Algerian brandy, called *tako*, meaning "rough," and indeed it was rough. In the American messes and post exchanges there was plenty, which caused bitter jealousy (the G.I.'s were not too tactful), particularly on the part of the British Tommies who occasionally erupted in bottle-swinging riots.

The black market flourished. There were clandestine restaurants where those initiated could reserve places and eat a strange variety of foods, minute birds like sparrows, rice in many guises, and the beef everyone knew was horse meat. Over a period of time there developed a kind of quasi-social life. Refugees poured in from a variety of countries. The Allied diplomats brought their ladies. The Hotel Alleti and the Cercle Inter Allies were noisy and dressy. Gathering places for artists were popular. André Gide, with his beret on to cover the baldness, Vercors whose *Silence de la mer* (*The Silence of the Sea*) had already been published and acclaimed, and other writers of the resistance press, discussing more politics than literature.

Among the Allies political tension was high; from the start Russians were aloof and uncooperative, the French, torn by inner strife—all of which spelled evil for the years ahead.

It was in early August, 1943, that Jeff arrived in this feverish center of the Allied Command. He was to perform at a gala in the Opera House which had not long been reopened. One could read in the American Press that the Mediterranean was clear of air attack, but this was not true; and for some time after, sporadic and vicious raids took place. In spite of this, it was decided to open the Opera. For the first attempt, a performance of *Carmen* was announced, but warnings of a possible bombing were received and it was postponed.

[270]

Later, there were many galas, plays, operas, visiting bands, orchestras, and concert artists. One of the most memorable was a performance of Beethoven's Ninth Symphony, for which a refugee orchestra and chorus was gathered, and the "Ode to Joy" was triumphantly rendered by the multi-languaged singers as the audience wept and then hurrahed.

The night Jeff was to play his own accompaniment and sing, appearing as the Tan Troubador but in his sergeant's uniform, was to be a gala for the benefit of the families of those who had been killed or wounded in the air bombing of a prison fortress at the southern end of town.

Every seat had been sold. The military were there, of course, and the diplomats and their wives, refugees and their wives, some bedecked in Parisian finery preserved from the old days, others in makeshift costumes. The gala was under the patronage of General Giraud whom Ambassador Robert Murphy and the U.S. supported as head of the French forces, but General de Gaulle, the popular favorite, was also to attend.

There had been no opportunity for Jeff to rehearse. He and Bones Cobb, who had somehow wangled a ticket, were held up by the crush of people. When they arrived in front of the opera, General Giraud had already gone in. A mass of people were in the square outside. Suddenly there was a glare of lights (against all the regulations), a tempest of trumpets, cheers rising and breaking from all directions. A scarlet carpet was rolled to the door, two lines of huge Spahi guards, armed and ferocious to behold, black limbs and scarlet tunics glittering, formed a lane. The legendary hero, pale, serene, almost as tall as they, mounted the steps as flowers were showered around him, and entered the building.

As Jeff and Bones managed to follow, the tumult inside joined the tumult in the square. Back stage, they found themselves surrounded by native dancers from the French colonies, by members of the Foreign Legion Band. They could look out now to where Giraud sat in the left-hand grand box with Ambassador Murphy, and de Gaulle in the right-hand box, alone.

The dancers performed first, brown and sinuous, all male, their weird instruments accompanying a series of figures, some slow and dreamlike, some frenetic. They had been brought here to impress the Allies with the variety of French culture and power throughout the world.

During the pause that followed, the audience became engrossed in staring at the two generals, who sat resplendent in bright uniforms and medals, ignoring one another.

As the piano was rolled out, there was a brief introduction, applause, chiefly from GI's who had heard Jeff in the USO's before. Then Jeff ran his fingers over the keys, and for a moment he was terrified. He had an impulse to put his head down and weep. The piano was out of tune. It jangled. Keys stuck. Then Jeff realized that this piano was a survivor too. Perhaps it was the only playable piano in Algiers. The North African climate had wrecked it, and there were undoubtedly no replacements for strings. Certainly no tuners. He must sing. He must improvise.

He sang a medley of French tunes. He sang southern lullabies, the Preacher's Sermon from the ballet, "One Quiet Night," and all of it caught together by the pattern he could always charm them with. Then he ended with "Return Ride" and they cheered him. Jeff knew he had managed to turn the trick. He had meant it all and they realized it.

The Foreign Legion Band played military marches, and more folk songs. As they closed with the "Marseillaise," the audience turned to face the saluting generals. de Gaulle rose to leave, with a barely perceptible nod to Giraud. The roar of the crowd outside mingled with the roar of the crowd inside. As Ambassador Murphy escorted Giraud from the box, there was only a fluttering of applause.

A messenger invited Jeff and Bones to the reception the American ambassador was giving for Giraud in the crystal-heavy salon back of the opera boxes. Jeff and Bones made their way there. In spite of the regal refreshments, the champagne, the American Colony, and the obedient representatives of the Allies, it was a pallid scene.

"We are proud of Americans like you," Ambassador Murphy said as he presented Jeff to the General.

When they were outside, Bones said, "You did fine, man. I got transportation. Let's go. And you'll get a real meal now, and I mean real."

Over steak, french fried potatoes, all the trimmings, they talked until morning at the observation post.

"I respect that man Giraud," Jeff said. "We've got a lot in common. It's a lonely business. Those generals, they're two lonely men, but Giraud's the loneliest!"

IV

The Back Door was beginning to fill up now as it was getting toward six o'clock. It had stopped raining and the sun was shining; it was a beautiful evening, cool for June. Charlie Himes had come in. He was one of Gil's boys, very young, spectacular at the piano and with a fine tenor voice. Perky had a combo only over the weekends this summer. Before he began his stint on the stage, the entertainer asked, "Well, how's our boy Jeff doin' now he's back in town? I don't see him often."

"He's fine," Fess said. "Busy, Cartwright keeps him going at his teaching job at Juilliard. He's cleared the bases of almost everything else, hasn't he, Gil?"

"Yeah. Concentrating on work and courting."

"What's the gal doin'?" Perky asked as Floyd quietly set down fresh drinks.

"She's got a teaching job here in a school not far from mine. She's a fine teacher."

"Will she go on teachin' after they's hitched?" Perky was being his usual practical self. "What they gonna live on? Where's they gonna live?"

"Jeff's rented a big apartment on Edgecombe Avenue. He's

[274]

staying there now. He's got back some of his trappings, not too many, you know. Doesn't want those ghosts playing around. It's real swell. Grace is hanging out at the Y.W.C.A.

"They'll be O.K. when they decide to get married and she quits her job. Jeff's in demand to do orchestrations and, why, Perky, you'll even be getting more percentages again! Jeff's got a new album coming out with parts of the ballet, 'Return Ride,' his songs for Grace, and some other stuff. It's good. It'll sell. It's called 'The Troubador's Return.' Also he's pulling away at his own composing. He's made notes for a quintet for soprano and small orchestra. Course he's got Dolly-May in mind."

"Look's like he ain't gonna be no thin cat. What's you two men mess around wid when you don' have him to baby no more?" Perky was pleased at the thought and laughed loud and high.

"We've got our own games to play," Fess said. "There's plenty rough innings ahead."

Gil smiled his best cynical smile. "Oh, well, we know him, don't we? Jeff'll be in and out of plenty trouble and we'll be around like mommas and papas."

Jeff was laughing as he and Grace Caldwell came in. His arm was around her, and he was dressed again as the troubador, cream-colored shirt and trousers, scarlet scarf around the neck. He carried a white raincoat.

"They sure make a purty pair," Perky said as they stopped to greet Jake at the bar. "She's some looker."

The friends stood by, waiting for the couple to join them. Charlie Himes played "Return Ride." The other patrons stared pleasantly at the handsome couple.

"Same old Jeff," Gil said, "making an entrance per usual. Maybe he'll go into a dance now."

It was an entrance, yes, but it was a relaxed entrance. Gil was pleased by what he saw and what he sensed. He was pleased, too, by Grace's appearance. It was characteristic that she had made concessions to the "new look," but she had kept her autonomy. Her pale yellow blouse was not as full in back as some, the sleeves only slightly bulged, her matching skirt not too long and her nylon stockings were in the mode, dark bottle green. She carried a short green jacket and a large green straw hat with a golden yellow ribbon. The dark veiled eyes were livelier than usual.

Gil was abruptly conscious of the tableau they made, of the setting, of The Back Door. For a moment he felt as though Deborah were there, or about to come in. This was a turning point in Jeff's life. It was a turning point in his own. He was determined to change, to find some peace from his marauding forays in business and in sex, but even as he felt, genuinely enough, his determination, he knew that it was late to change. Regretting Deborah, he would take Zabee back, he would take others; but at least he believed that Grace and Jeff would find the peace he craved, that they would be an oasis of trust and friendship for him. He had not really meant his cynical remarks of a few minutes before.

"So you are 'Perky' Sparhawk and this is The Back Door. How good to be here at last!" Grace said as Perky held a chair for her.

"Mighty fine! Mighty fine! It's good to have you, Miss Grace. This goin' to be your home away from home. An' this is Floyd. He's gonna fix you an' that good-for-nothin' boy friend some drinks."

She greeted Floyd. As they made small talk around the table, Jeff went over to play. The crowd was delighted. Some of them had heard him at USO shows and knew of his travels. They joined in. They yelled for "Return Ride." He sang it and then "War's End." Gil noticed that Grace's eyes filled, and he thought, "This is a moment she has dreamed of for a long time."

—2—

"Guess it's no news to anyone we're going to get married," Jeff said when he came back to the table.

The proper sounds of delight were made. Grace showed them her ring, a square-cut emerald with small diamond clusters at each side.

"The wedding's to be the first week in July, probably Saturday," Grace said. "Everybody's to come. Everybody."

Perky looked solemn. "I'se afraid Mr. Kirby he won't cotton to me bein' there."

Grace reached over and patted his hand. "He'll want you very much. He's already told me so."

Perky's face shone, his gold tooth glittered. "We's all gonna have a big blowout here. The Back Door'll be poppin.'"

Jeff frowned and looked as though he was going to object, but Grace quickly reacted.

"Of course. Thank you, Perky. That will be wonderful."

"Where's the weddin'?" Perky asked.

"At the new apartment," Jeff said.

It was clear that Grace was excited over her plans. "My family's coming from Charleston, so we can have all our friends. They'll give us the wedding, of course, but the Edgecombe Avenue apartment is big enough. The Reverend Robinson's going to marry us. He married Cass and Priscilla. Dolly-May and Priscilla are going to be my attendants. Friends are coming from Chicago, Dave is coming in from New Mexico."

"Yes, I'm going to be tied up good and plenty," Jeff said. "And she's going to give up teaching."

"We'll miss you." Fess said to Grace. He meant this deeply. There were few teachers with Grace's sensitivity to the increasingly complex problems of the Negro in school, few who combined with it a fine education and a natural ability to teach.

"I shall miss it. Perhaps they'll let me come in and substitute now and then. We're all going to have to help. There's trouble ahead. Harlem is going to change."

"It'll get better," Jeff said.

Grace frowned. "More trouble, worse trouble, before it gets better. We have many things to face, many things to do."

Jeff looked around the table. He raised the glass.

"Come now, let's drink to all the things she's got to do first at home."

Gil noticed to his satisfaction that Grace was not embarrassed. She spoke quietly.

"I can drink to that, too. We do want a family. Not just a child—children."

Perky was glowing again. "But you wants a boy fust, I reckon. Hope he looks lak you, Miss Grace. Then it'll sure be a pretty baby."

Grace smiled. Jeff took her hand.

"We'll be happy with whatever we get," he said. "We only hope he or she will be happy with us."